A Deadly Deed Grows

by

Kathryn Long

A Deadly Deed Grows

Cover Art by *Kim Mendoza*

The Wild Rose Press, Inc.
PO Box 708
Adams Basin, NY 14410-0708
Visit us at www.thewildrosepress.com

Publishing History
First Crimson Rose Edition, 2015
Print ISBN 978-1-62830-854-9
Digital ISBN 978-1-62830-855-6

Published in the United States of America

She felt the buildup of tension on the trip back. And she knew it came from an obvious source, that anticipation of a goodbye kiss. She didn't know what to expect or how she would respond. Her feelings were conflicted with the person sitting next to her being so friendly, so engaging. She couldn't keep that nagging voice in the back of her head away for long. And it kept warning her that not everything was as it seemed. Still, she liked Sean, couldn't help but like him. She forced that thought to stay with her as they said goodbye.

"Well, it's been nice, Mira Stanley. I enjoyed your company despite the ugly conversation about your view of my partner's notorious brother. But we won't go into that again," he said.

His words touched her face with short brushstrokes of his breath as his face came within inches of hers. Closer and closer it seemed. And each inch pushed her heartbeat to race faster and faster. "Um hmm," she answered, since her thoughts refused to form into words.

"And I hope you feel the same way," he whispered and came closer, backing her against the door.

Now, Mira could only see parts of him, but she focused on his lips as they brushed against hers, his voice drowned out by the pounding of her heart. But when he touched her, the beating stopped. His kiss made her stop everything. All thoughts and feelings focused only on one subject. That kiss. And whether foolish thinking or not, she wanted it to last forever.

Dedication

I dedicate this book
to all the people and events in my life
that have inspired my desire and passion
for the written word.
Such is the way stories are created.

Chapter One

"What do you mean he won't see me? I drove all night to keep this damn appointment." Mira cut off her verbal lashing to take several gulps of coffee. After three hours of driving through the torrential rain in Georgia, her nerves, like frayed wire, were exposed and vulnerable, ready to ignite.

"We understand, Miss Stanley, but it can't be helped. Mr. Lane was called away to an emergency meeting at one of our branch offices."

"Tell me. What am I supposed to do? Maybe he'd like to explain to my client why he has failed to take the time to deal with her problem when she'll lose her home any day now."

"I understand, but it can't be helped. Mr. Lane is in a meeting."

"I heard you the first time." Mira gritted her teeth. She waited to calm down and to convince herself that rescheduling remained her only choice.

"Miss Stanley?"

"Yes, okay. What time?" Mira managed to ask.

"Pardon?"

"What time can he meet?"

"Oh. Well, I'm not sure how soon. His schedule is full and…"

"Forget it," Mira snapped and ended the call.

At this point she wanted to drive to Lane

Developers and sit in his office until he returned. She certainly had nothing else to do and no other place to go.

Mira glanced at the number of missed calls and the name attached to them. She sighed and shook her head. She wanted to forget all of it, the whole pathetic, twisted mess. "Leave me alone, Alex, will you?" She said aloud what her heart and mind had felt for weeks. This trip and the distance it brought should work. "If only you'd stop calling." She shut her phone off before tossing it on the seat.

She pulled back onto the highway and headed south into town. Port Saint Joe, like a blip on the radar, still offered a few motels. She'd try to book a room for the night, maybe for the next two or three. She didn't know how long her agenda might take, but assuredly each hour made a difference. If Claire Peterson lost her home, it would be Mira's fault. And to make matters worse, she'd be fired. Well, maybe not fired, but she could forget that promotion to become a partner in the firm. Mrs. Peterson was not her client; she was the senior partner's aunt. Rob Peterson entrusted the situation to Mira to investigate matters. He assured her she was the most accomplished, and that she was the only one he trusted. Of course, he planned to come himself, but a major client's future was in jeopardy. A billion dollar deal, he'd explained. Not something to turn his back on.

As far as this case, all she knew was what Rob had told her. His aunt claimed Lane Developers cheated to get her property. Though Mrs. Peterson and her lawyer battled the case for the past year, as far as the court was concerned the deal was ironclad. Rob wanted Mira to find evidence that proved otherwise. Mira felt apprehensive right from the beginning about what she could accomplish. To make matters worse, she faced less than a week to solve the problem. And of course the other detail left more pressure on Mira. Rob warned her, but she still felt uncomfortable. His aunt, to hear him tell it, was a tad bit eccentric. In order to help her, Rob bought Mira a book on gardening. When she raised an eyebrow, his explanation was to advise her that in order to gain his aunt's trust she should talk about flowers. And that's all he mentioned. With a quick study on the subject, a crash course done in two days, Mira packed and was on her way south.

She drew a deep breath and sensed the feeling of panic as the image of her promotion faded. She was drowning, and Lane Developers was the hand that held her under the water. The image of the peculiar Aunt Claire with a trowel in one hand and her prize roses in the other did nothing to help.

"I *can't* lose."

The palm of her hand slammed against the steering wheel and without meaning to she sounded the horn. The car in front of her put on the brakes. Mira did the same and, with a squeal of tires, tapped the back bumper.

"Great. This day keeps getting better and better." She sighed and grabbed her insurance card from the glove compartment. Once out of the car she found herself confronted by an angry-faced driver.

Mira winced and forced herself to study the back end of the man's car. Sure enough, the crumpled metal was more than she expected. It had sounded and felt like such a tiny bump. Mira shrugged her shoulders and attempted a smile. She didn't trust her voice to speak, yet.

"I hope you have insurance, because this is a Mercedes, you know, and the parts for it are *not* cheap," he snapped.

Mira nodded as she extended her arm and spoke with caffeine and nerve-induced speed. "No need to get so upset. I have insurance. Doesn't everybody? I mean, you'd be a fool not to, don't you think?"

He took the card from her hand and studied it. It was at that point Mira caught sight of movement from someone seated in the Mercedes' passenger side. He turned around to look back at them. Rather than the expression of impatience Mira expected, the man smiled and waved. She tilted her head to the side and nodded.

"Okay, here is my business card. It has my insurance information on the back. And I'm sure someone will contact you within twenty-four hours. Are you from—oh, God."

"What?" Mira looked up from reading the card to see what the man, Justin Waverly, referred his "oh, God" comment to when his passenger exited the car and now stood alongside him.

"Why the hold up?" He tapped on the damaged bumper. "Looks like no more than a ding to me. Seriously, Justin, why don't you let it go?"

Waverly's face blushed to crimson. His friend suppressed a laugh as he stepped back to lean against the rear end of the sedan.

"Let it go? Are you insane? That's at least five grand worth of repairs, Thorndale. I'm not about to let it go. She with all her horn-blowing, bumper-crushing should pay."

"Oh, for God's sake. You own the dealership. Your guys will fix it for free if you tell them to, and the cost will be soaked up in the next sale you make." The man, Thorndale, glanced at Mira with apologetic eyes. "Don't worry. He can handle it. He likes to put on a show every time something goes wrong."

"I do not." Justin turned back to Mira. "My insurance company will call by this…"

"Seems to me I remember a certain incident in the mall parking lot last year, after the Christmas party, wasn't it?"

"You bring up the Christmas party? That's hardly the same—oh, forget it."

Mira's eyes grew wide as Justin Waverly walked to his car, his steps agitated and hurried. She shifted her gaze back to Thorndale, who laughed.

"It's okay. You don't need to call your insurance. Lucky for you the damage is all on Justin's car. A little rubbing should take out that mar on yours, Miss, ah…"

"Oh, sorry. I'm Mira, Mira Stanley." She managed to hold out her hand, which he took at once and cupped in his own. She guessed his height to be well over her five-foot-ten frame.

"Glad to meet you, Mira Stanley. I'm Sean. You already know the Thorndale part."

Mira looked down at her hand that he still held and smiled. "Well, thank you for the rescue."

"Justin needs a lot of redirecting at times. He's lucky to have a buddy like me."

She laughed. "Good to know. Um, do you think…?" She tipped her chin downward. "My hand?"

"Oh! Sorry." Sean let go. "First time to Port Saint

Joe and the Cape?"

Mira looked surprised. "How did you...?" She looked behind her to follow his gaze. "The license plate. Yeah, it's my first. In fact, I drove all night from Ohio to get here, and then I find out...Skip it. Not your problem. Know of any cheap motels close by?"

"You'll find a Best Western up the road a couple of blocks. It's pretty reasonable." Sean drew a card and pen out of his pocket and then wrote on the back. "Here's my number. If you need any help getting around or anything, give me call."

When he smiled his blue eyes seemed to turn from pale to deep turquoise, like the ocean water she had stared at moments ago. His tanned skin contrasted with the blond hair, cropped short the way she always liked men's hair cut. She sighed. A tiny twinge grew inside, causing her to shiver. She was tired. That's all. Tired and needed lots of sleep.

"Okay, Sean Thorndale. I'm going to check into that motel and sleep the day away. Thanks for your help." She pointed toward the Mercedes. "And if he changes his mind, I'll be in town for a few days."

Sean laughed and shook his head. "Don't worry. The reminder of the Christmas party incident will keep his mouth shut for months to come. And you should get out on the beach. Soak up some sun before you leave. Cape San Blas has been rated one of the best resort beaches in the country."

"I might do that. Thanks." Mira walked back to her car. When she slid into her seat she glanced up to discover Sean watching her. The twinge in her stomach surfaced again, but she ignored it.

As she pulled around him and the Mercedes, she

waved, but didn't beep. No more beeping, she told herself and headed for the Best Western.

Chapter Two

The afternoon sunlight broke through a slit in the shades. It formed a line across Mira's face. She squinted at its bright interruption and threw the covers up over her head. After a moment she poked an arm out from underneath, and her hand patted around the surface of the nightstand until she found her cell phone.

"Great," she mumbled and threw the covers back off. The day passed five o'clock. Too late for a meeting with Lane. She had planned to sleep only a couple of hours. Now, she'd need to wait until tomorrow. In her head she heard the clock tick, a loud and annoying beat that reminded her how valuable time passed with every second for Rob's aunt. Besides, Mira was to be evaluated next spring, maybe offered an associate partnership. One more step up the ladder. She hated the game, but how else was she to gain job security?

She sighed as she went into the bathroom. After a shower she'd feel better. She could plan for tomorrow, after some well-deserved rest and maybe a peaceful hour or two on the beach. She needed a witty tongue and sharp mind in order to tangle with Bradley Lane.

For the first time since this morning, she recalled her encounter with Sean Thorndale. It brought a smile to her face. No doubt, his good looks attracted her, even if it was impulsive to think it. She had no evidence to validate her feelings, other than he was nice enough to offer his help while she stayed in town.

Glancing in the mirror, Mira scowled at her reflection. "Face it, Mira. What would a great looking guy like that want with a girl like you?" Her long brown hair with its untamed curls remained disheveled most of the time. She considered chopping it off, but with the wide angular features of her face, short locks weren't flattering. Besides, the dark brown mane accented her green eyes. She gave herself a confident smile. Once she freshened up, Mira grabbed her bag and sunglasses and went out the door.

The tourist brochure she'd perused offered a choice. Either take the shortcut across the road, which led to Saint Joseph Bay, or choose the longer car ride around to the gulf side, along the barrier peninsula called Cape San Blas. It was more upscale than Port Saint Joe and almost commercial-free with one small grocery store and a restaurant called Surf and Suds. The photo of the eatery showed a building painted a loud, tangerine orange and was no doubt pretty easy to find. Her stomach rumbled enough to let her know it was past dinnertime.

"Gulf side it is." With a firm nod she walked out to her car. When she got to the parking lot she was surprised to find someone loitering next to her vehicle. With cupped hands he leaned in to peer through the window.

"Excuse me. Can I help you with something?" Her hand reached inside her bag to grab hold of the pepper spray she stashed there. Her breath held as he turned to step sideways several feet from the car.

"Ah, sorry. My girlfriend told me to come outside and see if she left her bag in the backseat. She told me it was a gray Mazda. I guess I was in too big a hurry to recognize this isn't it."

It sounded like a reasonable explanation, but her hand wouldn't release its grip on the spray. A big city attitude left her cynical about strangers. She nodded and kept her voice steady. "Yeah, definitely not it."

The man hurried away without another word. Mira scowled as she quickened her pace to reach her car. After she locked the doors and pulled out of the parking lot, the tension in her muscles relaxed. With all that happened since she came to town, the cancelled appointment, the fender bender, and now this, Mira remained on edge.

Route 30 took her out past impressive condos and homes the size of mansions—those cape properties with seven-figure price tags. Mira read that people who lived in the area for more than twenty or thirty years found this a more profitable investment than ever imaginable, people like Rob's aunt. However, Mrs. Peterson needed to deal with the likes of Bradley Lane who seemed to focus on ways to swindle the old woman, to take away the only security she possessed. Time remained short, and it pushed her to find the opportunity to speak with Lane. If she figured out what went through the man's head, it might help Mrs. Peterson keep her home.

Mira spotted the bright orange monstrosity of Surf and Suds half a mile ahead. She slowed and turned into the nearly empty parking lot. The few patrons who stopped by sat outside on the patio deck. Some of them brought their dogs along. One pet in particular didn't seem too happy to see Mira as it growled when she got out of the car. She glanced at the owner who frowned and put a finger to her lips. She looked up to give Mira an apologetic smile.

"Sorry. He's very friendly but maybe a bit too protective. Aren't you, Samson."

Mira nodded. "It's okay. I love dogs. I own one myself."

"And you didn't bring it with you? They allow pets here. In fact, most of the Cape's rentals allow pets. One of the draws for many tourists to this area."

Mira took stock of the woman while she talked. She spoke with a bit of a drawl to her voice, and her face shone bronzed and tanned. Mira wondered if she was a local. "Oh, I couldn't imagine leaving my pet behind in a strange motel room while I carried out my errands. Do you rent in the area?"

The woman shook her head. "No. I live in Apalachicola. I don't know where my manners are. My name's Nadine Wiggins. I own a real estate agency in Port Saint Joe." She reached out to shake Mira's hand.

"Real estate? That must keep you busy in a place like this. Glad to meet you, Nadine. I'm Mira Stanley."

"Vacationing?"

"Sorry to say, I'm here on business. At least it's a warmer place than Ohio." Mira looked around for the nearest empty table.

"Why don't you join me? It's not often I get a chance to chat with a Yankee." Nadine smiled.

"Thanks. That would be nice. So how are sales?" Mira pulled up her chair and raised an arm to signal a server to the table.

"Slugging along, I'd say. The economy, you know."

"I can imagine. Though it does appear a lot of building is going on. I see signs for Lane Developers all over the place." Mira hoped to get some inside information about Bradley Lane's business habits.

Nadine wrinkled up her nose and rolled her eyes. "Bradley Lane. Yes, he seems to do all right for himself. Of course, if everyone behaved like he did, no one would trust anyone, if you get my drift." She paused to take a sip of her beer.

"Sounds like you don't approve of Lane's business etiquette."

"No, I guess I don't." Nadine leaned in closer to Mira and added in a low voice, "I've heard things, rumors about shady deals and bribes."

Mira matched Nadine's tone. "You mean he has friends in the court system?"

Nadine smiled. "Let's say he knows who to call when he wants a deal to go through without all the red tape."

Mira reflected on Nadine's comment. To size it up, facing Lane weighed heavily on her. If she failed to handle the Peterson case, the promotion opportunity disappeared, but even more significant, Mrs. Peterson would lose her home. Mira hated the idea of Lane as the winner in this true to life game of Monopoly.

"Do you happen to know about the residence of a local by the name of Claire Peterson?"

"Ah, yes. The Flower Queen." Nadine smiled and nodded.

"Flower Queen?" Not only did the woman grow flowers, she wore a title.

Nadine laughed. "Claire Peterson has been the top contender in area gardening events for as long as I can remember. Hence, the Flower Queen."

"I had no idea."

"From what I hear, those gardening fanatics take their hobby seriously. In fact, it can get rather unpleasant."

"How so?"

"Let me think…" Nadine shifted in her seat while she stared past Mira's shoulder and out at the Gulf. "It was three, maybe four years ago when someone who came in second place at the Northern Florida Spring Bloom contested the results. Claire Peterson and the other contestant churned out more than a few colorful words, I tell you. Neither one let it go. And people took bets whether it would go to court. It was front page news for days."

"But Mrs. Peterson won?"

Nadine nodded. "No one has questioned the judging since. In fact, I think the judges are afraid to give her less than top prize."

"Sounds like a scary lady." Mira shuddered.

"Not at all. In fact, to hear people around the Cape and Port Saint Joe tell it, Claire Peterson is the nicest, most generous person you could meet. She'll invite anyone who's interested to visit her garden. She loves to show it off, but I'd say it's not wise to question those flowers and her talent to grow them."

"And her property? What happened to—?" At that moment her phone rang. Alex's name lit up the screen. Mira scowled at the sight.

"Aren't you going to answer it?" Nadine took a sip of her drink, but kept her gaze on Mira.

"Just one of those telemarketers." Mira shrugged and ended the call before she dropped the phone back in her handbag.

Nadine narrowed her eyes and nodded. "Yes,

indeed. Those telemarketers sure are a pesky lot, aren't they? Now, where were we?"

"You mentioned the property?" Mira took a relaxing breath as she changed the subject.

"Oh, yes. I remember the Peterson estate. It was a listing with a rival Realtor a few years back. It stayed on the market for a few months but never sold. I think it's out on Route 30 east, heading Apalachicola way. In such a secluded stretch, you can't see those homes from the road. Most of them were built around the early nineteen hundreds. Anyway, the Peterson place has a colorful history. Many locals claim it's haunted."

Mira's brows shot up. "Haunted? Are you kidding?"

"Haunted. Neighbors claim they've heard screams in the night, eerie sounds, and glimpses of glowing white in the windows." She shook her head and tossed Samson a doggie treat.

"You don't believe it's haunted, do you?"

Nadine laughed. "Do you think people would come near the place to see those beautiful flowers if it were? It's bull. All of it bull. But it works well for the local economy and the tourist business. You know how it goes. Make a brochure of several local homes. Claim they're haunted. Sell the tour to folks for twenty bucks a pop. Bingo. You've got a cozy setup to bring in money. I don't know too many who'd object to it. Everyone is scrambling to make ends meet. Times are tough."

Mira scratched the top of Samson's head. "Sounds like harmless entertainment. Can you think of any reason why Bradley Lane is desperate to own the Peterson property?"

Nadine looked puzzled. "Lane? No, can't say I do. By reputation, Lane Developers goes after big land deals with lots of acreage. The Peterson place is a little over two acres and the land is situated at very low elevation. In fact, when the ocean swells during a storm, most of the property in the back is flooded. It started years ago. Owners along that stretch of beach continue to fight this problem. I can't imagine it's worth much to anyone except Mrs. Peterson."

"Sure is puzzling." Mira stood up. "Thank you for sharing lunch with a Yankee. Maybe we'll run into each other again before I leave."

After they shook hands Mira walked back to her car. On the way back into town, Mira attempted to sort out all of Nadine's comments about Lane Developers and the Peterson property. She suspected Bradley Lane's motives before this conversation because of what Rob had told her. Now, she grew more certain. Maybe it was personal and never about business development. Whatever it was, Mira needed to meet with both Lane and her boss's aunt before she managed to explain any of it.

Mira steered into the turn lane to head east on Route 30 and away from Port Saint Joe. She'd risk it and stop at the Peterson estate without calling. Hopefully, Claire wouldn't be upset at the intrusion. Her eyes strayed from the road for a second to glimpse the ocean. It looked peaceful. She smiled at the sight of seagulls gliding and swooping above the water. They seemed content, so carefree; it somehow made her feel sad.

The beep of a car horn brought her gaze and attention back to the road. She swerved to avoid crossing the center line and a collision with the oncoming car. "Real sharp, Mira," she mumbled.

This time her vision stayed glued to the road ahead. It took a second to realize there were no other cars ahead of her. A look in the rearview mirror showed one vehicle, a gray pickup truck. She frowned at its fast approach. A plastic tarp covered the bed, and the sides flapped and rippled in the wind. For some odd reason Mira shivered and the tiniest hint of anxiety traveled through her body. Still, she found no time to dwell on it. Her eyes widened. Too fast and too close, the truck barreled toward her.

In the next instant, it rear-ended her car with such a blunt force that Mira's head and shoulders shot forward. Another glance in the mirror gave her a close-up view of the truck's headlights and grill. It resembled a face with an angry smile and wild eyes glaring at her. She gripped the steering wheel and pressed down on the brake before she lost control and careened off the road.

"What the hell is wrong with you?" she yelled out the window, even though the crazy driver couldn't hear and didn't seem to care. This time, the truck gave her another shove, not as hard, but enough to send jarring pain through her neck and back.

A mix of anger, fear, and confusion overwhelmed her mind, but the anger pushed to the forefront. Whatever and whoever this was about, Mira wouldn't make it easy. "You want to play? Let's play." She stomped down on the gas pedal. Her tires screeched as the Mazda distanced itself from the pickup.

When she approached within several yards of the grocery store parking lot, Mira jerked the wheel to the right and made the turn. The tires spit gravel, and the dust took a few seconds to settle after she stopped. Her eyebrows knitted together as she scowled. Without any attempt to follow, the pickup flew by. At that point she didn't know whether to be relieved or annoyed. However, the sense of what happened settled inside and left her with a tremendous sense of fear. Not knowing the identity of the driver and why he engaged in a game of bumper cars didn't sit well with her.

Mira's hands trembled as she tried to grip the steering wheel. She stared out the window and didn't trust herself to move. At last, she yanked the keys out of the ignition and exited the car. She gave one cursory glance at the minor rear-end damage to her vehicle. This rated as an unlucky day for driving. She unlocked the trunk and searched through her suitcase until her hand touched cold metal. Once uncovered, she studied the handgun, a gift from her dad who believed in the strong arm of self-defense. Her heartbeat found a calmer rhythm. Reassured, she placed the gun back in its hiding place. Maybe she overreacted, but what she'd faced in the past made her cautious.

Back inside the car, Mira took a couple of deep breaths and started the engine. She needed her mind to focus all its energy and attention on Claire Peterson's case, not be distracted by some maniac truck driver. No matter how bizarre the incident, she refused to let it rattle her.

The next move, which she doubted would amount to much, made her grab the phone. "Yes. Hello. My name is Mira Stanley, and I need to report a traffic incident."

Chapter Three

Mira sat in front of the Peterson estate for several minutes trying to block out any remainder of unsettled nerves left inside. She needed to appear like the strong, rational person she was most of the time. Who knew how agreeable the woman would be to welcome a stranger into her home, especially when that stranger claimed to have a supposed plan to save her day. Add a distraught and nerve-wracked personality to the mix... Well, Claire might send her out the door without so much as a hello and how are you.

She'd debated on whether or not to call Rob and let him know about her run-in incident with the truck driver. However, without any real proof that it somehow connected with her investigation, she couldn't follow through. The last thing she needed was to sound like some hysterical female. Not with her boss. As it was, she promised the officer she spoke with on the phone she would stop by the precinct to file a report. She still didn't hold out much hope for police to find the maniac driver. She hadn't been able to provide more than a description of the vehicle. Without a license plate number, the search was next to impossible.

Mira sighed and got out of the car. "Oh well, here goes," she mumbled. Once in front of the Peterson door, she gave the bell a forceful push.

"Who is it?"

Mira caught sight of someone peering through the door's window pane. The face looked anxious.

"Mrs. Peterson? It's Mira Stanley. I work with your nephew, Rob Peterson." She tried on a cheery face and it worked.

Claire smiled and opened the door. "Good morning, Miss Stanley. It is Miss, isn't it?"

Mira nodded. "I hope this isn't a bad time." She stepped inside.

"No, of course not. I was finishing my after dinner tea." Claire hesitated and then added, "You're awfully young for a lawyer." She squinted her eyes.

Mira suppressed a laugh. "Yes, well, I've practiced for a few years. In fact, Peterson, Jared, and Sloan is the second firm I've worked for."

"What happened at the first one? Did they fire you?" Claire looked skeptical and worried.

Mira bit down on her lip. "Let's say I wanted more from my career, and the first place didn't deliver. Your nephew's firm is at the top of the list. And it's a good fit for me."

"Okay. I'll give you a chance." Claire nodded and led Mira to the kitchen.

Mira smiled. "That's fair." She walked past the corner table to peer out the window and spotted the garden. The vibrant colors of roses, carnelian, persimmon, Mikado yellow, and cherry blossom pink, erupted among the dark green foliage like a spray of fireworks.

"Although, I must say, you better be prepared to take on Bradley Lane. He's a snake oil salesman. Slick and slippery as seaweed. Don't trust a word he says. Tea?" Claire poured them both some and set sugar and lemon juice on the table.

"Do you feel that way about him for a particular reason, Mrs. Peterson? I mean, can you explain how he managed to get a hold of the deed to your property without you agreeing to it? I need details in order to understand how that happened."

"Do sit down before your tea gets cold, and please, call me Claire."

Mira did as she was told. If Claire's memory was as sharp as her tongue, she should be able to give an accurate account of this whole ordeal from start to finish.

"I tell you as the God's honest truth, the first I heard mention of this deed was the day a lawyer called and claimed he possessed papers I needed to look at, papers which proved Mr. Lane was the new owner of my property. It's been a year, and I've been fighting this ever since. I can't seem to lick it."

"You mean to tell me you had no clue?"

"I'm afraid so." Claire nodded. "It makes no sense to me, but according to the lawyer and Judge Thorn, Charles signed the contract. Now that he's gone, Lane Developers inherits this property, *my* property." Claire's teacup shook as she brought it to her lips. She paused to add in a softer tone, "And my garden." She turned to gaze out the window, quiet once more.

Mira studied the distraught woman. "Mrs. Peterson…Claire, I'm curious. Why isn't your name on the original deed?"

Claire shook her head. "It's such a shame. Charles inherited the property, and we never worried enough to go through the hassle of getting my name added. After all…" She shrugged her shoulders and gave Mira a weak smile.

It wasn't her place to judge, so Mira kept quiet. No matter how much the Petersons loved and trusted each other, as a lawyer, she knew the importance of a legal document in today's world.

"Did your husband ever mention Lane Developers?"

"Charles and I talked about everything. We kept no secrets between us. That's why this feels odd. Of course, the lawyer explained the document says I am to receive the fair market value for my home. But my Charles would never consider this, not when he knew how much it meant to me." The elderly woman stood up and walked to the window. Her shoulders moved up and down as she quietly sobbed.

Mira didn't know whether it was the right move to go to her, to comfort her, but she needed to do something.

"I know the situation is bleak, but I can assure you I will get answers. I plan to meet with Bradley Lane this afternoon."

Claire swiveled around. "And you think that will help? I've tried to deal with the man. He spins a clever tale about his meetings with Charles. Several of them, he claimed. He says Charles and he maintained a close relationship, but Charles never mentioned him to me. No, Miss Stanley, you will get nowhere by talking to that man. Nowhere."

Knowing how her visit and the topic of conversation agitated the poor woman, Mira got up from her chair to leave. "I'll be in touch as soon as I find information worthwhile sharing. Please, don't worry. I know you don't think I can do it, but I will.

Trust me."

Claire met her visitor's gaze with sad eyes. "I don't mean to sound negative. It's not like me. But if you only knew...since my Charles passed away, my gardening has been a blessing. To take that from an old widow, the one thing left to give me pleasure? It's cruel."

Mira didn't believe she was about to say it, but she felt too sorry for Claire. "Maybe next time I visit you'll show me your garden? I hear you're quite the prize winner."

Claire's eyes came alive. "Oh, yes. I'd love to show you. Do you garden, Miss Stanley? I grow some beautiful grandiflora. They're my best effort. It's a cross between the floribunda and hybrid tea."

Mira nodded without comment on the grandiflora, but remembered Rob's advice. "I can't claim to know very much since I have little time to garden. It is fascinating though. And I'd love to talk more, but I should go if I plan to visit Mr. Lane."

Mira was discouraged, but not beaten. Maybe Claire Peterson failed to get anywhere with Lane, but she was elderly, a vulnerable target in this situation. People like Lane were barracudas, and Claire was easy prey. Mira was not that soft. She held her own with the worst of them. And she'd make sure that included Lane. She would get answers. Maybe Claire's story didn't make sense to Mira. Not yet, but she still had plenty to investigate.

Before leaving, Mira told Claire Peterson to stop worrying. She planned to get this straightened out or else. She drove back toward Port Saint Joe and the police precinct. She tried to clear her mind of worries, but the possible "or else" element of this case refused to go away. If it came to that, several lives could be destroyed.

Chapter Four

"Gwen, bring me my agenda for the day. I must fit in lunch with Vivian, or she will nag me about how little time I spend with her." Bradley lifted his finger off of the intercom. His mother and her cantankerous ways worsened as she grew older. To place her in a private nursing home seemed attractive, if he could persuade doctors to sign the papers. They weren't as easy to manipulate as Judge Thorn. To that end, he put up with her complaints, her gripes, and her scathing criticism. Who needed a wife, he thought, as Gwen walked into the room.

"Here you are, Mr. Lane. You have an hour this afternoon to squeeze your mother in for lunch." Gwen backed away from the desk after she set the agenda down.

Bradley scanned the list of names and stopped when he got to Mira Stanley. "Who's this?" He pointed to the name.

Gwen leaned over to read it. "Oh, she's the lawyer who wants to speak to you about the Peterson property. She was scheduled for yesterday, but you were called away to…"

"Yes, yes, of course," he snapped. "Well, I guess you can pencil in lunch with Vivian for one-thirty, right after the Stanley appointment. But if she's even five minutes late, you'll need to reschedule her again."

Bradley was procrastinating. Continually putting her off in hopes that she would go away wasn't going to work. All the same, her agenda wouldn't win either. His document was ironclad. He'd made sure of it. The Peterson property was his. Why Claire Peterson continued to fight baffled and annoyed him. No amount of protest worked as far as he was concerned. She'd find no other recourse but to pack her belongings and move out. The sooner he tied up the estate matters, the better. He needed to relax and get back to a normal life.

****

Mira sat in the waiting room, tapping her shoe against the chair leg. Fifteen minutes had passed since her scheduled appointment time with Lane. The longer she waited the more anxious she became. This must be a tactic he used. Make the adversary nervous as hell before the meeting so you hold the upper hand.

"You're pathetic, Mira Stanley. You can do this," she muttered under her breath and closed her eyes. They popped open in the next second, though, as the image she'd conjured up was of Sean Thorndale, his warm smile, tanned skin, and friendly voice.

"Damn it, Stanley, focus." Mira gritted her teeth and looked at the clock once more. Twenty minutes late.

"Miss Stanley? Mr. Lane will see you now." Gwen got up to lead Mira to the door and motioned her inside.

Bradley Lane stood in front of his desk with what Mira suspected to be a disingenuous smile. At least her frame of mind was prepared—skeptical, on guard and ready to do battle. Lane extended a hand to shake.

"How do you do, Miss Stanley. I hope I didn't keep you waiting too long."

Mira smiled and knew well that Bradley Lane intended just that. "No, of course not. I had some last minute phone calls to make. Business calls to clients. My job seems to never end," she answered and gave Bradley's hand a tight-gripped shake.

Bradley laughed. "Yes, indeed. I'm all too familiar. So what in particular brings you to Port Saint Joe?"

Mira's gaze followed him as he retreated behind his desk, giving him a formidable barrier. Instead of sitting on the other side of it, she pulled up a chair alongside him. With little to separate them, a hint of disapproval formed his expression, and it made Mira smile.

"Let's try to be honest, Mr. Lane. You know very well why I came to see you." Mira leaned in closer and kept her eyes locked onto his. "Why are you trying to cheat Mrs. Peterson and take away her home?" Mira knew enough from courtroom battles to put her enemy immediately on the defensive.

"I do not cheat or take anything away from anyone. In this case, I gained legal possession of that property, and I have the evidence to prove it. Face it. You can't claim wrongdoing on my part. If this is all you've come for, I might as well save us both some time and end this meeting." He stood up as if ready to lead her to the door.

"Please. We're far from finished." Mira spoke almost too softly. But her tone did the trick as he remained in his place and eyed her in silence as if assessing his options.

"I don't know what you expect to accomplish or change. The legal document of the property transfer from Charles Peterson to me is valid. Judge Thorn agrees. Claire Peterson can do nothing about it. It's foolish for her to continue this fight."

Mira noted the stubborn set of his jaw. "May I see this document?"

"Why? What good will that do?" He frowned.

"Has Mrs. Peterson seen this document you talk about?" Mira leaned back in the chair, but her eyes and ears remained alert.

"Of course she's seen it. Why wouldn't I show it to her after all her rants and complaints, asking me for proof," he said, his voice rising to a loud irritation.

"And you yourself showed it to her?" Mira refused to let go because she suspected he tried to avoid any direct contact with Claire, especially if this was a shady deal. Leaving his team of lawyers to dirty their hands, she guessed.

"I'm a very busy man. My lawyer delivered it to her. He told me she refused to look at it because she claimed it was bogus. Preposterous, cantankerous woman is who she is. Absolutely unreasonable to work with. Why, her name wasn't on the original deed!" He went over to one of the file cabinets and pulled open the top drawer. Once he retrieved a file, he walked back to his desk.

"Here you are." He handed it to Mira. "You're a lawyer. I'm sure you recognize a legal document when you see one."

The remark hinted at deliberate sarcasm, but she let it pass. The document did look proper. The wording contained all the correct language, the embossed notary was stamped at the bottom, and it did indeed show Charles Peterson's signature. If that in fact was his signature. Mira considered the ways Lane could've forged the man's name.

Even if the papers were bogus, with Judge Thorn in his pocket who would question it? She read the witness' name below Peterson's signature and bit down on her lip. *Sean Thorndale.* How did Sean and Bradley, or Sean and Charles, fit together, she wanted to ask? Mira calmed herself to speak in a steady voice.

"How did this deal come about? Did Peterson approach you about his property?"

"No, I must admit one of my employees spotted it as a listing in one of the local real estate ads several years ago. He brought it to my attention. We worked for more than a year to acquire several properties along that stretch of road, you see. This was one of several. I contacted Charles Peterson to see if we could strike a deal."

"But Mrs. Peterson told me they decided not to sell."

"Yes. That is what Charles initially told me, also. But after a couple more visits I convinced him his wife would be well taken care of should he pass away first. After all, the man was getting on in years. And if you ask me, he didn't appear to be in the best of health. Anyway, he agreed, after I named an amount he found satisfactory. I called my lawyer to draw up the papers. As I stated earlier, all legal, witnessed, signed, and notarized."

"About the witness. Does this Mr. Thorndale work for you?" Mira tried to keep from sounding too eager.

"Thorndale? He works for our lawyer's firm. He's one of their senior partners. I don't know him personally. Lane Developers isn't one of his clients. I believe he happened to be at our office to drop off some documents at the time I needed a witness to sign the Peterson deal. That's all. If you'll excuse me, I'm meeting my mother for a luncheon date. She's impatient and doesn't like to be kept waiting."

Mira wanted to know more, but at the moment no other questions came to mind. Her thoughts were stuck in gear, like a video image frozen on the screen of Sean Thorndale and his possible involvement. She didn't want to believe he was party to a forged deal. Still, she didn't know him. One five-minute session did not give her the opportunity to size him up. However, he did rescue her from the accident, and chivalry did strange, unpredictable things to a woman's mind. No, she refused to let her judgment be impaired. She must stay objective.

"Fine. But I'd like us to meet again, if I think of any more questions. And perhaps Mrs. Peterson and I will make a trip to see your lawyer. What did you say the firm's name is?" Mira stared into Bradley's eyes. She didn't blink or waver.

He sighed. "Thorndale and Lane. It's located in Apalachicola."

Mira paused as she readied her pen to write the information in her notebook. "Lane?"

"Yes. Kyle Lane is my brother. Lawyers and doctors. That's what my mother wanted from her sons. Well, she got one out of the two, didn't she?" Bradley looked away to stare at his phone. After a quick search, he added, "The number there is two-two-eight, five-three-five-seven. Now, I must ask you to leave. Traveling across town to get to my mother's house takes a while."

Mira nodded and left the room. Her head reeled

with all she'd learned, much more than she expected. To add to it, her stomach reeled with queasiness at the idea of visiting Thorndale and Lane. On a hunch, she dug the card Sean gave her out of her bag. Sure enough she read the law firm's logo written on the front. If she'd looked at it earlier, she would've recognized the names. The number on the back, however, was different. She guessed it might be Sean's personal phone. Her fingers itched to call it, but she restrained herself. This wasn't the right time. In fact, she knew that to give him any warning about who she was and why she was in Port Saint Joe was not a wise move.

As she left the building of Lane Developers, Mira opened her phone to call her own firm's office. "Hi, Janine. Is Rob in?" In a moment she heard a click as Rob picked up.

"So, how's sunny Florida? You've made time to visit the beach, I hope." Rob's voice crackled over the phone. "Or maybe you had the pleasurable opportunity to explore the garden and see Aunt Claire's prize roses?"

Once again she considered relaying the story of her mini crisis on Route 30, but in the next second dismissed the idea. "Ha-ha, funny. Listen, since this is a horrible connection, I'll make it brief. Do you know anything about a law firm located in Apalachicola named Thorndale and Lane?"

"Ah, I see you've made progress. That's Lane Developers' legal counsel. Did you speak with them yet?"

"No, but maybe a little background knowledge might help before I do pay a visit." Mira didn't add how she also wanted to know more about Sean Thorndale.

"Okay, well, I did check them out when Aunt Claire first mentioned them. They are flawless, Mira. No wonder Claire's lawyer has been up against a wall to fight this. I tried, but didn't find a smudge on their record. At the very least you should get honest answers from them."

Mira wasn't sure. Anyone who agreed to do business and rub shoulders with Bradley Lane couldn't be all that squeaky clean. As far as their snow-white reputation was concerned, Mira knew there were lots of ways to hide any unethical behavior.

"All right, thanks. Say, do you recall if your aunt ever mentioned meeting with Bradley? Or were all her dealings through the lawyer?"

"Good question. I believe she spoke with him on the phone once. But she refused to be in the same room with the man, claiming she'd never endure the stench. Or some words to that effect."

Mira chuckled. "Sounds like your aunt. Well, I want to snoop around some more. Maybe a few of the locals can offer a story or two. Which reminds me, did you know your aunt's place has a reputation for being haunted?"

"Haunted? Are you serious? I don't recall the family telling any ghost stories about the place. Where on earth did you find that out?"

"Oh, some lady I met at the Surf and Suds restaurant. She sells real estate and told me your aunt's place is part of a ghost tour that visits favorite local haunts. She claims it's all in fun. Seems strange Claire never mentioned it."

"Hmm. Maybe she doesn't know. She's pretty much of a recluse and hasn't socialized with her neighbors since Uncle Charles died. Just talks to those curiosity seekers who come around to see her garden and maybe learn a few tips on growing roses. I told her she should broaden her interests, maybe join a knitting club or play bingo."

"And what did she say?" Mira smiled and figured she knew the answer.

"She told me those things are for old people," he laughed.

"Yeah, that's what I figured. Okay, gotta go dig up some dirt." Mira tried to keep her voice light and cheery.

"Good luck, Mira. My aunt and I are counting on you," Rob finished and hung up the phone.

Mira sighed. She already felt enough pressure. Rob somehow added that much more. She needed a pick-me-up and caffeine wouldn't do. As she headed for her car, Mira decided to put on her suit and go for a swim. It was no more than a little past one. Plenty of time for the beach and some sunshine.

Chapter Five

"Tell me what I can use against her, Tanner. I don't care how lovely her rose garden is or that she's a sweet, little old lady," Bradley snapped. His patience wore thin and made his nerves brittle.

"Sorry, boss. I hate to see anything or anyone cause her harm, I guess."

"Harm her? That woman you think is sweet is costing me thousands of dollars every hour of every day. Now, what can you tell me?" Bradley paced back and forth in front of his desk.

"Okay, when I was on the job today, I managed to get away from the crew and sneak up to the kitchen window. The voices I heard made me think she had company, you know. But when I took a peek, I found her alone and it was like she talked to the air. No one around, but her. Weird, huh?"

"Leave your feelings out of this and stick to the details, okay?"

"Right. Anyway this was where it got more than a little strange. She carried on this odd conversation. First, she'd say something, wait a few seconds, laugh, and say something else. But when she spoke the name Charles, I began to understand." Tanner nodded.

Bradley stopped and stared at Tanner. The implication of what he told him sank in. "Are you sure? This is no time to make mistakes. I can't afford them."

Tanner nodded. "Oh yeah, I'm real sure. She said—and I can quote this word for word—she said 'Charles. What kind of trouble did you get us into? You never kept any secrets.' After that, she tilted her head, as if she waited for an answer.

"I tell you, it got really weird when she laughed and shook her finger at no one, before mumbling how she'd already checked the shed.

"Before long, she sat down and held her head in her hands. I swear when her shoulders shook, I wanted to crawl through that window and comfort her. I felt bad for her and…"

"Tanner!" Bradley snapped.

"Oh, sorry. Anyway she asked Charles to help her decide what to do next. Then she left the kitchen."

"That's all? You're sure?" Bradley struggled to keep his voice calm. Things were looking brighter. With a little push in the right direction, he could get the judge to order a psychiatric evaluation. No doubt, they would find her loonier than, well it didn't matter. It was the ace up his sleeve. And he'd use it, if need be.

"And the talk with the foreman I told you about." Tanner shook his head and laughed. "I sure like her spunk. *Her* beach, she called it. She wanted us off of *her* beach. And I worried she'd blow a cork when the foreman told her to back off and that the property belonged to you."

"A whole lot of good that will do her," Bradley mumbled. "Gwen will have your check at the desk. I put a bit extra in it. For your discretion."

Tanner nodded. "Lips are sealed. But I sure hope you don't do anything to hurt her, boss. I mean, she's such a…"

34

"Sweet little old lady. Yes, I heard you the first time. You can leave now. I have lots to do."

Bradley waited until Tanner closed the door. Pulling open the bottom drawer of his desk, he removed the book and made a few notations. He smiled. It turned out to be a profitable day after all.

Chapter Six

Mira lay on the beach contented with splashes of sunlight like a warm bath washing over her body. The waves lapped against the shore, and she almost tasted their saltiness. In the distance, a mother warned her child not to wander too far out into the water, and Mira listened to the voice become a fading echo.

"Ah, this is how you spend your time. I like the idea though. Relax on the beach; soak up some rays; maybe go for a swim; all the best of the Cape experience."

Mira jolted awake and squinted into the sunny sky with its tall shadow in the middle towering over her. "What?" she mumbled and then her breath caught as she heard a familiar chuckle.

"Glad to see you took my advice." Sean sat down next to her and brushed the sand off her shoulder.

Mira flinched and regretted it at once. He leaned away from her with a puzzled look.

"Sorry. You startled me. And, yes, I took your advice. Nice beach. Thanks." She hoped her voice didn't hint at the suspicion she felt. Besides his signature on the Peterson deal, she still couldn't think of any reason to doubt Sean Thorndale's character or motives. Yet, she remained conflicted.

"I'm glad you found the time. Say! Are you hungry? I'd love to take you to a great restaurant up the beach a ways. They serve the best king crab."

Mira found herself caught off guard with his unexpected offer. His confidence was both alluring and intimidating. She hadn't been on a date since her breakup with Alex...Or maybe she should admit it and call it what it truly was. Her *altercation*. The blowout, the shouting frenzy, and near physical altercation that pushed her to extreme action. She told herself everything resulted for a good reason. And her priority should be her career, not personal relationships. After all, the job consumed most of her energy and time.

This was different. By the end of the week she would be almost two thousand miles away, a safe, reasonable distance from any relationship. Besides, she felt it wise to learn all there was to about Sean. What was the expression? Keep your friends close, your enemies closer.

"Sure. I'm starved, and king crab sounds scrumptious."

****

The Sunset Coastal Grill was a quaint upscale restaurant situated on Port Saint Joe Bay. Sean asked the maître d' for a table outside on the deck.

"I figured this offers a nice view of the bay." Sean nodded toward the window.

"It's beautiful, the water, all those boats. How do you ever manage to get any work done living in a place like this?" It didn't occur to Mira until the words left her mouth. She fished for information, and it felt deceptive.

"Oh, I manage somehow. Need to pay the bills, you know." Sean motioned for the server's attention.

"And what is it that helps you pay the bills?" Mira

couldn't resist, no matter how sneaky it made her feel. She knew what he would say and prepared herself to act surprised.

"I'm a lawyer who dabbles in business and corporate law."

"No kidding? So am I! What a small world." Mira shook her head.

"That *is* a surprise. Two lawyers. I wonder if that's the attraction," Sean teased with a smile.

"Ha, very funny." The server came and took their orders. It gave Mira a chance to regroup her thoughts and decide how to play this. She had settled for the honest approach when Sean's next comment stopped her.

"Law for me added up to a logical choice. My uncle is a judge, my brother is a legal secretary, and my sister finished law school this summer. Runs in the family, you see."

An unknown detail nagged at Mira, underneath the surface where she felt the twinge of it, but not enough to identify it. "Do they all live and work around here? That's a lot of clout and power, I'd imagine."

"Oh, my brother lives in Georgia. My sister wants to specialize in political law and she's headed for Washington in the fall."

"And your uncle?" Mira's heart beat a little faster as the twinge became a lot stronger.

"Ah, yes, the famous municipal Judge Thorn. Odd, isn't it? Thorndale. Thorn. I guess a branch of the family decided to change their surname. And it wasn't mine."

Mira's heart sank like someone piled a stack of bricks on it. Thorn being Sean's uncle was a connection, which led right down one road and to one explanation. If the judge was on Bradley Lane's secret payroll, then it was possible Sean might be, too. All of a sudden, the idea of king crab was nauseating. Her insides performed a dance of flip flops.

"Sean, I've got to be honest with you. My stomach feels a bit touchy. Must've gotten more sun than I should," Mira explained with a genuine expression of misery, both physically and emotionally.

"Of course, Mira." Sean got up from his chair. "We can come back again later in the week, if you like. I'll take you back to the motel right away."

"No! I mean, it's just up the street. I can manage." Mira stood up. "You can go on with your meal. With a little rest I'll be good as new." She stepped backwards as she talked.

"If you're sure." The frown on his face matched the disappointment in his voice.

"It's fine. Maybe we can get together tomorrow," Mira called over her shoulder as she walked away. A far from subtle exit, but after their conversation and her discovery, she struggled to maintain a relaxed demeanor. In fact, she wanted to shout and ask what the hell he meant by cheating little old women out of their homes. That feeling from yesterday, the one she recognized as the start of attraction, turned sour.

Mira tried to keep a professional distance whenever she researched a case. This, however, presented a challenge. How was she to know when she met Sean Thorndale he'd be involved with Bradley Lane and the Peterson deal?

As she approached the front of her motel, Mira spotted the same man from yesterday who peered into her car. He entered the room next to hers.

"Great. The peeper is my next door neighbor." She stopped and waited across the street until he disappeared inside. Instead of going to her own room, she headed for her car. "Time to move on this case."

And it was. She headed east on Route 30, toward Claire Peterson's house.

Chapter Seven

"I don't care how you do it, but make sure she doesn't catch you following her. And I want a report from you every few hours. Got it?" Bradley ended his call with Sean. He then turned to speak to the contractor from Howell Excavation.

"All right, I think that covers it. The work orders will be ready by Saturday for you to start the excavation. I want the house leveled and the lot graded by next week. My schedule is tight with no room for delays."

"I'm still waiting on the soil report, but it should come in tomorrow. We'll be ready to move on Saturday. Don't worry about your schedule."

The two men shook hands before the contractor went out the door. Left alone in the room, Bradley found the time to think. He concentrated on what needed to be done. Mira Stanley presented a minor inconvenience, but she was still a problem. He'd found out after one day she didn't scare easily. Even so, he had a strong hunch she bought his story about Charles Peterson. He knew as long as she remained in Port Saint Joe to snoop into the Peterson case, she was a threat. And threats weren't acceptable. Though some might consider his actions callous, Bradley approached his business ventures with serious intent, and personal business was no exception. He walked over to his desk and pressed the intercom button.

"Gwen? Call Kyle's office. I need to speak with him. Then get a hold of Judge Thorn's secretary and see if the judge is free for lunch today." Bradley drummed his fingers on the desk while he waited for his brother. When Gwen buzzed his brother through, he grabbed the phone.

"I need you to do me a favor. I want you to research our lawyer from the north and find me something that will hurt. You get whatever I can use against her. Got it?" The call ended after a debate on whose turn it was to take their mother to lunch. Kyle lost, and it left a smug smile on Bradley's face when they hung up.

"Even the tiniest details make my day." He leaned back in his chair with his hands resting behind his head as he waited for Gwen's word on the judge.

Chapter Eight

Mira received at least one phone call from Sean on the way to Claire Peterson's place. She started to answer, but texted him instead. She didn't feel like talking. Not yet at least. Not until she talked to Claire and asked about Sean. Claire may have crossed paths with him at some point. A small chance, but still possible.

Want to sleep this off. Talk to you tomorrow.

She hoped he'd be satisfied and leave her alone for the day. Her breath held when the phone buzzed.

Good idea. If you need anything, let me know. And I promise it won't be king crab!

She smiled at the message.

"Dammit! Why is it when I meet a nice guy, complications threaten to ruin it?" She almost slammed the steering wheel again, but her hand froze when recalling yesterday's fender bender. She recognized the line of trees ahead and put on her signal light to turn. Thoughts about Sean Thorndale needed to wait until later.

****

"Hello, Mira. How nice to see you," Claire greeted and motioned Mira inside.

"I'm sorry I didn't call ahead, but what I want to talk about won't wait," Mira explained as she followed the elderly woman back to the kitchen.

43

"Oh? Well, I guess this calls for a fresh pot of tea. Will you join me? We can sit out on the patio. It's not uncomfortably sticky today."

Mira agreed and situated herself outside while her hostess busied herself with the tea. She sat and watched a couple of playful gulls fly back and forth. In the next second, they soared up into the sky and toward the ocean until they were tiny specks. It was then she caught sight of several men on the beach. She turned away when she heard the rattle of cups and the patter of Claire's feet.

"Who are those men, Claire?"

"I don't know, but they've been around for a couple of days, measuring something, I believe." Claire poured the tea into the cups.

"Did you speak to them? After all, it's your property." Mira grew curious, even suspicious.

"Yes. I did. When one of them started this way, I asked him why he trespassed on my land."

"And what did he say?" Mira admired the woman's tenacity.

"He remarked it wasn't my land any longer." Claire clutched at her cup, both hands tightly wrapped around it. "I must admit his words startled me. I haven't allowed myself to believe all this is real. To me it's been one horrible nightmare."

Mira wanted to comfort the woman with some encouraging news that might cheer her. However, her mind drew a blank. Instead she asked about Sean.

"I met a nice guy yesterday. He's a local. Such a coincidence. He's a lawyer who works for the same firm that handles Bradley Lane's business. Sean Thorndale's his name. Do you know him?" Mira let her cup pause in front of her lips and waited while Claire seemed to search her memory.

"Sean Thorndale...hmm...isn't he related to Judge Thorn?" Claire's eyes widened as if the idea of what she'd said surprised her.

"Yes, he is." Mira deflated at the reminder.

"Well, I can't recall ever meeting him, but I've heard talk about him."

"Oh? Like what?"

"I'd say gossip, some rumor about a falling out with his family. They're all lawyers and such, you know."

Mira nodded.

"By all accounts he fell into this heated argument with his father. This put such a strain on their relationship until they no longer spoke to one another. And of course there was that woman."

"Woman?" Mira's focus shifted.

"The woman they argued about," Claire explained while she poured more tea.

Mira sat, perplexed by her hostess's story. Claire managed to take some quick turns and left too much unsaid. "Okay. Who is she? And why argue about her?"

"I guess Sean and this woman—her name is Jessica—were married for no more than a few months when they announced their plans for a divorce. Everyone in his family was disappointed, not to mention embarrassed. Especially given the relationship Sean carried on with the Lane family."

Mira was interested to learn more, but the warning in her head to keep a professional distance echoed its reminder. "You mean Sean's decision whether to partner with Kyle Lane?"

"No, dear. Kyle Lane and Sean Thorndale became partners well before this happened. Of course, after the failed relationship with his wife, I'm surprised he stayed partners with Kyle."

"Why's that?" Mira leaned forward.

"It's understandable, I guess. I mean if your wife carried on an affair with your partner, how do you go to work every day and see his face, knowing all that? And to top it off, your partner goes on to marry the woman."

Mira nearly spit the tea out of her mouth, but choked on it instead.

"Oh, my. Are you all right? Let me get you a glass of water." Claire hurried into the kitchen.

Mira struggled to compose herself. This played out like a soap opera. And Claire was right. How did Sean manage to stay in the partnership? If she were him, she'd be behind bars for murdering the bastard. And his wife? She thought of several choice words to call her, but refused to waste her time. She engaged in a heavy dose of supposition at the moment, and it wasn't fair to Sean. If she confronted him with Claire's story, she might get answers. But was her motivation for professional reasons or personal ones?

"Let me ask you, Claire. Do you think Sean Thorndale is capable of being a party to cheating you out of your property? I mean, I know you don't *know* him, but you know of him."

"That wouldn't be fair of me to say, would it?"

Mira silently agreed. Most likely she tried to clear her own suspicions by putting all of it on Claire's shoulders. Not the right thing to do. She needed to bark up another tree. She'd pay a visit to Kyle Lane, but not before she spoke with the guys on the beach.

"I'll be just a minute." Mira walked off the patio. She approached the worker who stood off to the side and a short distance away from the others.

"Excuse me. Can you tell me what's going on here? You do know this is private property, right?" Mira kept her voice pleasant.

One of the other men heard Mira's comment and walked over. He held up a paper for Mira to see. "We're employed by Lane Developers. Here's the work permit, which allows us to take some measurements for excavation purposes. And this private property happens to belong to our employer."

Mira sensed the defensive attitude building. She tried to defuse it. "Sure. I understand. And when is this excavation and building supposed to happen?"

The one guy shrugged. "Soon, I guess. We only do the excavating. Lane contracts out most times with Howell's."

"Will they leave the house standing, do you know?" This time he shook his head.

"Big plans for this lot, along with a few next to it. I guess a professional complex will go up. You know, doctors, lawyers, and such."

Mira's brain kicked into gear and mulled over the possibilities. "Do you know if the law firm of Thorndale and Lane is one of the tenants?"

"Maybe. Don't know those kinds of details. Look, we need to get back to work. And tell Mrs. Peterson she can stop with the stares. We aren't going away."

Mira nodded and walked back to the house. It was obvious Bradley Lane planned to move ahead without expecting any setbacks to his deal. His smug, pompous attitude riled her. The satisfaction of taking him down torched in flames seemed the ultimate coup. She only hoped Sean Thorndale didn't burn along with him.

****

Mira finished her visit with Claire. When she got outside and approached her car, she stopped short. She bent down to get a better look and found the flat tire in the front. At this point, though common sense told her it was the paranoia talking, it didn't take much to suspect foul play. Not after the rear-ender incident. With hands on hips she glanced up and down the road but didn't spot any unusual or suspicious signs. Of course she had spent over an hour with Claire, which allowed plenty of time for someone to damage her tire. But why bother? Other than a minor nuisance and the work of a childish prank, what did it accomplish? If it was meant to discourage her, whoever did it, *if* someone did it, possessed no imagination and didn't know her very well.

She pulled the jack out of the trunk and placed it next to the wheel when the crunch of tires on the drive caused her to look up. At once, she recognized the man behind the wheel grinning at her.

"Great," she mumbled and put up a hand to wave at Sean Thorndale.

"What a coincidence. I was heading back to Apalachicola when I found this familiar car in the drive. Looks like you've got a flat." Sean bent down to take a look.

"Yes, hence the reason for the jack."

Sean laughed. "Yeah, I guess it is." He came over and held out his hand. "Why don't you let me take care of it? After all, you're not feeling too well."

Mira raised her brows and shrugged. She felt like a

kid caught in a lie and put in a corner for a timeout. What started out yesterday to show promise now played out like a bad dream. All she experienced when around him, for the most part, was uneasiness. Still, it wasn't all her fault. He was the one caught up in a shady deal.

When he finished replacing the tire, Sean placed the jack inside the trunk. "Anything else I can do for you? Or do you need to return to your nap?" A smile struggled to stay under the surface.

"Jeez, give it a rest, will you? I tried to sleep, but after a half-hour I…What? Why are you shaking your head?"

"You don't give up, do you, Mira Stanley? Why don't you admit you didn't go back to your motel room? You see, I found your room key on the ground outside the restaurant, right after I called you. I approached the maître d', but since my drive would take me past the motel, I decided to stop and drop it off there. I figured you might go to the manager for another key to get into your room. What a surprise when I found out you hadn't. Mira, if you didn't want to dine with me, you could have been honest about it."

The guilt rested like a heavy weight pressing down on her; the look of sadness on Sean's face was too much. Either she was the biggest pushover, or he was hurt by her actions. In either case, she refused to give in.

"Okay, I didn't sleep, but I did feel sick to my stomach." And not because of too much sunlight, she admitted to herself. "I didn't want to hurt your feelings after you ordered and I assume paid for such an expensive dinner. After all, a bright and cheery date I was not." She took a deep breath. She actually used the word date.

"Date, huh? Well, it's okay because you can make it up to me tomorrow. No, don't you shake your head at me. You owe me. I know a place over on Saint George Island. No seafood. Just plain old American cuisine. How about steak? And a baked potato? That should appeal to anyone's appetite. Say around five? I'll pick you up outside your door. No need for both of us to drive."

Mira tried to protest, but found no opportunity during his long-winded invitation. Instead, she smiled, a half-hearted effort, and waved as he backed out of the drive. How did she manage to get roped into dinner with someone she suspected? And why did the twinge inside of her return?

Muttering under her breath, she got into her car and headed back to the motel. A sudden realization made her swear. "Damn. What about my key?" Without caring she slammed her hand against the steering wheel once more. That man stirred her up in more ways than one, she admitted.

Chapter Nine

"No, she's still there…Yes, all afternoon. She left the restaurant early, claimed she didn't feel well, and then went straight to the motel," Sean explained on the phone as he drove.

"Are you sure she didn't go anywhere else? What about calls? Did she make any calls?" Bradley's anxious voice resonated through the receiver.

"How am I supposed to know? I'm not the telephone company." Sean was annoyed with Lane's questions. He approached the turn off to his office and slowed down. With nothing more to add, he wanted the conversation to end.

"Well, if she happens to mention anything worth checking into, you let me know. And try to keep her busy so she won't snoop around. I tell you, if she pumps Claire Peterson for information, that's a hornet's nest I won't have disturbed. Not without consequences. You understand?"

"Sure thing, Lane."

"And you better report back to me every few hours like I asked. Or your uncle will hear from me." Bradley's harsh words carried no hint of respect.

"Yes, sir. Now, I need to go take care of my clients, if you don't mind," Sean announced, not caring if the sarcasm was obvious. He ended the call before Bradley uttered another word.

He walked into the building and grabbed his mail out of the tray on the way into his office. As he shuffled through the envelopes he noticed one of them with a California postmark and Stedman Law on the return address. Another useless report, he guessed, and set it aside.

He went over to close the door and lock it. Once seated, he rubbed his eyes with the palm of his hands. How long he managed to dance to the tune of Bradley Lane's demands was anybody's guess, but it put a strain on him. He neared the breaking point. He pictured Mira's soulful green eyes and her sensuous smile. It made him want to quit the game. Quit and walk away. It wasn't worth the sacrifice. Not even for his family's sake. But who else would help? Besides, he felt a strong sense of chivalry toward Mira. He refused to leave her unprotected, subject to the devious ways of Bradley Lane who'd stop at nothing to carry out his agenda. No, the closer he stayed by her, the safer she'd be. This seemed clear enough. The sad part was, he admitted, he couldn't tell her the truth. Knowing placed her in danger.

When he added up the pros and cons, Sean knew he must keep to the plan, despite the obvious. To play on both sides grew more dangerous with each day. Bradley was too perceptive and too intelligent. It wouldn't take much longer before he discovered where Sean's loyalty lay. Yet, he'd made a silent promise to someone who was no longer able to carry out the deed. And when Detective Guárico made it clear nothing would get solved without someone on the inside, someone who tracked every one of Bradley Lane's actions, Sean knew he had no choice. No matter what the risk, he was in it until the end. After all, a promise was a promise.

Chapter Ten

Mira left the motel office with key in hand and let herself into the room. The temptation to go to sleep— for real this time—made her reconsider the next step. She wanted to visit Kyle Lane but suspected he'd be gone for the day. It was after six, and unless he was a workaholic, most likely he'd be at home, ready to wine and dine with Jessica, the two-timing ex-wife of Sean's.

When the knock on the door came, Mira never imagined the decision of whether or not to see Kyle Lane this evening was about to be made for her.

"Hello. Are you Miss Stanley?"

A gentleman who looked to be around sixty or so stood there. He held an envelope in his hand. Mira considered him a bit too old for playing messenger boy. "Yes, may I help you?"

"I have an invitation from the Lanes." He held out the envelope.

"Invitation to what?" Mira tore it open to read the contents. No doubt because of her recent thinking about Kyle Lane, she expected the message to be from him. As it turned out the delivery came from his wife, Jessica Lane. The invitation to a dinner party at the Lane house, tomorrow evening, with a few personal comments.

I hope you will come. Earlier at lunch, my brother-in-law mentioned to Kyle that you were in town. I wanted to somehow show you we Lanes can be hospitable; though I'm sure Bradley hasn't given you that impression. I'm afraid he can be sour and uninviting most of the time. I apologize for his behavior, and I do hope you will attend my party.

Until tomorrow…

Jessica Lane

Mira wasn't sure how to respond. The courier stood there waiting for her answer. Even though she didn't know the woman, she didn't like her. In fact, from what she knew about Sean and the way Jessica played him, Mira could say she despised her. How was she supposed to endure an entire evening in her presence?

Still, she agreed she might learn some things, information to help out Claire Peterson and put Bradley Lane and Lane Developers out of a deal. That proved worth spending a miserable evening at the Lanes. She scribbled some words on the RSVP card included with the invitation and handed it to the man.

"Good day, miss." He nodded before turning to leave.

Mira closed the door and laid the invitation on the table. "What in the world are you up to, Jessica Lane? Or maybe it's Bradley who put you up to this." In either case, she knew it was at least a way to learn more about her. Of course, it worked both ways as far as she was concerned.

She'd pay no visit to the Lane and Thorndale law office this evening. With time on her hands, she opted to visit the town library. A quick history lesson on the Peterson property might lead to something more than ghost stories.

****

The Port Saint Joe library was no more than a large room with several shelves of books and two computers, which from appearances looked like they were pioneered in the eighties. Mira wished she'd brought her laptop along. Being in such a hurry, she left the motel room without it. Within seconds, she found the local history section and scanned the titles. Nothing snagged her attention or interest until the words *Florida's Best: Scandalous Stories of the Murderous, Mysterious, and Famous.* Mira gave it a skeptical eye but lifted the thick volume off the shelf and went to find a comfortable chair and began reading.

After a few minutes and several pages, she was disappointed but not surprised. Not a single detail about the Peterson estate was mentioned. As the title suggested, the information read like gossip more than fact. The contents involved stories based on numerous accounts provided by local residents, even some relatives who no doubt wanted their moment in the limelight, and from snippets in the newspaper society page. Still, it was all she managed to find. She scanned through the index and hoped one of the entries might prove useful. Her finger trailed down the column and stopped halfway.

"Well, I'll be," Mira exclaimed in a low tone. The words Lane and scandal on one line stood out like a neon sign to grab her attention.

The subject covered close to ten pages, but it was the first few sentences that gave her enough curiosity to devour the entire entry in minutes. It suggested Bradley and Kyle Lane's father maintained quite the reputation with the ladies before as well as *after* his marriage. Their mother, Curtis Lane's wife, always ignored his extracurricular activities. The source claimed her behavior was an acceptable compromise since Mrs. Lane profited from an estate worth tens of millions. Whatever her reasons for staying with Curtis, it all ended after Bradley and Kyle went away to college.

Mira struggled to believe the next part of the story. With more soap opera antics, the story wove an incredible web. An employee who worked as a concierge for a local hotel claimed Curtis Lane frequented the establishment with different women. However, he remembered one woman in particular. Lane's ongoing companion, Lois Thorn, was the sister of Judge Thorn. And as Mira realized, she was Sean's aunt.

The article's informant continued to elaborate on how some claimed the affair between Curtis and Lois carried off and on for a period of several years. When Vivian Lane discovered their lengthy liaison, she worried she might lose Curtis and all his millions. Vivian might regard Curtis as disposable, but not all those millions. She wouldn't give up a penny and she threatened Curtis with a scandalous divorce. She planned to walk away with everything he owned and make sure everyone knew about Lois and all his other affairs. She would make certain he lived out the rest of his days poor and miserable.

Mira flipped the page, anxious to find out more. Claire, not even Nadine, mentioned any of this, and again, it made her doubt whether any of it was credible. The next account came from someone who worked many years as a maid for the Lanes and who managed to overhear the most shocking stories. Divorce was exactly what Curtis wanted. He fell deeply in love with Lois and wanted to marry her. At least he felt this at first. The one problem, besides coping with the vindictive Vivian, was Lois didn't love Curtis. What Mira learned next made Sean's ex-wife look like an angel in comparison. During the affair, Lois Thorn recorded every detail about the Lane business and fortune.

Mira's eyes grew wider still as she read a story told by a close friend of Lois. She confided in her friend about her meetings with Curtis who tended to wag a loose tongue while in bed. She'd ask him questions about the business, flattered and coaxed him with comments about how fascinating it all was. She squirreled away all the important facts—the stock investments, the business deals, the what, where, and when of everything. Somehow she managed to obtain account numbers to foreign investments put away in various banks. With that information she managed to pilfer more than ten million dollars from the Lane estate. She invested every penny into European market accounts where Curtis could never get to it, if and when he discovered her thieving scheme.

Mira put down the book for a minute to rest her eyes. The implications were mind-blowing. Though it equated to a gossip rag, at least some of it must stem from the truth. And with such a history together, it came as no surprise the Lanes, Thorns, and Thorndales were connected. Like a den of thieves, Mira imagined they held many grimy details on each other, none of them able to turn his back and walk away. Despite her reservations, she had sympathy for Sean. He seemed like such a nice guy for someone with all those skeletons in his closet. Her thoughts about Sean were interrupted by the reminder that the title of the book was about murder. She hadn't read of anyone being murdered. Yet.

Another friend wrote her own account of Lois's final days in Port Saint Joe and the bittersweet love story. It was based on a letter she had received from Lois who by this point could only vent her anger about how badly events were turning. As Vivian pursued her threat of divorce, Curtis found the push he needed. In a brave effort he became courageous and asked Lois to marry him. However, Lois said no. In fact, she laughed in his face and told him she would never marry such a cheating, disloyal man. Curtis reeled from her cruel rejection. Stung with hurt, he became angry and bitter.

Soon after, Lois made a foolish mistake, according to the friend's account. After all her careful planning to steal close to ten million dollars of Curtis Lane's money, she stumbled. She despised how he shouted at her with his pompous attitude and words. Lois blurted out how he may be rich, but she was, too. And that was her undoing. With a bit of investigating, Curtis figured out her scheme, and with his connections and unscrupulous means, he managed to get all the money back into his greedy hands.

Mira went on to read that after the blowout between them, Lois Thorn disappeared from town. Most everyone believed she fled to Europe to be with her millions. However, a few couldn't help suspecting that Curtis Lane murdered his lover out of revenge and dumped her in the Gulf ocean waters. They found no proof, of course. Curtis and Vivian stayed married, though it was a bitter, cold relationship. Curtis died a short time later, leaving Vivian with the millions she cherished. And Lois Thorn had never been heard from or seen by anyone since.

Mira sat back and emitted a soft whistle. She found the whole story unbelievable, until she considered all the players. Bradley Lane was unscrupulous. And with that genetic line, why not Curtis Lane? As for Lois, Mira figured if she asked around town, someone might know more. The book was published five years ago. The name given as editor: Stanley Thomas. A local resident? And Mira wondered if someone had seen or heard from Lois Thorn recently.

She knew where her mind led her. She didn't want to go to him, but the opportunity presented itself in a neat, little package. If she asked the right questions, she might learn all about Lois Thorn from her nephew. The one she had arranged a date with tomorrow. Mira sighed. Fate kept bringing them together, no matter how much her suspicions told her to stay away.

While she continued to study the cover, Mira got up from her chair and moved toward the local history section once more. She traveled only a few steps before bumping into someone.

"Oh! Sorry, I didn't see you," Mira exclaimed as she looked up. Her eyes widened when she recognized the same man who'd been looking in her car. The peeper. He scowled at her without uttering one word.

"You." She backed away several steps.

"Why don't you look up when you're walking? Most people do, you know," he snapped.

His attitude put her on the defensive. "Well, why don't you keep your nosy self out of other people's business? Like the inside of my car, for instance."

The man's face turned from annoyed to angry. Maybe he didn't know who she was. "The motel? My Mazda? You were looking inside when I caught..."

"Look, I told you it was a mistake. Give it a rest, lady."

He was back to being annoyed, but hurried away before saying more. Still, Mira mumbled a few unkind words he probably didn't hear. Feeling exhausted after the day's events, she elected not to spend any more energy on the unpleasant encounter. Go back to the motel room, take a long hot shower, and get into bed, she told herself. That seemed a wiser choice. With lots to do tomorrow she wanted to be well rested.

****

Mira failed to concentrate on anything but the story of the Lane and Thorn families. She had gone to the library to find out information that helped with the Peterson case. Instead, she opened a different can of worms and failed to determine if the Lane scandal was in the least bit useful. An affair between Curtis Lane and Lois Thorn revealed very little. Mira felt deflated. She needed evidence, but where to look?

She pulled into the parking lot, grabbed her things and went inside the room. A moment's glance as soon as she flipped on the light switch told her something was out of place. Mira walked from one end of the small bedroom to the other. She checked her luggage, and then moved on to the bathroom where she made the same careful search.

As soon as she re-entered the bedroom she stopped. Her eyes darted to the table where her laptop sat with the lid open. Mira hadn't left it that way. She was sure of it. Taking quick, long strides, she reached the table in seconds. The tiny green glow of light told her the computer was on. She pushed down on the enter key and the screen lit up.

"Mind your own business, or somebody might get hurt." The words were typed in large, bold letters across the screen. Mira let out a small gasp. She reached over to the nightstand and in a minute had her phone in hand. Her thumb paused over the keys. Who should she call? She dialed the manager, first.

"Hi. This is Mira Stanley in room 215. Did you happen to see anyone go near my room this evening? Or maybe someone asked about me?"

"Nope. Can't say I did." The words came out in a yawn.

If he'd been sleeping, how could he know? "Well, someone's been in my room and gone through my things. I'm going to call and report it to the authorities."

That seemed to get his attention. He protested and told her there was no need to involve the police. Mira suspected he was afraid of an insurance claim or bad publicity.

"Nothing was stolen. At least I'm fairly certain. But someone got into my laptop and wrote a threatening message. Are you sure you didn't notice anyone?" Mira hoped to get a better answer this time.

"Well, come to think of it, a guy stopped by to ask about you earlier today."

"Oh? Did you recognize him? Maybe know him from somewhere?"

"Sure do know him," he answered, his voice lifted, sounding pleased.

Mira smiled. *Bingo, we've got him.* "Then we can

get the police to question him. What's the name?" Mira waited.

"Sean Thorndale. He wanted to know if you were in and what room 'cause he found your key. Sounded kinda fishy, if you know what I mean."

Mira's elation sank right back down. She'd forgotten Sean stopped by the motel, and it left her still wondering who wanted to do her harm. "No, it's okay. He's a friend, sort of. Anyone else you can recall?"

"Nope. That's it. But if I think of someone, I'll let you know. Ah, ma'am?"

"Yes? What is it?" Mira was ready to get off the phone. She needed to make her next move.

"Are you still going to call the police?"

"Oh, for Pete's sake," she muttered and hung up the phone.

It took less than a minute to convince the Port Saint Joe police to send an officer over to take her statement and check out the computer, and another five minutes until he arrived. She wasn't certain if he believed her story or not. He gave a suspicious stare at her computer and questioned if maybe she typed those words herself and had forgotten about it.

"Okay, let me get this straight. You think I typed the words to myself, threatening myself. Does that sound right?"

The officer nodded. "It's possible, isn't it?"

"No. It's not possible. In fact, that's so impossible, it's downright ridiculous," she snapped. "Now, do you plan to investigate? Someone just threatened me."

He shut his pad of paper along with her report and shoved it into his pocket. "Yep, of course that's what I'll do. It's my job. If any more incidents occur, be sure to call the precinct. And we'll be in touch if anything develops." He tipped his hat and left the room.

Alone now, her mind started to work. Mira couldn't decide if she was more angry or scared. She leaned toward angry. And curious. Her poking around had worried someone enough to threaten her, which meant she was closer to the truth. She simply needed to figure it out.

She picked up her cell phone and called the office. Janine left work every day by this time; however, she knew Rob's habits. He worked too hard, and too many hours spent away from home left him a divorced man.

"Hey! If it isn't my favorite female lawyer calling from sunny Florida," Rob sang out in his cheery voice.

"I'm your only female lawyer, you putz. How are things?" Mira smiled. She missed him more than she expected and a sudden desire for home overcame her. A long pause silenced the moment before he answered. Mira frowned. "Rob?"

"Since you ask…someone has been calling every day looking for you."

Mira gripped the phone as her heartbeat picked up speed. "I hope you didn't…"

"Of course not. Everyone in the office knows the drill. That psycho ex of yours will get squat from us." The defensive edge to his voice was evident.

Mira cringed at hearing the name "psycho." Alex once had a gentle side, but later the meaner, angrier, and plainly out-of-control personality surfaced and refused to go away. "Thanks," she whispered, ashamed of what she failed to recognize in the beginning. When they claimed love is blind, Mira knew firsthand how dangerous that could be.

"Don't you worry, Mira. He can't touch you. I won't let him."

She detected the protective edge to his voice. She didn't want anyone else to be hurt by this. Especially not Rob. "I'm not worried. He's in the past. Besides, after one phone call he'd be behind bars in seconds." She forced the confidence into her voice.

"Good. We've gotten that ugly business out of the way. How are things going with you?"

Mira knew he meant to hint at the well-being of his aunt Claire. She also realized he cared for the elderly woman and would do anything to protect her. If it came to that, he'd fly down to Florida in a moment's notice. Mira simply needed to ask. But she wouldn't. Not yet.

"Not bad. I came across some juicy gossip on the Lane family. The father of Bradley and Kyle wore a roaming eye when it came to women, I guess."

"That *is* interesting. Maybe we can somehow manage to use the information to blackmail Lane into giving back Aunt Claire's property."

Mira bounced up from her seat. "You might be on to something, Robert." Excitement welled in her chest.

"Mira, I was kidding. Blackmail isn't what we do. Not even for family."

"It is if you're in Bradley Lane's family." Mira paced across the room.

"What?"

"What if the Lanes were being blackmailed? I mean, Curtis Lane's lover, Lois, tried to blackmail him. People blackmail people all the time. And sometimes they are successful, but sometimes they may end up with nothing but a bundle of troubles."

"Lois? I think you've lost me. Is this something

that will help Claire? If it is, you should get on it right away."

"You're right. I have lots to do. And we're quickly running out of time." Mira regretted her words as soon as they left her mouth. She hadn't wanted to mention the excavation plan. Rob couldn't do anything about it anyway.

"Running out of time? Of course, we are. I'm sure Lane has plans for the property, and soon as he can, he'll develop it. He's like the blitzkrieg of the construction world."

"Yes, well, since you mentioned it, he has plans to tear down the house as soon as next week."

"Then you better get out there and see what you can do. I'm counting on you, Mira."

"Yes, I know." Her shoulders slumped as she told him goodbye. All she wanted was to climb into bed and sleep, but common sense told her it wouldn't come without trouble. She'd toss and turn, worry about Claire Peterson, think about her date with Sean Thorndale, and fret over all the possible outcomes haunting her about that dinner party with the Lanes. No, it was destined to be a poor night for sleep.

As Mira slipped into bed and pulled up the covers, she heard her phone buzz with a text message. It was from Sean, saying how he looked forward to tomorrow. Mira sighed and wished she felt the same.

Chapter Eleven

Morning came with sunlight peeking through the window and resting its rays on Mira's cheeks. One look at her watch told her she'd slept later than she wanted and better than she expected. After throwing on her clothes and running a brush through her hair, she decided on a quick visit to the donut shop she'd passed by earlier. Coffee and a cream stick would hold her for a couple of hours, even if it wasn't healthy. She needed to hurry and do some more sleuthing before lunch with Sean.

As Mira got into her car, her phone rang. A strong hunch hinted it was Sean. However, she was surprised.

"Hello, Miss Stanley. I hope you don't mind my calling."

It was Nadine Wiggins. Mira recognized the deep, husky voice. She had forgotten they exchanged numbers. "Hi, Nadine. And please, call me Mira."

"All right, Mira. I won't keep you long, but something you mentioned the other day got my attention and hasn't let go."

"Oh? What's that?"

"Claire Peterson and Bradley Lane."

Mira sat up straight in her seat. "Yes. I asked if you knew anything about them."

"And I told you what I was able to think of at the time. But since then, I kept having this little twitch in the back of my mind. You ever get one of those? It bugs the hell out of me, such a nuisance. Anyway, I kept thinking, until it hit me. I did a little digging in my files. I keep files from years back. A real pack rat is what I am."

"Nadine?"

"Oh, yes. My reason for calling. I found a detail about the two of them, which might interest you."

"Oh?" Mira hoped it wasn't information she already found.

"I guess it's newsworthy. You'll be the judge. It seems I was wrong. Claire Peterson's husband sold the property when he put it on the market several years ago, but the deal fell through."

"Does your information explain why?" Mira didn't remember Claire mentioning any deal Charles made. That by itself seemed odd.

"It doesn't, but I do have a name. A friend of mine, Glenda, who works at another agency, keeps me in the loop. She lets me know about their sales and such."

"And she gave you the name?" Mira urged. Nadine possessed a true agent's gift of gab.

"Oh, sorry. I tend to run on too much when I'm excited. The name of the buyer was Jason Thomas."

"Jason Thomas." Mira wondered why this Jason Thomas backed out of the deal.

"Yes. I'm sorry I can't tell you any more than that, but I figured the name might help."

"Yes, Nadine. Thanks." At once, Mira added, "Didn't you also mention Bradley Lane?"

"Oh! Almost forgot. This may not be much. It's a news article from the society page. Let me see, hmm... here it is. It says Bradley Lane and the Lane estate donated ten million to the Peterson charity foundation."

"I didn't know a Peterson foundation existed," Mira commented.

"Being the prima horticulturist, Claire Peterson thought of this brilliant idea to host an annual event, which would reach out to all of Florida. Growers from the Keys to the Panhandle came to enter their prize flora. I tell you, the entry fees brought in a million or more every year. Afterward, Claire and Charles donated the proceeds to local charities. Sad to say, it no longer exists. I believe Claire Peterson had to dissolve it after her husband's death. Or perhaps she lost interest. Whatever the reason, it's curious Lane did that, don't you think?"

"I'll say. From what Claire tells me, her husband found no kind words to comment about Bradley Lane. What pushed Lane to donate money?" Mira wondered aloud.

Of course, Nadine didn't have the answer. The possibility of Lane buttering up Peterson to get his property seemed more probable than an act of generosity. He didn't seem the philanthropic type.

"Did you make time to kick back and relax yet? I'll bet you haven't. You seem the eager-to-get-things-done type. Am I right?" Nadine laughed in her husky voice.

"It just so happens I'm meeting someone for lunch and then attending a dinner party this evening." She sounded more enthused than she felt.

"Good for you, Mira. Well, I better let you go. You've got a busy day ahead of you. Maybe you can work me into your agenda somewhere and we can do lunch again. This time I'll take you to my favorite seafood spot."

"Sounds nice. I'll be staying until the end of the week, I think. I'll give you a call when I'm free."

Mira hung up and headed her car in the opposite direction. After the conversation with Nadine, it was more urgent than ever to talk with Claire Peterson and ask about Jason Thomas. With any luck, she might shed light on his story. Maybe she'd get the opportunity to speak with him, if Claire knew anything, that is.

****

"Hmm...Let me think a moment. I'm sure something will come if I..." Claire wrinkled her forehead and drummed her fingers on the table.

Mira didn't feel too confident. When she arrived earlier, no one answered the doorbell. After a peek in the front window, Mira understood why. Claire sat in the living room, staring at a painting on the wall. The look in her eyes seemed dreamy, as if her mind carried her somewhere far away. Mira tapped on the glass and got the woman's attention. Claire glanced her way and looked at Mira as if she were a stranger. A few seconds later, she smiled and hurried to let her in.

"Jason Thomas. Wasn't he the man who lived a couple doors down from us?" Claire asked, situated on the sofa once more while Mira found a place in the chair across from her. The older woman stared into space and directed her question to no one in particular.

Mira puzzled over the strange behavior because each time Claire voiced her thoughts aloud, she kept her eye on the painting over the fireplace.

"No? Well, was he the one who visited the club and golfed on the league? Perhaps..." Claire placed a finger to her lips.

Mira had the distinct impression Claire Peterson

completely forgot she was in the room, yet she carried on a conversation with herself. At least it's what Mira figured until the elderly lady's next comment.

"Charles says Mr. Thomas did belong to the club, and he offered to buy our home when we put it on the market. However, the deal fell through."

Mira's mouth dropped open. She was stunned into silence.

"Oh dear, I'm so sorry. I forget this shocks people. Yes, I do speak to my husband. And strangely enough, he answers. I don't know how, but we can hear each other. Odd, isn't it?" Claire chuckled and turned to stare at the painting once more.

Mira's eyes followed, and she finally spotted the large gold urn on the mantel. She nodded toward it. "Is that your husband's, ah...?"

"Yes, dear. That is my sweet Charles. I wanted him to be with me for the rest of my days, you understand."

"Of course." Uncomfortable, Mira focused her thinking on Jason Thomas instead. "Did you hear anything about that deal later on? For instance, if your husband contacted or met with Mr. Thomas, maybe said something about him? Perhaps he mentioned seeing him at the club?"

"No, I'm afraid not. You see, Jason Thomas died not too long after from a heart attack. I do remember that. I'll admit I can't escape this terrible habit all elderly people seem to possess. I look through the obituaries every day. Many of my close friends or acquaintances have passed on. I go to pay my respects, if it's someone close, you understand." Claire gave Mira a wizened look. Her eyes reflected the tired fear of mortality and an unfamiliar future.

Mira stood and walked over to sit down next to Claire. "How about some tea? I know my way around your kitchen. I'll brew you some."

"That's nice, dear. Yes, I'll drink a cup." Claire smiled.

"All right. I do have one more question, though. Do you happen to know why Bradley Lane donated ten million to the Peterson Foundation?"

In an instant, Claire's eyes lit up, as if awakened from a trancelike depression. "Yes! I do remember. Charles was furious at the time. He endured a constant battle with Lane Developers over property to be used to build a hospital for cancer patients. Lane wanted to build a shopping complex. Somehow, Bradley Lane managed to work his evil dealing, and the property became his. My Charles wanted Judge Thorn and Lane Developers investigated for fraud. The police wouldn't touch it. After that, Charles hired a lawyer. We spent so much." Claire's voice trailed off.

"And did you win?" Mira waited while Claire shook her head.

"No. It's funny, but he changed his mind. As if it came out of the blue, Charles stopped fighting. He told me the case was impossible, and we couldn't afford to keep the lawyer any longer."

A sudden notion came to Mira. "Was this before or after your husband put the house up for sale?"

"The battle with Lane? A few months before, I believe. The lawyer fees got expensive. We didn't want to lose everything. Of course, things changed and we didn't need to sell after all. It's funny how things work out sometimes."

Like a prickly thorn, something tried to get Mira's

attention, a detail which didn't make sense, wanting to correct itself. "And where do the ten million in donations come into the story?"

"That's the funny part that worked out! When Lane donated to the foundation and gave Charles the credit for persuading him to do so, the director of the cancer wing at the hospital in Apalachicola paid our lawyer fees as a way of appreciation."

The pieces were falling into place. Mira wasn't surprised. An unscrupulous villain like Lane didn't change his colors. To get Charles off his back, he must have made the donation. Besides that, it wouldn't surprise Mira if he paid the lawyer fees.

"Let me get you that tea, Mrs. Peterson." Mira patted the woman's hand before heading for the kitchen.

Chapter Twelve

Firehouse 9 Bar and Grill was located on Saint George Island. Mira stared out the window while Sean drove on the four mile bridge over the Gulf. She worried her suspicions caused an awkward beginning to their date. She couldn't be her usual talkative self, not without asking what was actually on her mind. Each time she got close, her lips froze into a smile. *He must think you're an idiot.*

"You sure you don't want to say something? Like how beautiful the ocean is? I don't think you've mentioned that." A grin spread across his face.

Mira loved the way he looked when he smiled, his mouth somewhat crooked with one corner higher than the other. And his dimple on the left side. She laughed. "No, I think I covered the ocean, several times. Anyway, sorry. I'm too distracted with this case I'm investigating. Got a lot on my mind. You see, I need to find out why some guy cheated my client out of her property."

"Gee, that's too bad. Anything I can do to help? Being a local has its advantages."

Mira shuddered. They both played their parts well; anyone watching would believe their stories. Nevertheless, it was time to do a little fishing. "I can't think of anything right now, but maybe—oh, wait! Have you heard of Bradley Lane of Lane Developers?"

She gauged his reaction carefully.

His hands blanched as they gripped the wheel tighter. "Yes, I know him. He happens to be one of our firm's clients. Why?" He gave her a quick side glance and then returned his focus to the road.

Of course he told her the truth, she reasoned. He figured she already knew about Bradley Lane. He wanted her to trust him.

"Oh? I didn't realize. Well, this is awkward," she said with a shrug. The car slowed to a stop as they reached the island and the Firehouse 9 parking lot.

Sean leaned over. "Okay, let's be honest, Mira." He spoke in a low tone. "We both realize you know very well who I am. Lane told me you asked about my signature on the Peterson contract."

This was not what she expected. Somehow she sensed relief. She hated being deceitful, especially with people she liked. She tried not to let her feelings cloud her judgment, but it proved to be a losing battle. Maybe if she learned the answers to the questions playing pinball in her head she'd feel better about it.

"Fine. What *is* your relationship with Lane?"

"Which one?"

"Bradley. Because I must tell you, I don't like him, don't trust him, and any friend of his is…" Mira shrugged her shoulders.

"Fair enough. I get it." He chuckled. "Let's say it's an acquaintanceship. We do business, but don't socialize. That goes against my principles."

"Principles? Don't your principles warn you not to trust people like Bradley Lane?" Mira tried to keep the sharp tone from her voice.

"I don't try and change things I can't control. My

partnership with Kyle Lane means Bradley Lane is part of the picture. Get it?"

"I get that part, but as you said, let's keep it honest. How could you sign a bogus contract? The Peterson deal was in no way legal."

"To tell you the truth, I don't remember signing it. Believe me." He reached over to touch her hand.

She pulled away. "Okay, maybe you don't, but I believe it's bogus. From what I've heard, Bradley Lane makes a habit of unscrupulous dealings. And with Judge Thorn to sign anything Lane wants, Lane Developers can't lose. Of course, I suppose you'll deny knowing that, too. Isn't Thorn your uncle? Kind of hard not to know when your relative is in bed with sleazy scum like Lane." The words shot out in short, quick jabs. She was quickly losing her appetite and interest in Sean's company.

"Look. I'm not my uncle's bodyguard. I couldn't stop him if I tried. It doesn't mean I always agree with what he does. Or what Bradley Lane does. What I do know is I would never cheat someone out of their property. I wouldn't sign a contract that wasn't legal. You can believe me or not. Your choice. But I hope you do believe, because I can be your greatest ally, if you let me." Sean grew silent and once more with a slow, tentative move he reached out to touch her hand. She didn't move this time.

Mira nodded and didn't speak for a while. They went inside the restaurant and ordered a steak dinner. After the seafood fiasco, it was a welcome relief. They began their meal in silence, but Mira needed to say something. The quiet was torture.

"I want to believe you. I need to," she confessed

with sadness in her eyes.

Sean studied her face for a short time. "I suspect you're struggling with that, aren't you?"

Mira sensed his disappointment. Maybe he was hurt by her doubt. Yet, what was she to do? Force herself to trust him? Not without more, something they forgot to discuss or bring to the surface, which might help put her at ease.

"You claim to hold a professional obligation for all your clients. I feel the same way, but I draw the line at corruption. I won't cover or condone any client who practices unethical standards knowingly. Nor should you."

Sean shook his head. "Who says Bradley Lane does that? I can't find any evidence of his business performance being anything but shrewd and aggressive attempts to close his deals. All those rumors about him bribing my uncle are nothing but pure conjecture, in other words, bullshit." He set his fork down on his plate and cupped one hand under his chin. "Like I told you, I've committed no wrong. I may not like Bradley Lane, but he is our client. Kyle may deal with him directly, but I'm aware of all his client activity as he is with mine." He leaned across the table and reached for her hand once more.

"Mira, I like you. In fact, I like you more than a little, if that's possible in the short amount of time I've spent with you. And I respect your feelings. But can't we put this aside and enjoy our time together? Like this lunch, for instance?"

Again, the charming, sweet look and seductive voice of his struck her. Like a magic spell, Mira was drawn into it. She relaxed and smiled at him. "Okay.

I'll call a truce, but you should decide whether you, in fact, believe Bradley Lane is honest, or if maybe you are turning a blind eye because it's convenient. No, I see you want to argue, but don't. I only ask you to consider the possibility. And if you still come up with the same answer, so be it. I'll accept it." Mira looked down at her plate. "Finally, I can eat. And this steak is delicious. How long did you say this place has been here? I adore the view."

The next hour or so passed with a great meal and pleasant conversation. Mira found Sean to be not only attractive, but also witty and intelligent. Not just book intelligent, but street wise, too. She learned though he had both a father and a mother, he was left a lot on his own. For the first several years of his childhood, before his parents became successful and able to move elsewhere, Sean's neighborhood was rough. He'd learned at a young age to defend himself in the only way his underdeveloped, small frame managed: with words.

"I charmed my way out of every problem with any thug or gang member who backed me into a corner. It became quite the art form. It's no wonder I was drawn to become an attorney. To this day, I get an adrenaline rush in the courtroom when I defend a client. Business law doesn't give me the meatier cases, like murder for instance, but I make the best of it."

Mira nodded. "I can see that. I guess you don't find much time for a personal life?" She remained discreet and didn't mention how she knew about his ex-wife, but at the same time hoped her question might get him to discuss his brief relationship. But she was disappointed.

"Nope. Not much. Of course, when a pretty lady such as you comes along, I make time." He teased her with his engaging smile.

"Seriously, your attraction toward me is probably based on the fact that in a few days I will be a thousand miles away." She narrowed her eyes at him in a challenge to deny it.

"Right. That's my sole agenda." He laughed. "If you knew me better, you wouldn't suggest that. But since you did, how about you? Is that why you agreed to this date?"

"No, of course not," Mira defended.

"Ah. I think you jumped on that one maybe a little too fast." Sean raised his brows and held his lips together.

"You are a troublemaker, Sean Thorndale. I can see that much." Mira pointed her fork at him. "I'm not afraid of a relationship, if that's what you're suggesting." She protested but her stomach rippled and turned as she tried to block out thoughts of Alex.

"No?" He let his mouth relax and form a smile.

"No. In fact, I've recently gotten out of a long-term relationship," she explained.

"Oh? And why is that, if I'm not intruding." Sean brought his hands up to rest under his chin.

Mira chewed on her bite of steak to give herself time to make a decision. At last, she lowered her fork onto the plate and shrugged her shoulders. "We didn't see eye to eye on the important things, I guess."

Sean nodded, his expression transposed to a serious one. "Good to find out before making that final commitment. A lot less hurt."

Mira studied his face as Jessica Lane came to mind

and how much hurt she may have caused Sean. And at that instant, Mira sensed how much she liked him. The idea of it scared her more than a little. She forced a smile and shrugged her shoulders once more. "It's okay. I'm not hurting as much any longer."

"I'm glad because I'd hate to see a good steak meal go to waste," Sean quipped. "Certainly not over ex-boyfriends. And I must say he's one stupid man to break up with you."

"Hey! Who said *he* broke up with *me*?" Mira scowled. When Sean laughed, she tossed her napkin at him. "Very funny." All at once, her mood lifted, and warmth filled her to replace the cold uneasiness from before.

****

The date ended with Sean leaving Mira outside the motel room door. The buildup of tension on the trip back had troubled her. She knew it came from an obvious source, that anticipation of a goodbye kiss. She didn't know what to expect or how she would respond. Her feelings were conflicted as the person who sat next to her managed to be friendly and so engaging. She couldn't keep that bothersome voice in the back of her head away for long. It persisted with its warning that not everything was as it seemed. Still, she liked Sean, couldn't help but like him. She forced that feeling to stay with her as they said goodbye.

"Well, it's been nice, Mira Stanley. I enjoyed your company despite the unpleasant conversation about your view of my partner's notorious brother. But we won't go into that again."

His words touched her face with short brushstrokes of his breath as his face came within inches of hers.

Closer and closer. And each inch pushed her heartbeat to race faster and faster. "Um-hmm," she answered, since her thoughts refused to form into words.

"And I hope you feel the same way," he whispered and came closer, backing her against the door.

Mira saw only parts of him, but she focused on his lips as they brushed against hers, his voice drowned out by the pounding of her heart. Yet, when he touched her, the beating stopped. His kiss made her stop everything and focus on one subject. That kiss. And whether foolish thinking or not, she wanted it to last forever.

****

Mira took a shower and thought of Sean. She dressed and pictured his smile. She put on her jewelry and makeup and felt the warmth of his kiss. And it frustrated her.

"Dammit, Mira, stop." It wasn't relationship issues. Sean misinterpreted that one. However, she might confess to the insane knack of falling, without the slightest hesitation, head over heels for the wrong guy. It impaired her judgment and was unlike her. In the work place they called her the barracuda. She was scrupulous in her research and a brilliant litigator in the courtroom. She went to the heart of the case and attacked the jugular. She hadn't lost a case since her second year of practice. That's why she'd make partner earlier than anyone she knew.

If only she acted that way when making decisions about her personal life. Yet, she was the one who always got her heart broken, or in this last situation, her heart bruised and battered. She shivered at the memory of those details, that frightening night when Alex made his final attempt to keep her in their relationship.

Afterward, it left her alone and leery of any intimate moment. Now, after one day, Mira sensed that she and Sean shared something that, contrary to reason, brought them closer. They'd both experienced broken hearts. It was a wonder they tried speaking to the opposite sex.

"Well, *he* seems to be over it and doing fine," she muttered and finished putting on her earrings. At least one good thing was true. She glanced at her phone to make sure. Alex hadn't called in over twenty-four hours. Maybe he'd given up. She certainly hoped it was true.

Less than an hour to get to the dinner party left her anxious. She didn't want to arrive late. The idea of walking into a room full of the Lanes and their friends, who all stared at her, was enough to make her stay in the motel room. Still, she needed to go for Claire's sake as well as for Rob's. She owed them. If she mingled after dinner with other guests it might reveal information she'd otherwise never get.

Chapter Thirteen

Intimidated by her surroundings, Mira grew uneasy. The front of the Lane estate—more like a mansion than a house with its pillars, balcony, and ornate stained glass—expanded the width of what looked like more than a block. As she got out of her car, an attendant took her keys. She walked with slow, deliberate steps up the wide marble stairway, dreading each one as it brought her closer to meeting Kyle and Jessica Lane.

She didn't need to ring or knock since someone opened the door to greet all the guests. He motioned her over to another who took her wrap and gave her a ticket in return. She read the ticket's gold letters engraved on a black background, ornate like the mansion.

"How nice of you to come, Miss Stanley. Welcome to our home." A tall, well-groomed woman close to Mira's age approached and held out a hand.

"Thank you for inviting me." Thinking of Sean, Mira couldn't help but size up the beautiful woman in front of her with hair the color of wheat and eyes a deep, azure blue.

"Come meet Kyle and the rest of the family." Jessica led Mira into another room where a couple dozen people stood while others sat, all of them engaged in conversation.

Mira studied the room to get a better idea of the

type who attended a function given by the Lanes. She figured Judge Thorn to be one, and someone else who she hadn't considered. When her eyes caught sight of him she gasped. Jessica Lane turned around to look at her.

"Are you all right?" Her pleasant voice grew anxious.

"Um-hmm, yeah, got a tickle in my throat." Mira scrambled to find the excuse before she blurted out the truth. She saw Sean in the far corner, talking with an elderly woman. He was dressed in a dinner jacket and tie, and he looked better than she remembered. Her heart leaped. She rubbed her arms that all at once chilled her.

"Would you like me to get you a drink? A warm brandy for instance? You look rather pale."

Her hostess seemed genuinely concerned for her well-being. It caused Mira to feel guilty. Her chills and pale complexion had nothing to do with illness. Not unless you call falling for someone an illness.

"No, I'm fine, honestly. This dress isn't as warm as I thought it might be. Perhaps I should go get my wrap." Mira wanted an excuse to escape. No longer did it seem crucial to coax information out of the party guests.

"Nonsense. One of the staff will get it for you." Jessica motioned to a man who took quick strides across the room and reached them in seconds. "Please get Miss Stanley's wrap for her."

Mira held out her ticket and tried to keep her hand steady. The hurried movement of the servant caught Sean's attention. Mira swallowed nervously as his eyes followed, led across the room until they landed on her.

Instead of looking shocked as she was, he smiled and waved.

"It figures," she murmured.

"What was that?" Jessica looked puzzled.

"I'm sorry. I spotted someone I know. Sean Thorndale?" She anxiously waited for Jessica's reaction. When her eyes narrowed and her mouth formed a rigid line, Mira wasn't sure what to make of it.

"Ah...Here is my husband. Kyle, come say hello to Mira Stanley." Jessica's voice resumed its lilting tone.

"Mira Stanley, I've heard so much about you already," Kyle said and shook Mira's hand.

"And I've heard about you, too." Mira nodded toward the corner. "From your partner, Sean."

"I'm certain my ears should be burning and Sean's told you all my terrible secrets. Don't believe half of them." Kyle smiled.

"And the other half?" Mira didn't resist the quip. She already disliked the man. He was glib, but it seemed to be given in a deceitful way with a sugary sweetness as he stood ready to pounce on his prey like a cat on the hunt.

Kyle threw back his head and laughed for a full minute. "That's good, Mira. In truth, I am a nice guy at heart. Just ask my wife."

"Hmm. I think I'll leave the conversation right where it is. It's about time for dinner." Jessica left the room.

Though it was slight, Mira detected Jessica's glance over to the corner before she disappeared through the doorway. And Sean seemed to meet her eyes. His face held no expression, neither happy nor sad. Not even angry, Mira realized. Jessica Lane must've hurt Sean Thorndale deeply.

Dinner was an elegant affair with eight courses, two wines, and for those who wished it, an after dinner brandy. Mira wasn't one of them. Her eyes grew heavy with fatigue after the huge meal and the full day of events. Besides, she hadn't managed to get much out of the conversation with her neighbors seated next to her at the table. Mrs. Doddling had never met the Lanes; she came because she was a client. In fact, she had moved to Florida only months ago. Mira also spoke with an elderly gentleman, Trenton Caudwell. He was the long lost relative from across the Atlantic who came to spend a few months in the States. He wasn't any help either.

It didn't matter. Most of the time, thoughts of Sean managed to occupy Mira's mind. He hadn't attempted to talk to her. Of course, no opportunity arose since he sat at the opposite end of the twenty-foot long dining table. The signal to get up couldn't come soon enough. Everyone filed into the living room, but some headed for the foyer to leave. Mira chose to follow the second group.

"Leaving already?"

Mira turned when she recognized the voice. "Hi." She smiled and wanted to say more, but felt awkward, as if she only imagined their close encounter earlier today.

Sean reached up to move a stray lock of hair from her cheek. "Oddly enough, I can't manage to get a certain beautiful lady off my mind."

"Well, I…" She blushed and turned to give the valet her ticket. The touch of Sean's hand on her arm made her weak enough that she worried her legs would collapse. This was ridiculous. She needed to get control. Two days? A person didn't feel this way after two days, she reasoned.

"Let me give you a ride back to the motel." He leaned sideways and whispered close to her ear.

Mira struggled with her emotions. She wanted to say yes, but if she did, she knew where it would lead. And she lacked the will power to resist. She needed distance.

"I need to get up early tomorrow for an appointment. Maybe some other time, okay?" She gave him what she hoped was a convincing smile, but inside her composure unraveled at a reckless speed.

"I see," Sean answered.

Mira sensed she hurt him, but she refused to change her mind. "Call me tomorrow?" Her hurried steps found their way to the door with her feet almost tripping over one another. And she wouldn't look back, afraid once she saw his disappointment she'd change her mind.

"Not tonight. Not this time," she mumbled as the valet brought her car to the curb.

As she got behind the wheel her phone rang. "Hello?"

"Hi, Mira." Rob's voice came across.

"Rob! This is a surprise. I figured you'd be in New York by now. Didn't you arrange an early appointment with the business mogul whose case is scheduled for next month?"

"Something more important came up."

"Oh? What could possibly be more important that it took you away from business with a multi-million dollar retainer?" Mira laughed.

"My aunt is missing."

Mira barely heard his voice. "What? Did you say someone is missing?"

"Claire. I think Claire is missing. I got the phone call a few minutes ago."

Mira sat there, though a repeated tap on her window urged her to move along. After the valet began shouting at her, she put down her window and yelled back for him to wait.

"What do you mean you think she's missing? How can she be missing?" Confusion kept her mind from accepting Rob's words.

"The call came from her neighbor. He told me a car with two men pulled into the drive. They went to the door, and a minute later they led Aunt Claire to the car. Afterward, they drove away. And my aunt along with them. God, I knew I should've sent someone to stay with her when all this started."

"You didn't know. Stop beating yourself up and think. Why would anyone want to take her? Maybe those men are friends of hers and she went with them voluntarily. Did you try calling her?"

"She doesn't carry a cell phone. I'm telling you, something is wrong. She wouldn't go with anyone like that. She doesn't like riding in a car. Avoids it as much as possible. Ever since my uncle Charles died in that car crash."

"Wait a minute. I thought he died of a heart attack," Mira interrupted.

"Yes, but the heart attack caused the accident. It doesn't matter. Mira, I feel it in my gut; she wouldn't go with those men by choice."

"When did it happen? I mean when did the neighbor say the men and Claire left?" Mira refused to say kidnapped. Not yet, anyway.

"This evening around seven. If any harm comes to her, I will blame myself." Rob's voice trembled.

"Please don't think like that. Maybe she'll call or return home before the evening is over. You shouldn't panic," Mira warned. She was frustrated. She wanted to be there to comfort him. "I'll head over there. Maybe I can find out something that tells us where she went."

"No, I don't think that's a wise idea. What if those men return?"

"I'll be fine. Call the neighbor back and tell him I'm coming. I want to talk with him."

"Mira, I don't…"

"Bye, Rob. I'm hanging up. Call me after you speak with the neighbor and let me know which house it is." Mira ended the call and put her car into gear. It took ten to fifteen minutes to get to the Peterson place, if she went over the speed limit. She did a U turn and headed toward Route 30 and Apalachicola.

Chapter Fourteen

Five more minutes, she thought. Her eyes detected the familiar signs—the thrift store on the left, the road sign for Spruce Avenue on the right, Indian Paw seafood bar—all of them flew by in a blur. Mira's mind raced just as fast. She brainstormed to hit on the reason why anyone would take Claire Peterson. Bradley Lane wanted her property, but enough to engage in foul play? If Mira hadn't learned the neighbor's story, she'd believe Claire wandered off on her own. Claire talked and reminisced about her late husband, but Mira recalled her last visit and the odd conversation in the woman's living room. Claire acted in such a strange manner. Why not accept the possibility she'd left to go in search of Charles? Mira suspected she wanted to make excuses and avoid a more serious explanation. After all, the notion of any harm inflicted on the vulnerable woman scared Mira. She'd become fond of Claire.

As she pulled into the drive, Mira spotted several lights in the front windows. The sight gave her encouragement. Maybe Claire had returned home. She took quick steps to the front door and rang the bell. She leaned against the door listening for footsteps, but heard nothing. Going to the window, she peeked inside but found no movement whatsoever. Not even Claire's cat, Delilah, slinked passed.

To be thorough, Mira headed for the back of the house. Instead of focusing on the porch and the box windows framing the kitchen, her eyes were drawn to the shoreline of the Peterson property. In the foreground Mira could see Claire's garden with even rows of clustered yellow roses aglow in the moonlight. Behind them, the backhoe resting on the beach formed a pale silhouette. Without a doubt Lane Developers was anxious and ready. At last she turned to approach the rear windows and leaned over to peer through the glass. Her mood deflated to see no one or any sign that Claire might be inside.

The return call from Rob told her she'd find the neighborhood witness, Mr. Warner, in the house immediately to the left. The bright pink stucco was hard to miss. Mira walked up onto the front veranda. Finding no doorbell, she grasped the flamingo-shaped knocker and tapped it several times against the metal plate. Within a few seconds the door opened.

"Hi. I'm Mira Stanley. I believe you called my partner with a story about your neighbor, Claire Peterson?" She held out a hand to shake, but the man who answered simply stared down at it. In a moment he lifted his eyes once again to focus on Mira.

"Yeah, Mrs. Peterson left with those two men. I can't imagine why she'd do such a thing. You can't trust people nowadays." He finished with a curt nod.

"Can you tell me what they looked like? Or what the car looked like?" Mira waited while he tilted his head and focused his eyes at some point behind her.

"Both men are rather large, I'd say six-five maybe. One had on an overcoat, the other a windbreaker, both wore dark pants and shoes. The hair was cropped short, you know, like a serviceman's haircut. The car was a luxury model. A Lincoln town car, I think. Fairly new, dark brown color." He brought his eyes back into focus, leaving them to rest on Mira. His look told her he was finished.

"Well, that's an accurate description, Mr. Warner." Mira met his stare without blinking.

"To be honest, I'm a little rusty, but after thirty years on the force, the knack never goes away," he explained.

"I see. Did you come to Florida to retire?"

"I worked for the Port Saint Joe precinct most of my career. My wife passed on a few years back. Never saw a reason to leave."

Mira knew she should move on and call Rob back or go visit other neighbors to see if they'd witnessed the event, but then she recalled Lois Thorn.

"I guess you were on the force when Lois Thorn disappeared?" Mira carefully studied the expression on Warner's face. The change was subtle, but Mira's trained eye detected the tense muscles pull at the corners of his mouth.

"Lois Thorn. Yes, I remember. I remember how many folks in town believed it was fishy when she left. They blamed us for not following up with an investigation. Bad press in the paper and all. I was head of homicide at the time. I used to get a dozen phone calls a night from people and their complaints. Even got threats to fire me. Shoot. What were they thinking? Too often the public doesn't give us enough credit. We do our job."

"You think it was her choice she wanted to leave?"

"Well, of course it was. We found no reason or

proof to believe otherwise. Curtis Lane spouted off enough accusations about her cheating the family business. He made things plenty ugly for her. Why would she want to stay?"

Mira puzzled over what the retired homicide detective told her. And she wondered if he realized what it implied. If Lane showed that much anger in public, who knew what he'd resort to in private?

"Mr. Warner, did you ever suspect Curtis Lane of doing harm to Lois Thorn? I mean, if he was that bitter and expressed such strong feelings in public…" Mira left the comment unfinished and shrugged her shoulders.

"Like I said, we did our job. Nobody found evidence of foul play or reason to conduct an investigation."

"Did anyone ever try to contact Lois after…?" Mira started but didn't get to finish.

"If you'll excuse me, Miss Stanley, I have soup cooking on the stove. I called your partner, trying to do a neighborly deed. I don't need to be given the third degree by you."

With that he slammed the door in Mira's face. She'd hit a nerve. Whether the nerve attacked his professional pride or struck a chord elsewhere, she didn't know. A hunch told her Detective Warner hid something, and if it leaked out it might destroy his reputation. Still, this panned out to pure guess work, not the facts. Maybe her imagination ran wild at this point. Who knew?

Mira spent the next half hour visiting and talking to other neighbors about Claire's whereabouts, but got no more information. She faced the uncomfortable task of calling Rob with the news. How could she reassure him nothing alarming or suspicious happened to his aunt? She wasn't certain herself. And the worst part was they must wait. Authorities wouldn't consider Claire missing until twenty-four hours passed. She didn't have the inside contacts like she did back in Ohio. She didn't know where else to turn.

As she walked back to her car, Mira tried to ignore the name that nudged its way into her head. The fact was, she didn't want to find out how close he might be to the whole sordid mess, or how involved. Keeping a professional distance, she discovered, proved a challenge where Sean Thorndale was concerned. All objectivity disappeared as her feelings for him took hold. Yet, she had to admit he might be able to pull some strings with the authorities. Mira sighed and made a decision to avoid all personal or intimate thoughts of Sean for the time being. Besides, she needed to call Rob.

As soon as she was back on the road, Mira opened her phone. "Hi. How you holding up?"

"Not so good. What did you find?"

Mira heard the strain in his voice. She hated being in this position, leaving her so helpless and frustrated. "No news about where she is or who she's with, I'm afraid."

"I guessed as much. I called the authorities down there, but as you know they can't move on this yet."

"We must do something. *I* need to. I can't sit and wait until tomorrow." In an instant, Mira was consumed with the serious weight of what possibly happened to Claire. "Look, I'll talk to you after I find out more. There has to be someone I can call. Let me at least try.

Okay?" She hung up before he started his protest all over again.

The next call was to Sean. She heard his phone ringing, but no answer. She had settled on leaving a message when he picked up.

"Well, if it isn't my favorite snowbird," he quipped.

Mira smiled, despite the serious of the moment. "Hi there."

"Let me guess. You miss me and called to suggest a late night rendezvous. Well, it just so happens I'm free."

"No. I mean that sounds nice, but it's not why I called." Mira explained Claire's strange departure and asked Sean if he knew anyone on the police force who might agree to ask around and help identify those men who took Claire Peterson for a drive.

"Maybe an acquaintance of mine at the police station would, but I can't make any promises. Sorry, Mira."

"That's all I ask. I know we can't do anything else, yet." Suddenly, the full impact of the situation hit her. Bradley Lane's sleazy business dealing ranked as trivial compared to this. If Claire Peterson was harmed…Mira wouldn't finish the thought.

"Why don't you come to my place and we can put our heads together. Maybe we can come up with some ideas," Sean suggested.

Mira was tempted, but too exhausted. "I think I'll head back to the motel. I need some sleep. This day has been more than I can handle, I guess."

"I understand. If I find out anything tonight, I'll call you. Okay?"

"Of course," Mira answered before hanging up. As she drove back to Port Saint Joe her mind struggled to stay positive. She wondered about Claire Peterson, if she was alive and safe, and prayed that was the case.

Chapter Fifteen

"Yes, she went back to the motel to get some sleep. Don't worry. I'm sure she doesn't suspect anything." Sean assured Bradley.

"I have a bad feeling about that woman. She's nosed around enough. I got a call from Warner. He claimed she asked questions about your aunt and suggested my family had something to do with her disappearance. I don't like it, I tell you," Bradley snapped.

"Calm down, Bradley. She may be fishing for dirt on you, but she won't find any. Let me handle it, okay?" Sean tried to diminish Bradley's paranoia. He clutched his phone in a tight grip until Bradley grew silent and ended the call. This couldn't last much longer. If Mira discovered his scheme and what he planned to do, she would be more than a little angry with him. But he didn't see any other choice. To keep her in the dark remained a priority. She mustn't know or suspect anything; that was for her own safety. He held his phone once more and punched in another number.

"Guárico. Can I help you?"

"I sure hope so," Sean started.

"Thorndale. I didn't expect to hear from you for a while." Guárico kept his voice low.

"Yeah, well something came up. We have a

problem."

"Oh?"

"I think they took Claire Peterson."

"That *is* a problem. Do you have any information, any details I can move on?"

"Not much. We've got two men in a Lincoln town car and a missing Claire Peterson. It's too coincidental not to point fingers at Bradley Lane. Who else wants her out of the picture?"

"Man, I understand your point. But without squat to go on, my hands are tied. We'll have to wait twenty-four hours, like any reported missing person case. It's the best I can offer."

"That's not good enough, Guárico. We can't waste time on this. If Claire gets hurt or maybe worse, I won't accept that. Now, you owe me because I've done plenty to help you." His anger and frustration simmered right below the surface. The longer he remained in this position, all to bring Bradley Lane to justice, the more dangerous it became. With Mira involved, he recognized other emotions entered the picture. Ones he hadn't let himself feel since Jessica. No doubt, his agenda needed to move along faster, and that meant putting Bradley behind bars where he couldn't hurt anyone, especially Mira.

Sean heard silence on the other end and had to push one more time. "Will you help me or not?"

Chapter Sixteen

The phone rang and Mira reached for it across the sofa, but her hand couldn't grab a hold. When the front door slammed she turned to watch Sean walk into the room. He asked her why she didn't answer the call. A frown crossed her face as she looked back to the table where the ringing continued, but she didn't spot a phone. "I can't find it. I can't even see it, Sean," she mumbled as her mood grew irritated.

In the next moment she woke, startled to find she didn't recognize anything at first. Her body relaxed as she recognized the familiar blue wallpaper on the walls. She calmed herself with a mental checklist: motel, Port Saint Joe, and her cell phone. It was still ringing.

She picked it up off the nightstand; it was three in the morning. It had taken a sleeping pill and more than an hour to relax enough to fall asleep. Now, she struggled to clear her head and read the number on her display. Finally, she answered the call with a long, drawn out greeting. "Hello?"

"Sorry, Mira. I know it's late, but I thought you should know the police found Claire."

Mira sat up straight and gripped the phone tighter. "Is she all right?"

"She's a bit shaken up, but that's all. The police found her wandering around Cape San Blas, nearby the park. At first, she didn't answer their questions, only repeated how she wanted to go home to feed her cat."

"Thank God, but does it mean she couldn't tell them who took her? I'd hate to think they might get away with it."

"This is where you come in. One of the officers told me after they got her home she recovered enough to ask someone to find Mira Stanley."

"That's odd."

"No. The odd part came when she told him Charles was angry with those—and I quote—scoundrels who kidnapped me. When the officer wanted to know who Charles was, she told him he was her husband. Of course, he asked to speak with him."

"Oh boy." Mira sat on the edge of her bed.

"Yeah, oh boy. Funny how Claire came up with a reasonable answer. She told the officer Charles wasn't around at the moment."

"Well, at least she's back home. Did she say why she wanted to see me?" Mira couldn't figure that one out, but if Claire's adventure with the mysterious abductors connected somehow, why not tell the police?

"Nope, but I can't wait to discover why. Do you feel like taking a ride to see her? I'll drive you," Sean offered.

Mira pulled her jeans on as they talked. "I'm already dressed. And driving me would be a great favor. And please, bring coffee."

Within five minutes, Sean knocked on the door. Mira didn't take the time to fix herself up. She pulled her hair back in a ponytail and grabbed her sweater off the chair while calling Rob back to let him know his aunt was okay. She gave Sean a nod as she ended her phone conversation.

"Let's go." She took the large coffee he offered. Then, they hurried out to the car.

The drive to Claire's took half the normal time with Sean's foot heavy on the pedal. Mira's mind was too occupied with worry to notice. A strong hunch told her this evening's event connected to Lane's suspicious deal with Charles Peterson. All of what happened so far did. She was sure of it. Mira failed to imagine the reasons why someone took Claire, though.

****

They discovered all the lights shone in the front windows. Sean pulled the car into the Peterson drive. The police cruiser sat with the engine idling near the garage. One of the officers exited the vehicle as Sean pulled up behind him.

"You should know she still seems a bit disoriented. While I waited inside, I heard voices come from the kitchen. She explained she needed some tea. Anyway, I went to check it out and found her talking to herself. But at the same time it's like someone was with her. I know that sounds crazy."

"Talking to herself, huh?" Mira didn't want to sound like she believed him, even though she knew exactly he what meant.

"Yep. And after she'd say a few words, she'd tilt her head and pause, like she waited for someone to answer. Real strange behavior, if you ask me. Maybe someone ought to get a doctor to check her over. She might have a concussion."

Mira deduced the officer was worried. "It's okay. We'll take care of it." She smiled at him. "She didn't happen to mention why she wanted to talk to me, did she?"

The officer shook his head. "She insisted on speaking with you only, like this was confidential. You need to let us know if she reveals information about what happened this evening, though," he advised.

Mira thanked the officer. Sean took her hand and they walked to the front door. Claire opened it at once, waving them inside. In the next instant she shut and locked the door. Without a word, she went to each of the front windows and pulled the drapes shut.

"Can't be too careful." She motioned for them to sit down in the living room.

Mira and Sean gave each other a worried glance, but kept quiet and waited for her to explain why she acted mysteriously.

"I want you to know..." Claire turned to study Sean and then looked over at Mira. "Is it okay to talk in front of him? I mean he may be the enemy."

Sean's eyebrows arched. "Mrs. Peterson, I assure you I want what's best for you. With that said, can you please tell us what all this is about?"

After a long sigh she sat back in the sofa and began her story. "Two men came to my door earlier this evening. They told me they were detectives from the Port Saint Joe precinct. Why would I doubt them? They wore badges and looked very professional."

Mira studied Claire who seemed to deliberate over what to say next. "Mrs. Peterson, Claire, I do understand. Can you tell us what they wanted?"

"Oh, I'm sorry. Where was I? Ah, yes. They told me something quite dreadful. At least I all but fainted at the news. They believed my husband's death dealt in foul play and claimed they had the evidence to prove it. Can you imagine how I felt? The very notion of

Charles, well, anyway, they wanted me to come to the police station with them to look at the evidence. Of course I said yes. Wouldn't you?" Claire's expression pleaded with them.

Mira was overcome with sympathy for the old woman. The idea of how painful it must be for her to imagine such an end to her husband's life was difficult for Mira to handle. She left her chair and went to sit next to Claire on the sofa. She patted her hand.

"It's all right. You acted from the heart. We don't blame you for trusting them and the lies they tried to sell you. Can you describe what happened next? If you need to take a break, maybe I could get you some tea?"

Claire shook her head. "No. I need to say this while I manage the courage to do so." She stared at the mantel with the urn displayed in the center. She appeared to sort through her thoughts. All at once she returned her attention to them and smiled.

"I know some might think I'm crazy, the way I carry on conversations with my Charles. It gives me peace somehow. It's the only way to explain it. I know he's gone, but he stays in my heart. That part never goes away."

Mira shifted her eyes to Sean for a moment. She imagined a love like Claire's, the relationship she cherished with her husband with emotion strong enough to last forever, even after losing that person. Mira knew she wanted to experience that with someone.

"Anyway, I've made you wait long enough. You want to know what happened to me. I guess I feel foolish for believing those men were who they claimed to be, but after they mentioned Charles my mind lost all sense of reason. Later, I began to suspect. I know where the station is in Port Saint Joe. I've been there several times over the years. And I doubted the car was headed there.

"The men kept silent during the entire ride in the car. I tried to get them to speak and asked them one question after another, but they wouldn't budge. This moment of dread crept in. You know the kind where you realize something bad will happen? And I knew in that instant, I needed to act, even if it were a desperate move." Claire shifted in her seat and squeezed Mira's hand.

"I must admit it thrilled me, though I was terrified at the same time. I told them I needed to use the restroom and an old lady like me couldn't delay such things or an accident might happen. I expect the idea of me creating a mess in their car prompted a decision because we stopped at the next gas station."

"You must have been scared," Mira suggested.

"Yes. Yes I was, but the alternative? Much scarier. I got out of the car, expecting one of them to follow me. He started to, but another man interrupted to ask for directions. It proved the distraction I needed. I figured if God provided the opportunity, I should be brave enough to act on it. I hurried away to the back of the station and good luck stayed with me. I found the service door open. So I slipped inside and closed the door behind me, praying he wouldn't figure out where I went. I hid among some boxes in the storage room and waited for an hour or more."

Mira felt the trembling in Claire's hand and became aware how she breathed heavily. "I think you should take a break, Claire. The stress of all you've gone through is too much." The woman straightened her shoulders and gave a curt nod.

"I'm nearly finished. After a while I mustered the courage to peek out the inside doorway and found no sign of those horrible men. I risked the chance and went out the back door once more. I lost no time starting my walk back to town. That's where the kind police officer found me. I was exhausted and upset. You know, I couldn't remember my name when he asked. All that came to mind was my poor cat and how hungry she must be. Strange, isn't it?" Claire smiled and reached over to pet Delilah.

Mira noticed how Sean remained quiet during Claire's story. She wondered what occupied his mind. Some doubts about his motives lingered and she worried he might be sulking over the fact that Claire got away. It surprised her when he made a suggestion.

"I think you should go down to the station and look through the mug shots. Maybe you can identify your abductors."

"Not such a bad idea, but if they work for Lane, we might not find any criminal record on file," Mira warned.

"And no mug shots," Claire added. "Well, don't look surprised. I watch those detective shows. And I also know the station has a sketch artist. Maybe I could give a description. I certainly won't forget those faces any time soon."

Mira glanced at Sean and he nodded. "I think you should get some sleep, and we can ride over there later this afternoon." Mira got up from the sofa.

"You're right. I'm so tired I could fall asleep right on this sofa."

Mira observed how her trembling ceased, but

Claire's eyes carried the dark shadows of fatigue. "All right. I'll give you a call around two or so. Unless…" The sudden notion of whether Claire would be safe alone in the house came to Mira.

"I'll be fine. You're here to protect me, aren't you, Charles?" Claire smiled.

Mira shivered. "I guess we will be leaving then?"

"Don't be alarmed, dear. Charles read your mind. No need to worry about me. They won't be back. And I won't be driven away from my own home by the likes of them." She started for the front door.

"We don't mind staying, if it makes you more comfortable," Sean offered.

Mira narrowed her eyes at him. *We*? Okay, that was forward, she thought, but didn't comment aloud. Instead, they said their goodbyes and left Claire Peterson to her cat and deceased husband. Though somewhat bizarre, Mira had begun to accept the old woman's behavior.

The ride back to the motel was done in silence. Mira was too tired to carry on small talk or even important talk. Sean didn't seem to care. His eyes stayed focused on the road and the way back to town. At five in the morning, it seemed pointless to go back to bed.

"You want to grab breakfast?" Sean spoke at last.

"Hmm. If I wagered a guess, I'm too exhausted to chew. All's I want is a nice warm bed and the covers pulled up over my head." Mira yawned and stretched out her arms.

"Yeah, bed sounds good," Sean murmured.

Mira's eyes shot a glance at Sean. The soft timbre of his voice left Mira a little unsettled. She took in a few deep breaths as she stared out at the lights of cars passing by them.

When they reached the motel, Mira was the first to get out of the car. She took quick steps to reach the door and waited for Sean to catch up. She prepared a brief word or two to say goodnight and end the evening. However, as Sean approached, her heart raced again. He smiled at her, a lazy but sexy smile. She groaned. This would *not* happen, she told herself. When he stood inches from her she grabbed hold of the door handle.

"I should probably go inside and get some sleep. Have to take Claire to the station in the morning, you know." Mira spoke the words, but it was like someone else's voice, far away and distant. Her heart beat faster as Sean shook his head.

"Not yet, Mira." His hand reached up to stroke her cheek before his fingers trailed down to her shoulder and back up again until they found their way around to the nape of her neck where they lingered.

The gentle caresses made her moan, too tired and aroused to stop him. His soft breath touched her ear and his tongue traced her lobe, followed by his kisses. They traveled across her face, mapping out a course to cover every inch.

Mira knew she was aroused and she wanted him, though her mind told her it was foolish. "Sean, I don't think this is a good idea." Her voice came out small and weak. She made a feeble attempt to push away from him, but he held her tighter.

"Of course, I understand," he said in a muffled tone between kisses, but he didn't stop. Not yet. He stroked her arms and back. His hands traveled down and caressed other parts of her, causing her to whimper, but then he backed away with slow, deliberate steps.

"What? No. I mean, thank you." Mira stumbled over her words and wore a confused expression.

"I'll call you later, after you've gotten some rest. We can take Claire to the station together. I have a few connections. Maybe we can get her in and out quicker." He stepped one foot inside of his car. At the last second, he stopped to gaze at her for a moment. "I enjoy your company, Mira Stanley."

Mira sighed deeply as he smiled once more before getting in his car to drive away. She didn't know whether to cry or scream. She puzzled over whether his behavior was sincere or manipulative. Men like Alex had taught her to be that insecure. Still, what she did know was how it felt great, thoroughly, remarkably great. And she wanted to feel it again.

Chapter Seventeen

Bradley Lane loved his job. He savored every deal and boasted about every building, complex, and park, all the testimonials to Lane Developers. What he didn't love were deals gone sour. To admit it, he was a sore loser. At this instant, the taste of it tainted his mouth, just a hint, but there to worry him all the same. Whenever possible, he did things legally, but other times called for more creative measures. Still, he pursued this deal without tainting the reputation of the company. And he refused to let a simple lawyer from Ohio ruin it all.

The Lincoln cruised up the front drive. Bradley spotted the light in the kitchen straight through the dining room window. Once inside, he called out for Vivian but heard only the echo of his voice.

"Mother, must we play this game?" Bradley left the front of the house and continued his search by entering the den. He knew she'd come out or answer when she was ready, and not before then. That is what infuriated him. It was her obsession to control others, above all, her sons.

"I'm not in the mood for this either, Bradley. I've a terrible migraine from listening to all the racket this morning. If you'll sit down, I'll get right to it," Vivian instructed. She sat in a chair at the far side of the room and her narrowed eyes followed Bradley as he paced.

"I suppose you summoned me to complain about your neighbors again? I told you neither the police nor anyone else can do anything about their loud behavior. If that's all you needed, I'll leave." Bradley abruptly turned to walk out of the parlor before he revealed the disappointment in his eyes.

"No. You're wrong as usual. I asked you over to talk about your brother's wife."

Bradley sighed. "I am not responsible for Jessica and her behavior. What has she done to upset you this time?"

"I know you aren't responsible, but your brother won't listen to me. Perhaps you might convince him to change his mind about the matter."

"What matter?" Bradley had tired of his mother's complaints a long time ago. Yet, he endured this because he felt obligated. Also, the large portion of the family fortune in her hands, which she continued to dangle in front of him as a reward for his attentiveness, helped keep his loyalty. Money, their one true relationship, he admitted.

Bradley studied Vivian as she rose from her chair. Her hands gripped the arms to keep from falling. She looked the full years of her life as the weight of old age plagued her emotions and made her mean. He recalled how she never wanted to become one of those whose days passed in misery, yet here she was.

"I don't want any more trouble, Bradley. I believe Jessica is stirring the pot a bit. Why was she foolish enough to invite that young lawyer to be a guest at our dinner party? God knows who she spoke with to learn things which are none of her business." Vivian walked across the room to stand closer. "And if she manages to destroy what we've accomplished, I will hold *you* responsible. I expect you to take care of it."

Bradley watched her leave the room, but turn as she reached the doorway.

"And tell Kyle to keep his wife on a shorter leash. Or in time the foolish girl will be the death of us."

Chapter Eighteen

Mira got the call from Claire at noon. She explained how the ordeal of the night before left her sore and tired. Mira suggested they go to the station after dinner around six.

"Do you mind calling Sean about the change in plans?" Mira pulled her jacket tighter as her stomach churned.

With time on her hands, Mira paid a visit to the library to research some more. She spent the entire afternoon scanning through news articles in the local newspapers. Her backside stiffened as she sat in the metal chair, and her eyes burned from hours at the computer screen. The Port Saint Joe library provided all the resources she needed, but not the comfort. She'd asked if it was possible to set up a temporary account in order to access all of their resources from her motel room and laptop. The library aide's face formed a confused expression, and she shook her head.

Three hours later and she still hadn't found one detail worth remembering. Not unless she considered all the social events written about the Lanes and the Thorns. She discovered plenty regarding those families, their relationships, their philanthropic acts, their deaths, but no mention, not one sentence, about Lois Thorn. Mira found that odd. Once more, she went through the past twenty years of events to make sure. She knew

Lois vanished from the picture within that time.

When she resigned herself to giving up, she came across a blurb in the local section under the police blotter. Mira read the report and again aloud to convince herself of what she saw there in print.

"June 12, 2010: Call from 47300 Cape Road to report an attempted robbery. The caller, Claire Peterson, stated she observed a man at the back of her property near her storage building. He appeared to be holding a tool of some sort and trying to break open the door. Authorities arrived to investigate but found no one on the property and no damage to the building."

Mira wanted to call Claire and find out more but figured talking with her in person might be better. She glanced at the date again. This occurred a few months after Charles Peterson passed away. Was it a connection or mere coincidence? Considering Claire's peculiar behavior, perhaps the person she saw sneaking around on the property grew from the woman's imagination.

She thanked the library aide as she left, glad to be on her feet again. Though it resulted in an uncomfortable, tedious afternoon with only a short break to grab a late lunch, at least the task took her mind off Sean. The slightest reminder of seeing him again left her weak. She couldn't deny such strong feelings any longer; she liked him, and more than a little. It took extra effort to remind herself why she'd come to Florida in the first place, to help Claire. That should be her priority.

Mira walked around to the rear parking lot and approached her car. The blistering heat of the sun hadn't taken long to send the temperature to an unbearable high. And that was on the outside. Inside her vehicle was worse. She struggled to grab hold of the steering wheel as she turned the key to start the engine. Once the air kicked on, she stepped back out until the interior cooled.

Her eyes concentrated on the view of the ocean. The water tempted and teased with its mesmerizing waves and lush blue color. Mira's dreamy state of mind took her away for a moment, left her relaxed and calm. The temptation to take a break, wade through the salty water and feel the sand between her toes was strong. However, she knew the time arrived to head east for her visit to Claire and their trip downtown.

Mira grew anxious to speak with her and Sean, as well. She needed to hear Claire's explanation about the nine-one-one call while gauging Sean's reaction.

She became irritated with herself. She obsessed over ways to prove Sean an honest person. Maybe because her feelings for him grew stronger each moment she spent with him. How anyone managed to get under her skin so quickly both amazed and frightened her. This wasn't like her at all.

When she turned into the drive, Mira noticed Sean's car. Her hands clutched the wheel tightly for a moment while she reminded herself to stay positive. Soon enough, she'd find answers. She needed evidence to help get this case moving in the right direction.

"Hello, Mira. I'm glad you're here. We were having the most pleasant conversation about you." Claire greeted her at the door.

Mira detected the sparkle in her eyes and the smile of mischief. "Oh? Should my ears burn or my nose itch?" Mira teased and listened to Claire giggle like a young girl.

"You wait and see. Now, come into the kitchen and join us for some tea and cookies." She walked ahead with a stiff gait.

"I hope you're feeling better. You got a great deal of exercise last night," Mira commented.

"Yes, but it will do me some good. I spend plenty of hours tending to my flowers, but I need to get out for walks more often. The ordeal I went through was traumatizing, but it made me realize exercise gives me energy. I think I'd forgotten that since...since Charles passed away."

"There you are," Sean greeted as they reached the doorway. He got up to pull a chair out for Mira. "We hoped you'd arrive soon, at least before I ate up all the cookies." He laid a hand on Mira's shoulder as she sat down.

The rush to her head left her dizzy. She smiled at him and nodded but didn't trust her voice to speak. It became deadly quiet in the room while all three sat and drank their tea. Mira took a few sips of hers. And after a brief moment, she forced herself to break the silence.

"I discovered a story while at the library earlier today," she started. Turning to Claire she added, "Do you remember a nine-one-one call you made to report a possible burglar on your property?"

Claire turned to glance out of the back window. "Yes, I do. It was in June and late at night. I couldn't sleep so I came down to the kitchen for a glass of warm milk. It helps me relax, you see. As I walked past the window, my eye caught sight of a shadow as it moved across my backyard to the storage shed." Claire pointed beyond the window.

"And you called the police?" Mira gave Sean a side glance to see his reaction. He showed little emotion, except for a slight frown.

"Yes, but not right away. At first I guessed maybe my eyes played tricks on me. It's my age. Can't say the sight works like it used to. Anyway, I went to get some binoculars I keep in the top cupboard above the refrigerator. It took a while because I needed the step stool to reach it, you understand." She nodded and took another bite of cookie.

"The burglar?" Mira reminded her.

"Oh! Yes, of course, the burglar. He leaned his face against the window of the storage shed to peer inside. Why ever did Charles want to build it with windows? In any case, he was peeking inside. I could see his hand jiggle the door handle. He didn't get in at first. And then he pulled an object, perhaps some sort of tool, from his pocket and slipped it into the lock. The door opened and he disappeared into the shed."

Claire went on to explain how she called the police to report it. By the time they arrived, a mere five minutes later, the man had disappeared.

"I don't think they believed me, to tell you the truth," she admitted. "Can't say I blamed them. An old woman with poor vision. Not the most reliable source, is it?"

"Did you check the storage shed yourself? Afterward, I mean," Sean suggested.

"Yes. And I was more certain after what I found inside." Claire walked over to the closet and brought out a bag. She reached in and pulled out a broken dish. "This is part of what I found on the floor, along with several other plates."

"And that's unusual?" Mira said.

"Oh, yes. It was only the day before I went in there to find some gardening tools. The plates were whole and neatly stacked on the chair." Claire explained.

"Maybe a cat or other animal got inside and knocked them over." Sean stood up to look out the window facing the backyard and the shed.

"Yes, I considered that. But how? The shed is locked with no open spaces for as much as a small animal to get through. It's a very solid structure. Charles built it himself."

"I think we've missed the point. The question is what could anyone want out of your shed? Do you keep valuables inside?" Mira wanted to know.

Claire shook her head. "Yard tools, patio furniture and a couple of storage chests, but no valuables."

"What's in the chests?"

"I stored some papers in there, along with some bric-a-brac I no longer use. Nothing worth much. I can tell you that."

Sean shook his head. "It doesn't make much sense, but then again someone did break in, wanted something, and maybe found it."

"Well, whoever he or she was, I haven't noticed anyone snooping around since." Claire placed the plate back in the bag.

"Why do you keep it?" Mira pointed.

"The plate? Oh, I guess it's foolish, but I keep it because it was part of the dish set Charles and I bought when we married."

Mira smiled as she looked over at Sean. His eyes met hers. The moment lasted only seconds, but the force of it stayed with her, wrapped itself around her.

Mira pulled away and looked at Claire once again.

"You know, I've been thinking ever since this morning when you told us why you went with your kidnappers. It's about Charles. You said he died of a heart attack, but your nephew told me about a car accident."

Claire nodded. "The police told me when it happened he must've lost control of the car. He passed out, you see. By the time they arrived at the hospital he'd died. Oh, they tried to revive him. My Charles was a fighter. As for the accident, the car ran off the road and landed alongside a guard rail without hitting any other vehicles. Thank goodness it involved no other victims. Charles wouldn't have liked that."

"I know this is difficult for you to discuss, but I hoped you might remember where they took him? And the attending physician?"

"Yes. It was Mercy Hospital in Apalachicola. And I believe the doctor's name is Faithful. I remember it because the thought of a doctor called Faithful seemed ironically appropriate. But why is this important, Mira?"

"I'm not sure, yet. But who knows?" Mira shrugged.

"I think we should get started. My friend on the force expects us at six. He's good at his job, but not a patient man," Sean explained.

They arrived at the Port Saint Joe police station in less than twenty minutes. Sean introduced Detective Guárico to Mira and Claire. Soon, another officer led Claire to a room where the sketch artist waited.

"I need to make a phone call to my boss. I'll be back in a few minutes," Mira announced and walked down the hall.

"Tell me, what do you think?" Sean kept his voice lowered as he stood next to the detective.

"I made some phone calls. Can't get anyone to talk," Guárico answered.

"Somebody has to, or this is going nowhere." Sean kept his eyes on the hall for Mira to appear.

"If you think you can do any better, maybe you should've been a cop, huh?" Guárico poked Sean in the side.

"The fat guy makes a joke. Didn't think you had a sense of humor. Nice to see though. It gives you a more well-rounded character."

"All jokes aside, if your friend can describe the guys well enough to the sketch artist, it might be the break we need."

Sean understood he'd need to give Bradley a call soon and let him know what was going on, but he wanted a chance to decompress. Then Mira came back into the room. Sean resisted the urge to reach out and grab a hold of her and kiss her. Deep and sensuous kisses to cover her mouth and face and neck and...He sighed.

"Well, I called Rob to let him know his aunt feels better and she might even help to track down her abductors. He's relieved, of course, but still wants me to pursue getting Claire's property back. I wish I could've told him this was the day to make that happen." Mira shifted to lean against the wall.

Sean understood the weight of all she'd faced, all in a matter of days, and it left her worn out. "I wish you could, too." He rubbed Mira's back and pulled her close enough to rest her head on his chest.

****

Mira felt the wetness of a tear trail down her cheek. She allowed Sean to comfort her, though she hated to appear weak. It was like giving up, and she refused to give up. When Claire walked out with the sketch artist at her side, Mira pulled away from Sean.

"Well, that was easy." Claire smiled with a gleam in her eye.

"She did great." The artist, Simone, nodded and smiled at the older woman. She held out the sketches of the two men.

When Mira caught sight of the faces, she trembled, not ready to accept the image in front of her. She recognized one of them, and the connection left her uneasy. The man outside the motel, the one in the parking lot who looked in her car window, the one who bumped into her at the library, the man who stayed in the room right next to hers, this was the face.

"I've seen him," Mira whispered.

Only Sean who was close enough to hear her reacted. "What? Where, Mira?"

"He's a guest at my motel, in the room next to mine as a matter of fact." She took a deep breath. "And once, when I left my room and reached the parking lot, I found him peeking inside my car. He claimed it was a mistake because his girlfriend's car looks the same. Later on, I saw him in the library. When I reminded him of where we met, he got all defensive and angry."

Sean, Claire, and Detective Guárico were stunned into silence. Too much of a coincidence, and it took a moment to absorb.

"It appears we have a lead. I'll send a deputy over to the motel to bring this guy in for a line up, if you'll come back?" Guárico looked at Claire, who nodded in agreement.

They gave the detective their thanks and left. No one wanted to say much. Even Claire who was ordinarily talkative kept quiet. When they got to the car, Claire slipped into the backseat this time, which left Mira to sit in the front next to Sean.

"This is getting too dangerous for you to stay at that motel alone," Sean said while he drove. His hands gripped the steering wheel. He chanced a look away from the road to wait for her reaction.

"I don't scare so easily. Besides, what am I supposed to do? I won't leave town until I get this matter settled. Claire deserves that much." Mira set her jaw and narrowed her eyes. She wanted Sean to understand she meant every word.

"I agree, but you shouldn't stay alone. Why not come and sleep at my place? It's not far from the motel. I own a beach condo along the Gulf, off the Cape road. You can't turn down a room all to yourself and a great view of the ocean."

He made it sound inviting, Mira admitted. Still, her instincts hinted at one inevitable outcome if she accepted the invitation. Her heart pounded out its warning with thunderous beats. She barely heard his words.

"I don't think it's a good idea. I mean, well, you know." She couldn't finish.

"I promise nothing will happen. I won't take advantage. It's not my style." He reached over to place his hand over hers and smiled.

Soft laughter escaped her lips as she stared out the window. "It's me I don't trust." At last she looked over at him and saw his jaw drop. It made her laugh once more, loud enough that Claire wanted to be let in on the joke.

"Not a joke, Claire. We were discussing possible ways to keep you safe from harm. And I have an idea, if you'll agree to it," Mira said.

"And what is that?"

"To make us both feel safe, why don't I come and stay with you? Neither one of us will be alone, then," Mira suggested. Even Sean acted as if it was a good idea, though Mira detected a hint of disappointment in his eyes. So much for total altruism, she mused.

"Yes, I'd like that. I'd like it very much indeed. But let me warn you, I will put you to work in my garden. And perhaps you can share your gardening secrets with me," Claire answered with a smile though her voice trembled a bit.

"Good. It's settled. Let's go back to the motel. I can pack my things and check out." Mira avoided the comments on gardening. She imagined the smirk on Rob's face when he found out. Maybe she should've taken Sean's offer after all, she thought.

Chapter Nineteen

Another note. Bradley didn't think the next would come so soon. He pulled open the desk drawer and reached for the bottle. Two pills fell into his hand and he took them without water. Then he pushed the button for Gwen.

"Try once more to reach him. I know I've interrupted your busy day, but once in a while I need to remind you who signs your paychecks." He stabbed at the button again before she could answer.

He walked over to the window facing the street and stared out at the stream of cars headed for the Cape. There were days he wished he could be someone else. Forget his zealous ambition, chuck the unreasonable goals he set for himself, and maybe drive to the beach. He could be like all those loafers who swam in the ocean, spent hours out on the water in their boats, without a care whether they'd made the top ten in the national business poll or if the Dow fell.

He walked back to his desk when he heard Gwen's voice. "Mr. Thorndale is on the phone, sir."

****

"I thought maybe you forgot about me," Bradley said.

"No, I don't think I could." Sean held the phone pressed tightly to his ear as he raked a hand through his hair.

"Good. Because it wouldn't be wise. Now, what's the news?"

"The Stanley girl is staying at Claire Peterson's. After the scare the old woman got, and when Mira figured out one of the abductors was the same guy who stayed in her motel, well, you can see where it led."

"Damn fool," Bradley mumbled.

"Yeah, damn fool is right. Both of you. You should have warned him not to be careless. Letting Mira spot him, not once, but several times? Rookie mistake."

"How the hell was I supposed to know the woman would recall so much detail? Most people end up scared out of their wits, too scared to remember a thing."

"It doesn't matter. I can keep a closer watch on them if they're together." Sean tried to efface Lane's fears.

"Maybe. Is the idiot aware of this so he won't be around when the cops come?"

"Why ask me? I'm not the one who gives him his orders." Sean let his words put the implication right where he wanted it—in Lane's face. He tired of the game and the deceptive part he played in it. Each day it became harder to do, but it was the only way. Bradley Lane had to pay for his deeds, past and present. They harmed or destroyed so many lives, and that included Sean's.

"Well, do something about it. Isn't this what I pay you for? If that idiot talks, which I've no doubt he will since he's a coward, we're all done. Make sure it doesn't happen."

****

Bradley ended the call without giving Sean an opportunity to argue. He expected his orders to be followed. They always were.

He studied the note once more, lingered on each word as if it might reveal a new meaning. *I know what you're hiding.* It was similar to all the others, though not as threatening. Whoever sent the notes knew intimate details about him, and it worried Bradley. What he did was confidential, known to a select handful of people who knew better than to share any of it with the public. Unless someone on his team was a traitor.

Bradley realized this left him in an awkward position. He couldn't tell anyone because he didn't know who to trust. He refused to handle his own dirty work. That's what employees were for. Of course, one person might be able to help.

He reached underneath his desk and pushed a button. When the drawer on his right slid open, his hand rummaged inside for the card. Turning it over, he read the number and dialed.

"It's me…Yes, I know, but I'm offering you a job, if you're interested in making a few bucks."

Chapter Twenty

"What do you think they want?" Claire sat next to the fireplace. The cool evening made for a perfect opportunity to light a fire.

"I think—and don't hold me to this because it's merely an educated guess—I think this is a tactic to keep us distracted so we don't find out how Bradley managed to cheat you out of your property. Not to mention a strong-arm move tossed in to make you too terrified to fight back."

"Then they don't know me very well. I don't back down." Claire crossed her arms and sat straight up.

Mira shook her head and laughed. "You remind me of my grandmother. Everyone used to tell me I was her little twin, how I acted just as stubborn and bold."

"Well, it's a good quality, in my opinion."

"Yes. It is." Mira picked up the poker and stoked the fire.

"What's next?" Claire said.

"I'll pay a visit to Mercy hospital and speak with Dr. Faithful."

"I don't understand. What do you expect to find there?"

"Call it a hunch, but when I consider your husband's heart attack and that car accident? I know it sounds paranoid, but I want to make sure the cause of death was truthfully what you've been told," Mira explained and viewed Claire with an anxious eye.

Mira felt relieved her honest yet blunt admission didn't upset Claire. Instead her dear friend relaxed. They sat and talked well into the evening. A sense of warmth, a closeness she hadn't experienced since childhood, filled her. She missed the feeling and hadn't realized it until she sat across from the elderly woman. In an instant, Mira made a stronger commitment to get Claire's home back.

"I think I'll go upstairs to get ready for bed. If you need anything, let me know," Claire announced.

Mira murmured goodnight and then opened a book to read. She needed to relax. A fire, a good book, and a glass of wine should do it. After several pages, she escaped into another world of romantic intrigue in the south of France. When her phone rang, she ignored it. When it rang a second time, she became curious and reached to pick it up. She didn't recognize the number.

"Hello?"

"Yes, Miss Stanley. This is Jessica Lane. I...I need to speak with you."

Mira wasn't sure why, but the woman's voice sounded sincere. Still, her usual defenses told her to say no. "Why do you need to? And how did you get this number?"

"It's not important, talking to you is. That's all I can tell you over the phone."

Mira waited for her to say more, but she didn't. "Look, I don't really know you, Jessica, and I can't— you'll need to give me more."

"But *I* know Bradley Lane. And I have information I believe will help you."

Mira admitted her words got her attention. "Okay. I

guess we can meet."

"Good, and I want you to understand, I'm doing this because he needs to pay."

They agreed to meet at Surf and Suds at noon the next day. As Mira got ready for bed she struggled to dampen the doubts that surfaced. Jessica enticed her with what she claimed to know. Mira was desperate to prove Bradley Lane guilty of fraud. So far, she found no evidence, merely supposition. For that reason she wanted to find out what Jessica had to offer. And Jessica knew it. If only Mira could be certain she was honest. After Claire's abduction, she remained somewhat skeptical.

Friday fast approached. The deadline—according to the surveyor Mira spoke with—was Saturday, the day the bulldozers would arrive to level the property. Today was Wednesday. So close. It made Mira nervous and the sense of panic set in.

She agreed to Sean's offer to walk the paths of St. Joseph Peninsula State Park and experience all the natural beauty of the Panhandle coast. Plus, he convinced her she needed to behave like a tourist at least once before she left Florida. Neither one of them dared to mention when her visit would end.

She considered postponing the invitation until after she resolved the case. Mira sensed the closer it got to Friday, the more aggressive she'd become. She called it her lawyer mentality to fight like an animal in the wild and win. The challenge in this instance was to remain on moral ground and not stoop to Bradley Lane's level and play dirty.

However, she refused to worry about it tonight. Tonight she needed rest. Tomorrow morning she would speak with Dr. Faithful about Charles. Not much, but at the moment it remained the one card she held in her hand.

****

Mira arrived at Mercy Hospital at seven in the morning. The hospital receptionist informed her that Dr. Faithful's full schedule started at nine, and Mira's best chance to speak with him was between seven and eight. Her heel tapped against the chair leg as she sat in the waiting room. A glanced at the clock showed ten till eight. Soon, it wouldn't matter. She knew doctors began to prep before the first surgery. Unless Dr. Faithful agreed to talk to her on the run, this might end up a waste of valuable time.

"Miss Stanley?"

Lost in thought, Mira almost missed seeing the tall gentleman in his white coat as he approached. She read the name tag on his lapel. "Good morning, Dr. Faithful."

He gave Mira a slight nod. "I must say I was surprised to learn you wanted to speak to me about a rather dated case. Charles Peterson, isn't it?"

"Yes. And I assume Mrs. Peterson contacted you?"

"Of course. I wouldn't speak to you about any patient without family permission. What would you like to know?"

"Okay, this may sound strange, but do you recall anything unusual? I mean, I've heard the cause of death was ruled a heart attack, but by all accounts this resulted in the car accident? Is that right?"

"Yes. When they brought Mr. Peterson into Emergency, I found multiple lacerations on his face and arms. The impact sent his head into the window and of

129

course the airbag caused some abrasion."

"But you determined the heart attack happened just prior to the accident?"

"I pinpointed the time of the attack minutes before, yes. But Miss Stanley, help me to understand. I don't see what is unusual enough that you'd come here to discuss it. Do you need to know something in particular?"

"I'm not sure." Mira tried to analyze why and what kept her in doubt. She went over all the facts earlier this morning, every event and every discovery connected to the case, but came up empty.

"Do you see this very often? Accidents caused by heart attack victims behind the wheel, I mean." Mira refused to give up on her hunch.

"Not in my experience. In fact, I can recall only one other case. It was a year before Charles Peterson died. Or maybe less than that, I'm not sure. Hmm, let me think…ah, yes, the man's name was Jason Thomas, from Port Saint Joe, I believe. Same circumstance. Heart attack and car accident. His resulted in a fire, which of course burned most of his body. Close to death when the ambulance arrived, but I was still able to determine the heart attack as the cause."

Mira's heart skipped. "Jason Thomas? Do you recall anything about him, like if any of his family lives around Port Saint Joe and the Cape?"

He shook his head. "I shouldn't talk about this. Still, the newspaper printed a write up at the time with all the details. So, I guess it doesn't matter after all.

"One of his relatives, a cousin, worked for the Port Saint Joe Tribune. He went on a crusade to prove foul play caused Jason's demise. However, as I told you, it was a heart attack. Plain and simple."

"Does this relative still work there?"

"I think so. Although I believe he was reassigned to the society section. The owner got a bit of flak from the Lane family for publishing Thomas' articles in the first place. I figured the reassignment was a way to punish Thomas without firing him."

"The Lanes? How do they figure into this?" Mira was puzzled but hoped this might be useful information.

"Thomas seemed to think they figured into all of it and spouted off his belief nonstop. He claimed Lane Developers pursued his cousin's property for years. When he refused to deal, they killed him. At least it's what Thomas suspected. You'll find it all in the papers and the court case."

"Court case?"

"Yes. Jason's cousin acted by taking the Lane dynasty to court. A civil suit against the family for claims of harassment that led to Jason's poor health and eventually the heart attack. Pretty clever move on the cousin's part, wouldn't you agree?"

Mira couldn't believe she missed it. Her thorough research made no mention of a court case or the reporter's claims against Lane Developers.

"How did the case end?"

"I believe they settled out of court. From what I heard, Bradley Lane became anxious enough to end it and get his company out of the spotlight. Every day, people talked and pointed fingers at him. He recognized the potential damage to his reputation, and hence to the company's. He's all about business."

"Yeah, I gathered as much. Did Jason's cousin

leave the matter alone after this?"

"I guess. At least I heard no mention of it since then. That was nearly two years ago. If you ask me, no one person alone can fight a dynasty like the Lanes. Not for long. Otherwise, well, the damage is not worth the effort."

"Damage?"

"Think of it. Besides Jason Thomas' ordeal with Lane—and you know how that turned out—there's Charles Peterson's situation. A healthy man with a healthy heart. I know this because his family doctor is a friend of mine. After a couple of years fighting against the likes of Bradley Lane, it took its toll on him."

"What fighting? I was told Charles made a deal with Lane to sell his property after his death so his wife was taken care of financially."

"You may be right. I don't know the details of that. A few others may tell you the particulars of his story better than I."

"Like who for instance?" Mira perused a mental checklist of those she knew and came up with nothing credible. Bradley Lane's opinion was slanted, and of course there was Claire who doubtless remained left in the dark about any trouble Charles encountered. He wanted to protect his wife from worrying, Mira guessed.

"Well, the reporter, Stan Thomas, for one. According to some, he has dogged every move Bradley Lane makes. I hear ever since his cousin died, he's kept his eye on that man, waiting for him to get careless, I guess, and reveal his true character."

"Who told you this?" Mira was amazed how much the doctor knew about the Lanes and Jason's cousin.

"Oh, my wife. She has far too much time on her hands between going to the club and gossiping with her friends who also tend to squander their lives in such ways, and to the salon where she hears stories. You know, who does what and where. A true wealth of information, all of which I am privileged to hear at dinner every evening."

Mira tried to suppress a smile. "I guess I should be going. I appreciate your help and taking time out of your schedule to talk."

"It's my pleasure. Given some time to have a normal conversation without all the medical jargon and with such pleasant company is refreshing. If you think of any other questions, please call."

As he walked away, an idea came to her. "Dr. Faithful, can you think of any way a heart attack involves foul play?"

The doctor turned around and faced Mira. "Well, I'd like to say none exists, but with drugs it can be forced. Not in this case though. Toxicology reports turned up negative for drugs."

"Okay. Thanks," Mira said and left the hospital. She still wasn't convinced. Anything was possible in her world. If someone wanted to and became desperate enough, it was possible. She was certain of that. And Bradley Lane was the type to want it.

Chapter Twenty-One

With all that happened in the past twenty-four hours, Mira grew apprehensive about the meeting with Jessica. Why should she trust anyone who was part of that family? True enough, she wanted more dirt on Bradley Lane. It was worth listening if Jessica possessed any valuable evidence, and if she was on the level.

It was a few minutes before noon and she still hadn't told Claire about her luncheon date. More than likely, revealing whom she planned to meet would prompt Claire to tell her she shouldn't go. At the last minute, she handed her some excuse; she needed toiletries from the drugstore. Then she rushed out the door.

Driving along the Cape made Mira relax, and the jitters from this morning faded. The view from her car window showed the ocean water sparkling in the sunlight as the waves played back and forth. She wondered if she could ever leave her home in Ohio and live where sunlight and warmth occurred all year long.

The bright orange siding of Surf and Suds appeared a half a mile in front of her. As she approached, once more she found few cars situated in the parking lot. Out of the handful, Mira guessed which one belonged to Jessica Lane. The late model Mercedes parked near the back edge of the lot.

When she stepped inside, she looked around but didn't see any sign of a familiar face. Jessica was tall and blonde with a model-like physique. It was hard to miss. Mira walked over to one of the servers to ask.

"Did you happen to notice a rather tall, attractive blonde woman come in recently?"

The man shook his head. "Maybe check downstairs? You'll find a bar down there. Many of our customers like the atmosphere better."

Mira thanked the man and descended the stairs to reach the first floor. The dim lighting gave the room an atmosphere of secrecy. She counted a handful of tables, but several stools flanked the entire bar and all were occupied. Seated back in the far corner was Jessica Lane. She nodded at Mira and motioned with a slight movement of her hand to come over.

"Miss Stanley. Thank you for coming. I was afraid you changed your mind."

Mira shook her head. "I did, several times, but I decided if there was a chance to learn something relevant, I didn't want to miss it."

"I understand. You want to help Mrs. Peterson. And I want justice. I want Bradley Lane to pay for his mistakes." Jessica took another sip of her drink. "And Vivian Lane. She is the worst one of all the Lanes. Don't ever let her fool you. She's good at that. Fooling people, I mean."

Mira waited while Jessica downed her margarita and order another. "Why do you want them to pay? They are Kyle's family and you're his wife. I take it you carry no family loyalty?"

Jessica threw back her head and laughed. "That's a joke. Family loyalty. You ever hear of the expression there's no honor among thieves?"

Mira nodded.

"Well, like a den of thieves we Lanes don't believe in trust or loyalty as much as saving our own skins, which includes making a profit. If my husband got in the way of business, for instance, I wouldn't put it past Bradley to cut him off. It's come close a couple of times. Believe me, I was there to see it." She took another few sips of her drink.

Mira sensed the bitterness. It seemed a shame for such a beautiful woman to be unhappy. And she wondered how often Jessica Lane regretted her actions from the past, the choice to trade Sean for Kyle Lane and his fortune.

"All right. I'm interested. What do you have that concerns Bradley Lane? How do you plan to help me?" Mira sat back and sipped her water. She declined the offer for a drink. She needed to keep a clear head.

Jessica reached into her bag and pulled out a bottle. She handed it to Mira. "I found these in Kyle's dresser drawer. He claims our doctor wrote the prescription for him. I didn't question him further, but I was suspicious. Kyle never takes pills. He's a health nut and only puts natural substances into his body. Anyway, I took this to a pharmacy for someone to check."

Mira looked at the bottle and and squinted at what left of the label. "What is it?"

"It's cisapride and is prescribed for nighttime heartburn. Or at least, it used to be. And I know Kyle suffers from heartburn. That part wasn't hard to believe. But get this. The drug was taken off the general market in 2000 when it was found to cause irregular heartbeats or arrhythmia, and in many cases heart attacks. Today, it's reserved for special patients with extreme health issues."

"But why would your husband hide this in his dresser?"

"I don't know. When I questioned him—I spun some lie about a health report on television I'd seen—he got angry with me and told me to mind my own business and quit asking questions or it would get me into serious trouble. His response made me more suspicious than ever and more determined to find out." Jessica's voice grew loud.

Mira figured the tequila and anger took over and did the talking. "Why don't we take a walk along the beach? It's such a nice day and it might be a way to blow off steam."

"No, I'm afraid I can't. If anyone I know sees us together, it will get back to the family. Trust me. I'd be dead along with the rest of them within a week."

"The rest of them?" Mira feared the woman had lost touch with reason and turned beyond coherent.

"Your friend's husband for one. And others." Jessica leaned forward and lowered her voice. "Let me tell you something, Miss Stanley. I like you, and I know Sean likes you. It's because of him I want to help you, even if it does put me in danger. This bottle wasn't Kyle's doing. He's not smart enough or cold enough to come up with a clever scheme. But Bradley Lane? He's smart enough, and he's the devil himself, if you ask me. I've seen him when he's at his worst. And it's frightening." Jessica tapped her fingernail against the bottle.

"The pharmacist is a friend of mine. He's filled my prescriptions for years, not to mention for other family members. He was able to trace this one from the serial number and guess what he found? The one who prescribed this was none other than Bradley Lane's doctor. And I'm certain that man doesn't experience heartburn. His insides are cold as stone and hard as steel. Nothing bothers him."

"What do you mean?" Mira didn't want to believe nor say aloud what Jessica implied.

"Why did Bradley possess a prescription for cisapride unless he intended its use for someone else? And why give someone a heartburn medication meant only for special cases unless it's intended to do harm? Harm to somebody like Charles Peterson, for instance? I know it sounds paranoid, but we are talking about Bradley Lane."

Mira didn't speak. Jessica's suspicions were outrageous if not implausible. The idea that Bradley Lane cheated Charles Peterson out of his property was conceivable...but this? This meant premeditated murder. Mira wasn't about to agree. Instead, she thanked Jessica and left. It came to mind the case led down a path more serious, more dangerous than she ever expected. She hoped she was able to handle it without becoming a victim herself.

As she pulled out of the parking lot and glanced in the rearview mirror she spotted the sleek Mercedes sitting there alone. Mira said a little prayer for Jessica Lane. She figured Jessica needed it.

****

"What the hell gave you such an idea? Meeting her might have been dangerous. No telling what she'd do," Sean said, an angry but worried look planted on his face.

"Well, it wasn't and I'm fine," Mira argued. She hoped he'd be more responsive to the suspicions about Bradley than focusing on the fact she met with Jessica.

"She's a loose cannon. I know her better than you do. And I wouldn't take much stock in her suspicions." He paced back and forth.

"And the bottle of pills?" Mira reminded him.

"It's simple. Bradley Lane got the prescription for heartburn and gave some to Kyle when he experienced similar problems. It's the logical explanation."

"Bradley doesn't get heartburn."

"How do you know? Just because Jessica says it's true? Why else would his doctor be willing to prescribe it?" Sean came over and sat next to Mira. "Don't buy into her paranoia. She's an expert at it, and it's easy to believe her. I used to, until I got wise."

"You mean when she left you for Kyle?" Mira didn't mean to be abrupt, but his demeanor showed it bothered him too much. She struggled to shake her suspicions he still carried feelings for his ex. It made Mira upset, and ashamed to admit, maybe jealous. However, the hurt look on his face made her regret the remark. "I'm sorry."

"Don't apologize. What happened is in the past. What you've tried to piece together to make a case for Claire is useless. You're moving in the wrong direction and losing valuable time. It's precisely what she wants. She's on *their* side, not yours. Even if it's by marriage, she's still a Lane through and through." He got back up and walked over to stare out the kitchen window in silence.

Mira didn't know what to think. She became confused once more and frustrated enough to hold plenty of doubt. Who was she to believe, Jessica or Sean? They both carried different agendas. How was she supposed to know with any credibility what those agendas in fact were?

She felt certain Sean cared for her and had no reason to hurt her with lies and deceit. As for Jessica, she gained nothing by lying to Mira about Bradley. Right? Bottom line, Mira didn't know the woman, but Sean did. She should believe him, though it deflated her mood. She'd lack evidence needed to prove Bradley cheated Claire and Charles. Mira sighed and massaged her temples.

"I need a drink." Mira looked in the cupboards for anything Claire might have stashed away. The elderly woman had gone upstairs to take a nap. The ordeal of the past couple of days left her weak and tired. Certainly, Mira would feel the same way if someone wanted to tear down her home.

"Here." Sean handed her a glass. "It's bourbon. I found it hidden under the sink."

Mira gave him a suspicious stare.

"A common place to hide liquor. My great aunt used to do the same. Here, drink." Sean leaned back against the wall and waited.

Mira sipped from the glass. It gave her time to let her nerves settle. When Sean's eyes stared once more out the back window hers followed his, straight to the storage shed.

"Is your mind focused on Claire's mysterious visitor?" Mira was grateful for the welcome change of topic.

Sean shrugged. "It's a mystery all right. If she did see someone, why didn't the cops find any sign? Not even a shoe print on the ground? Some evidence to show he or she might have been inside the shed. It doesn't follow."

"You mean unless she imagined the whole incident?"

"Well, she does talk to dead people, doesn't she?" Sean smiled.

"But that's her husband. I imagine lots of widows and widowers do the same. They miss their spouses and it's a way to stay close."

"If they believe the dead spouse is actually dead, that is," Sean added. His brows knitted together and he scratched his chin for a brief moment.

"You know, something puzzles me. Claire has never mentioned other relatives or friends, besides Rob. I wonder if she has anyone."

"Hmm. You're right. And it's easy enough to check out."

Mira gave him a puzzled look.

"Ask her." Sean laughed and so did Mira. Both relaxed after their tense conversation about Jessica.

"I think I'll go upstairs and check on her to make sure she's sleeping okay." Mira finished her drink and left the room.

She returned in a moment to find Sean quiet, his eyes staring absently out the window. "All peaceful and relaxed. I don't think she'll be up for a while. I'm rather tired myself. A nap sounds like a great idea."

"Are you kidding me? You plan to waste this glorious, sun-filled day? Night time is for sleep. You should come to the park with me as I suggested earlier." Sean winked and a smile spread from ear to ear.

His smile and persuasiveness worked on her. She

needed some relaxing time, and the fresh air from a walk would do her good.

"You don't give up, do you? Well, I'm tempted, but only a short visit. Maybe an hour or two? Then I need to be back here. I promised Claire I'd help out in the garden, doing gardening things like pruning and whatever else." Mira's eyes reflected the misery she held inside. With no more excuses, the moment had arrived to put her lack of knowledge to the test. Rob and his idiotic ideas, she thought.

"Great. Let's go. We can be back in plenty of time if we start right away." Sean grabbed Mira's sneakers from underneath the table and her jacket off the coat rack.

Mira laughed and reached down to put on the shoes. "I guess you've made sure I don't have time to change my mind."

"Exactly. Now, let's go. Chop, chop." He grabbed her arm and pulled her out the door. "You'll love this park. Because of all the unique wildlife, it's one of the best nature parks in the country."

"Oh, I can imagine." Mira smiled and tried not to feel guilty for experiencing a bit of happiness. At any rate, she deserved some pleasure. She'd worked hard all her adult life and paid the price. The time had arrived to get something back. She hoped this man could help her do that.

Chapter Twenty-Two

For almost an hour they walked the path. The snow white sand dunes spread outward along the sides, untouched by man's footprint, making it the perfect secluded setting. Mira felt herself relax. Flamingos waded in the bay water and Sean pointed out several hawks as well as a peregrine falcon flying overhead. The one moment to threaten her calm state was the mention of alligators.

"Well, let's hope we avoid the pleasure of that encounter," Mira quipped while she darted her eyes back and forth across the path.

Around the next bend they found a wooden bench carved with uneven and jagged lines situated off to the side. "Let's stop for a few minutes. I want to dump the sand out of my shoes. Besides, I'm a city girl and not used to this much walking."

"Weenie."

"Did you seriously call me a weenie? What are you? Five?" Mira teased back.

Sean rubbed his knuckles across the top of her head and then put his arm around Mira's shoulder. "I'm enjoying this. Aren't you?"

Mira leaned her head against Sean and remained quiet while she looked out over the bay. She felt at peace and didn't want it to end, especially the idea of leaving Florida. She quickly dismissed the unhappy reminder and tilted her face up to look at Sean.

"Yes, I am. And thank you. I feel at ease in this place."

"Good." He squeezed her arm and drew her closer. When she was inches from his face he moved in to brush his lips against hers. "And I hope you find the company enjoyable, too. I know I do," he murmured, and then kissed her.

Mira sensed the warm glow inside. His kiss left her wanting more and he gave it to her, one long and sensuous moment. Afterward, she didn't think she could move, until at last he stood up and pulled her to her feet.

"It's late. I think we should head back to the car." He led her down the path.

When they reached the parking lot, Mira discovered someone standing next to the car. His back was turned to them so she didn't see his face. Yet, Mira recognized something familiar.

She gasped and pulled on Sean's sleeve. "It's him. The peeper from the motel and Claire's kidnapper."

"Are you sure?" Sean picked up his pace to walk faster toward the car with Mira right beside him.

"Definitely. Same build, hair color, even the pants and the jacket are a match. I remember the Ohio Buckeyes because, well, you know. It's him."

Sean called out. "Hey! Buddy! What are you doing next to my car?"

It took a second, but once the peeper caught sight of Sean and Mira he bolted across the lot with Sean right on his tail. Left behind, Mira elected to call for help. If the peeper carried a weapon, he might hurt Sean. And she couldn't let it happen.

Once on the phone with the police, she relayed the information. Then, she started after Sean who had disappeared into the wooded area. She reached the edge of the lot and stopped to listen. She heard the shouts and scuffle in the distance; it came from the left of where she stood. A quick debate on whether to stay there or follow took her only a few seconds.

As she started for the path, her eye caught sight of another vehicle. It was situated behind a tree and clusters of tall grass where it hadn't been visible from the other side of the lot.

A gasp escaped her throat and her feet pulled to a halt. A familiar gray pickup truck with noticeable dents and dings on the front bumper made Mira's heart pound. In rapid succession her mind put the facts together for a clear picture. Her peeper had to be the driver who rammed her rear end out on Route 30. It didn't take much of a stretch to her imagination to figure out what or who came next. Bradley Lane. She'd bet on the connection to that and win.

Mira heard the sound of voices as they grew louder. She put her feet in gear once more and headed down the path. When she reached another turn and traveled a few more yards, she found Sean and the other guy wrestling on the ground.

"Stop struggling. I've got you pinned."

Mira heard Sean's muffled voice speak into the peeper's shoulder. He pinned him, but by the looks of it, that didn't mean the guy was giving up. Mira walked closer to them. "I called the police."

Sean looked back at Mira, but didn't loosen his hold. "I guess this kind of ruins the date, huh?"

"Are you kidding? A little excitement thrown into

the mix while my date shows off his muscle, what more could a girl want?" Mira teased.

Within a few minutes the Port Saint Joe police arrived and took the peeper into custody. Mira suggested to them if the gray truck belonged to the peeper, he was the guy who rear-ended her the other day. One look from Sean told her she'd have to explain later. They all walked back to the parking lot. Mira and Sean remained silent until the cruiser drove away.

"Now, you want to tell me about this accident of yours?" Sean spoke with a hint of irritation in his voice.

Mira shrugged. "At the time I figured it was no more than an unpleasant Florida welcome. I mean, I kind of suspected it might be something worse, but no way did I connect it to Bradley Lane." At least not at first, she admitted secretly.

"From now on, please let me know when any more unpleasant incidents happen, will you?" Sean left it at that and headed for the car while Mira followed close behind.

"I hope they can persuade him to talk. Maybe we can find out why those men kidnapped Claire." Mira attempted to lead the conversation in another direction.

They pulled out of the parking lot and headed back toward town. Sean kept his eyes on the road, never once glancing her way. The romantic mood from a moment ago disappeared, and somehow it bothered her. Not how the mood changed. She understood how that happened. Yet he grew distant, as if he guarded whatever crossed his mind, afraid she might figure it out.

"You know, I wonder what he was doing when we interrupted him." Sean's thumb tapped on the steering wheel.

"Huh?"

"Well, he must've been up to something. Why else stand by the car?"

Mira suddenly guessed why Sean had been so preoccupied. "Maybe he wanted to break in to steal it and leave us stranded."

"Maybe." Sean grew silent again and slipped back once more into silence.

As they left the park, Mira told Sean she'd like to stop for ice cream at Surf and Suds.

"A yummy treat. What do you say?" she persuaded.

"Fine with me, but when did Claire expect you? Five? It's almost that time."

"Let me give her a call. Besides, I need some comfort food after the peeper caper."

Sean laughed and pulled the car into the parking lot. They were the only customers by the looks of it. At the counter they ordered sundaes and then talked while they sat out on the back deck with its view of the bay.

"It still bugs me," Sean continued.

"You mean about the guy?"

"How did he know we'd be there? As far as I knew, nobody followed us into the park. And no other cars sat in the lot when we got there."

Mira shrugged. "Perhaps he saw you someplace else before? Look how he found me. Let's face it. You and I share one important person in common. Claire. And it so happens, the peeper has an interest in Claire. It's our common denominator. If he spied on me, why not spy on you? Makes sense, right?"

"I'm afraid it does. But this still doesn't explain

what he was doing."

As he made the comment, Sean and Mira heard an explosion, loud enough to shake the table and chairs where they sat. Both of them stared at each other, stunned. In the next second their server rushed onto the deck, ice cream sundaes in hand. He set them down and turned to go back inside. He threw out a hurried explanation as he went.

"Man, you should see it. Some dude's car is toast. Right out there in the parking lot, just blew up and— Wait!" The server stopped and turned to face Sean and Mira once more. "Awe, dude, I'm sorry. That must be your car."

Sean and Mira looked at each other once again. They scrambled out of their chairs to run across the restaurant to stare out at the parking lot. Sure enough, Sean's car sat engulfed in a pyre of flames. The sight of it left Mira ready to faint. Her knees buckled, and Sean caught her before she collapsed on the floor.

"Well, I guess we know what he was doing." Sean continued to look at the burning heap of metal while he held Mira close.

Mira glanced up to see his expression. She shivered. Though uncertain whether it was caused by the sight of the smoking ruins in the parking lot and their close call with death, the look on Sean's faced frightened her. The look which suggested he could kill someone. One thing she was certain of, though. She wouldn't want to be that guy.

Chapter Twenty-Three

"You messed up. I sent you to do a job and you messed it up. Incredible." Bradley tipped his glass and finished the whiskey. "That property needs to be leveled by the start of next week. And you better make sure no one gets in the way of my plans. Understood?" Bradley cut off the call and turned to look at his mother.

"I take it things aren't progressing smoothly," Vivian poured more into Bradley's glass. They sat out on the veranda. Clarice served sandwiches and fruit salad for their lunch.

Bradley recognized the look in Vivian's eyes, the one which sized him up every time she saw him. "I can handle it, Mother. Don't bother me with your sardonic jabs."

"Why, I'm offended, Bradley. I hardly use sarcasm where you're concerned. I'm always completely serious."

Bradley caught the true gist of her remark, but ignored it. She wanted control, and he'd never give it to her without a fight. "As I told you, I can manage without your input. If you'll excuse me, I need to get back to work." He got up to leave.

"Without eating?" Vivian stared down at his empty glass.

Bradley raised a brow and grabbed his sandwich off the plate. He turned to leave, but not before hearing her muffled laughter. Pompous old bag, he thought and went out the door.

****

The office was quiet with no one there to bother him. He sat back in his chair and brought his feet up to rest on his desk. A nap sounded nice. Any visit with Vivian left him exhausted. But of course he couldn't relax, not with everything left to finish before the weekend and his deadline. Still, he recognized the exhilaration, every time he closed a deal, every time he won, he got the feeling. It was what he lived for. No other aspect of his life, personal or otherwise, excited him anymore. Not even a beautiful woman. It should worry him, he guessed. Yet, it didn't.

He never intended to marry and share all of his wealth with a family. He'd seen how it complicated life and make people miserable. His parents and brother were testimony to such a debacle. And since he was in his forties, it mattered even less.

Bradley reached under the desk and pressed the button to release the drawer. He retrieved his black book from underneath the stack of files and studied the pages, read all the notations he'd made. The names, dates, and events he'd kept track of were all there, a collection covering the past ten years. If anyone in his employ breathed wrong, he kept a record of all useful information to keep them in line. Sure, they were threats he might not be able to carry out, but no one had called his bluff yet. No one wanted to take the chance to have their dirty laundry hang out to dry, as the saying went.

With the tables turned, he broiled at the idea of becoming the victim of his own game. He hadn't figured out who held the cards. When he did, Bradley resolved that person would pay dearly. In the meantime, he was taking care of the matter. And when it was finished, all those threats would be worth no more than the paper they were written on. The thought gave him extreme satisfaction. Once the book rested back in its hiding place, Bradley picked up his cell phone to call Kyle.

"I wanted to call and ask how things are going. We've had no chance to talk since the party...and, well, Mother wanted me to speak with you." Bradley tried to keep his voice cheery, though he imagined it sounded contrived or forced. It wasn't in his nature to be cheery.

"About?" Kyle also wasn't the jovial type.

"Your wife. Mother thinks she's attracted too much attention and has gotten chummy with the enemy."

"Enemy? Oh, you mean the Stanley woman."

"Yes, her."

"Don't worry. I've spoken to her. She'll keep her distance. In any case, I think it proved to be a clever move inviting her to the party. Makes her feel we've nothing to hide."

"I'm not so confident. However, if it will get Mother off my back, that's good enough. I'll let her know you spoke with Jessica."

Kyle continued the conversation to explain how during his investigation into her past, he'd found one noteworthy fact about Mira Stanley.

"Oh?" Bradley gripped the phone a little tighter and waited.

"My informant claims the Stanley woman had a nasty falling out with a former beau. Name's Alex Renfeld from Milton, Ohio. She had to put a restraining order on him. Not scandalous, but intriguing all the same. Don't you agree?"

The corners of Bradley's mouth turned up. "I imagine it has possibilities. Keep me posted." Bradley ended the call before Kyle could start a new topic.

A second later, the office door flew open. In stormed Sean Thorndale with Gwen right on his heels.

"I tried to make him wait until I called you, Mr. Lane, but he wouldn't listen," Gwen explained.

"It's all right, Gwen. You can go." Bradley waited for the door to close behind her before he turned to level his eyes at Sean. "What's happened?"

"That's the question I came to ask you. What the hell did you do? My car sits in a parking lot, burnt to ashes. Somebody rigged a bomb in it. If we hadn't stopped on our way back to town..." Sean ran his fingers through his hair, and then braced both arms on Bradley's desk. He leaned over. "Don't mess with me. I'm warning you." His eyes glared with hate.

"I don't know what the hell you mean. A bomb?" Bradley, for the first time in a long while, felt unsure of himself.

"If you sent someone to kill me, or Mira Stanley, I'll find out. Believe me. I will find out," Sean finished and with steps as pronounced as his words he marched out of the office.

Bradley leaned back in his chair and drew in a deep breath to relax. Though confused, he planned to get to the bottom of Sean's accusation. He refused to be blamed for something he didn't do, but he understood how Sean might make the assumption. If someone connected to him was responsible for a stunt like that, Bradley would discover who and bury him. No one under his employ made a move, unless he ordered it. Matters became too messy otherwise, like now.

He sighed and made yet another phone call. "I'm afraid one of your men thinks he's in charge of things. You need to talk with him, and soon." Bradley suddenly remembered the name Kyle had given him. "Oh, and I have one more task for you."

Chapter Twenty-Four

Mira sat next to Claire at the kitchen table after they'd spent the past hour in the garden, weeding and pruning Claire's prize roses. Mira worked alongside her while she listened to the knowledgeable woman's animated chatter about her hobby in how to crossbreed and fertilize to achieve the best flower. As if by magic, it transformed the old woman into an energized young girl. Mira kept quiet, with a nod or a smile thrown into the picture every so often. She hoped Claire's enthused accounts of gardening shows and tips continued to last without any probing questions, which might reveal Mira's secret. However, it wasn't to be.

"Most everyone around seem to think my flowers grow well because of the soil. They say it's special. Special ingredients in the minerals." Claire shrugged. "Tests at a lab turned up no unique qualities. Though I'll admit I needn't add bone meal or high doses of nitrogen when I fertilize. I prefer to use natural fertilizer mixed with cottonseed and alfalfa meal." Claire stretched her arms a bit and chuckled. "Maybe they're jealous. You think?"

Mira smiled. "Possibly. I mean, you *have* won plenty of competitions."

"Tell me, which do you prefer to keep away those pesky bugs? Summer oil or insecticidal soap? Personally, I like the soap. The oils are a bit harsh during the Florida summer heat. And neem oil works well on fungus. It stinks a bit, but it wipes out the mildew and black spots without all those chemicals." Claire stopped pruning to glance at Mira. She smiled and waited for her response.

Mira glanced down to concentrate on a stray weed and shrugged. "I guess the oil works fine where I live," she started, but hurried to add, "Of course, I can't speak from experience, not like you."

Claire nodded and went back to her pruning. "Most gardeners don't realize water is the cheapest and safest way to get rid of most insects. A good, strong spray will knock them off."

After a long torturous hour, Mira smiled gratefully when Claire suggested they go inside to freshen up. Any chance to get away from gardening and from Claire's questions, which Mira managed to stumble over when answering, was a welcome invitation. Claire may be elderly, Mira acknowledged, but not stupid. In fact, anyone with half a brain wouldn't be fooled.

Claire set a plate of sugar cookies and a frosted glass of lemonade in front of Mira. She seemed to study the young woman for a moment before speaking.

"You really don't know a thing about gardening and growing roses, do you?"

Mira coughed as she choked on the crumbs of her cookie. She swallowed large gulps of lemonade, set the glass down on the table, and then nodded. "Well, I guess you could say when God handed out the green thumbs mine was brown."

Claire leaned forward in her chair and laughed. "Brown, heh? I guess we need to work on that. A little gardening knowhow should help. But tell me…" Claire sipped from her glass. "Why claim you knew how to garden?"

Mira shrugged. "It was your nephew's idea. He recommended you might open up to me better if I talked gardening."

Claire chuckled and shook her head. "Sounds like Robert's squirrely logic. I can't imagine how he wins in the courtroom."

"Confuses the jury with his squirrely logic, I guess."

They both laughed and continued to chat about other things besides gardening. In a while, the heaviness of Mira's eyelids and a blanket of fatigue took charge. She missed more than one comment Claire made.

"I'm sorry, Claire. I guess I'm too tired to think," Mira confessed.

"I understand. This hasn't exactly been a typical week, has it?" Claire got up from the table and walked over to the counter to put away the cookies and place the pitcher of lemonade in the refrigerator.

"Hell, this isn't typical in anyone's lifetime." Mira didn't mean to sound blunt, but she couldn't help it. Little more than an hour ago, she and Sean almost became victims of a car bombing. If it hadn't been for her sudden craving for ice cream and stopping at Surf and Suds…She didn't want to dwell on it, but there it was. It played over and over again in her head. And the person closest to the situation, the one who experienced the same trauma, dropped her off at the doorstep and left. Sean's brief explanation told her he needed to attend to some business and would return, soon.

"I'm sorry I've gotten you into the middle of this."

Claire's voice trembled.

Mira looked up and found her eyes welled with tears. "Oh, Claire, don't you dare think this is your fault. I wouldn't have it any other way than being in the middle of it. I *want* to help you. I consider you a friend, a dear friend if you don't realize it, and I stand by my friends when they're in trouble."

Mira watched as Claire nodded and turned to wipe the crumbs off of the counter. She felt miserable and useless. This wasn't how the case was supposed to go. She should've been able to figure out a way to break the deal with Lane and hand Claire the deed to her property, all in a couple of days. Life, however, refused to turn out that simple.

"I think you and I should get out and do some shopping," Mira suggested and tried to inject a bit of cheer in her voice. "Shopping always manages to lift my spirits. You know, to buy something frivolous and splurge on a gift, which my practical self seldom does. What do you say?"

Claire turned and smiled at Mira, the tears dried away. "That's a lovely idea."

Mira and Claire heard the doorbell ring. "It's probably Sean." Mira hurried to the front of the house. She pulled open the door and gasped.

"Hello, Mira. It's been a long time."

Mira stared for second. She didn't trust her voice to answer, but the anger took hold. "What are you doing here, Alex? I've got nothing left to say to you, nothing left period." She tried to close the door, but he pushed back. She remembered her gun still in its hiding place, and cursed under her breath. Her mind struggled to regain confidence and not fall victim to the fear from the past. However, as if it were only yesterday she and Alex were a couple, all she managed to think was what a monster he'd become. "I told you, Alex. We are done." She gave an extra hard shove, but it had no effect.

"Oh, we're far from done, I'd say." He tried to step forward into the house, but something or someone pulled him back with a hard jerk.

"I'd listen to the lady, if I were you, bud. Now, get moving. As quick as you can before I decide to do something that will make you regret staying," Sean growled as he shoved Alex toward the drive.

"This is none of your business, *bud*," Alex retorted.

Sean shook his head. "It's very much my business. Get your ass out of here." He gave Alex another shove, much more forceful than the first.

Mira leaned her arm against the door frame, not trusting her legs to hold her up. Her heart resumed a calmer pace after Alex got into his car. If Sean hadn't arrived when he did, she didn't want to imagine what Alex might have done. She worried more about Claire's wellbeing than her own. Thinking of her made Mira turn around and gasp. Claire stood right behind her holding a cast iron skillet in both hands.

"I wasn't taking any chances," Claire explained.

Mira didn't know whether to laugh or cry. Instead, she gave Claire a hug. "You are too wonderful, you know that?"

Claire sniffed. "Hardly wonderful, but I carry a whole lot of sass. I can guarantee that."

Sean stepped back into the house, once Alex drove away. He studied Mira for a brief second. "You want to tell me what just happened?"

Mira bit down on her tongue. Her eyes darted from Claire and back to Sean. "Maybe we could talk later?" she suggested.

Sean seemed ready to protest, but finally shook his head. "Fine, but we will talk, right?"

Mira nodded and told Sean of their shopping plans, relieved to change the subject. Later, she'd have to explain. It wasn't fair not to, not after what happened a moment ago. The sinking realization that Alex had come to Florida sent a cold shiver of fear through her body. How did he manage to find her? It didn't make sense. However, she didn't have time to brood over it. They had shopping to do. And she refused to worry Claire.

They spent the next half hour primping. They planned their trip to Apalachicola to visit several stores Claire enjoyed. Mira expected Sean to make his exit and find more important things to entertain his afternoon, but he surprised her.

"I'll come along with you," Sean announced.

"You're serious? Most men I know can't manage the patience for the way women shop," Mira commented. She guessed at his motives, but wanted him to come out and say it.

He leaned closer and kept his voice in a low tone. "I don't want you venturing off anywhere alone. Not after what happened."

Mira sighed. "I can take care of myself and Claire. You have no reason to babysit us."

"Oh, I think I do. Besides, if anything happened to you..." He didn't finish the statement, but his expression did.

"Fine. If it makes you feel better, come along."

Mira grabbed her bag and keys, which she handed to Sean. "You might as well drive, too. Lord knows in my fragile state of mind I'd be too nervous to get behind the wheel." She hated the fact he might be right, and it showed.

Sean shook his head. "Go ahead and make fun. My motive is to be cautious. That's all."

"I certainly don't mind a little male security to come along and make me feel safe," Claire commented.

Sean gave Mira a smug look and then smiled at Claire. "Thank you, Claire. I appreciate it."

"Geesh," Mira mumbled and led the way outside to the car.

****

Their excursion led into late evening and near dark. They had time for a light dinner, but ended it with Claire's apple dumplings for dessert. By the time they finished cleaning up the kitchen, Claire was ready to turn in for the night.

"The day was quite enjoyable. Thank you again. It took my mind off things," Claire said before she excused herself and went upstairs.

Mira waited for her disappear before turning to face Sean.

"Maybe now you're ready to have the talk where you explain about the unwelcome visitor?" Sean kept a steady gaze on Mira.

Mira paused to think for moment. She needed to calm down from this afternoon's disturbing event in order to leave her emotions out of it when she told him the story. "I know it's not fair to keep you in the dark, but if you'll wait a bit longer? I promise. I'll tell you." Her eyes pleaded with Sean.

Sean smiled and shrugged his shoulders in defeat. "Well, I guess I should head for home. Unless you think your frail feminine self needs me to stay the night and protect you," Sean teased.

"Oh that's real cute. No, I think I can handle it. Me, my feminine self, and I will be fine without you."

Sean put a hand over his heart. "Woman, you've wounded my chivalrous spirit. I don't know if I'll ever recover."

Mira laughed and walked over to him. She placed her hand over his. "I think we can figure something out."

"Oh?" He pulled Mira to his chest and stroked her hair. "And what exactly did you have in mind?"

Mira rested her head against him. His heart pulsed. Its thunderous beat pounded in her ear. "The same as you do, I imagine," she murmured.

Sean placed his hand underneath Mira's chin and tipped it up toward his face. He kissed her; his lips soft and wet sent a shiver through her.

"Maybe I should spend the night," he whispered in her ear.

"Umm." She didn't answer, not while the blood rushed to her head and made her feel giddy.

When he led her to the sofa and they sat down, Mira surrendered her feelings to his incredible touch. His kisses and caresses stirred emotions she'd missed for a long time. But when his hand reached to explore more of her body she leaned away and found her voice.

"No, wait. Maybe we shouldn't." She stumbled over her words and looked up at Sean with an apologetic smile.

Sean smiled back and tweaked her under the chin.

"I'm a patient man, Mira Stanley. I can wait…at least for a while longer." He grabbed hold of her hand and pulled her up off of the sofa. With one final kiss, he murmured good night.

"Thank you," Mira whispered, though she suspected it might sound lame.

Sean laughed. "You're quite welcome, I think. Now remember, if you hear or see anything out of place, anything suspicious, call me right away. I'll keep my phone right next to me. In fact, I doubt if I will sleep while waiting for your call."

"Good. Serves you right for taking me on a date where your car gets blown up and frightens me out of my wits." Mira closed the door behind him. She peered through the window to watch as he got into his brand new Mercedes Roadster, compliments of pal Justin, and pulled out of the driveway.

She turned on the porch light and another in the living room. It was then she heard the clink of glass coming from the kitchen. She froze in her steps and listened. The impulse to call for Sean was interrupted by a soft sound, a woman humming a tune. Mira grinned and resumed her steps as she tiptoed toward the kitchen.

When she reached the doorway she found Claire. She was placing a pan on the stove and pouring milk into it. Suddenly, she finished her tune, tilted her head, and after a few seconds opened her mouth to speak.

"I don't think you should worry, Charles. Mira and Sean will figure things out. I'm sure of it…Yes, yes. I put it away in a safe place, exactly as you told me to do…What was that, dear?…Oh, it's been taken care of. I called someone out to look at it a few weeks ago…No, we put that away this past winter. Don't you remember?"

Winter? *We* put away? Mira admitted she was confused. She figured Claire spoke to her husband's spirit to keep from feeling lonely. This conversation gave her the impression there was more to it. And it worried Mira. Someone once told her dementia patients often mixed up reality and fantasy. If Claire believed Charles was still alive, what did it imply? Of course, she'd seen no other signs of senile behavior. Yet, could she be sure after spending scarcely a few days around the woman? Mira confessed the answer was no.

"Somebody having a hard time falling asleep?" Mira commented as she walked back into the kitchen.

"Oh, my! You certainly startled me. Yes, I figured a little warm milk might help." She turned back to stir the contents of the pan. "Can I offer you some, dear?"

Mira didn't answer at first. She guessed Claire might be asking Charles, until Claire glanced at her. "Ah, no thanks. After my day, I think I will sleep like a rock."

Mira did want to get upstairs to bed, but the idea came to her. Maybe she shouldn't leave Claire alone. It didn't seem right. She waited while Claire poured her milk and sat down at the table.

"You know, I couldn't help but hear your conversation before I came into the room a minute ago."

Claire nodded. "Yes, I still talk with Charles every evening. We always enjoyed our night time chats."

"Did you...have you ever mentioned your, ah, chats with Charles to anyone else?" Mira wondered if Claire understood this wasn't common behavior. Not to the extent she carried it.

"You mean such as a doctor, don't you?" She nodded. "I'm not crazy, you know. In fact, I'm saner than most people. Talking is my way of keeping Charles closer."

"Okay, but you mentioned how the two of you put something away this past winter. Didn't Charles die nearly two years ago?" Mira hated being forward, but knew it did no good to skirt around the issue.

"Oh, that. Well, I guess when I make a decision to do something...you see, I do feel Charles tells me things. I don't want this to sound insane, because it isn't. I do hear them; his words come to me."

"But Claire..."

"No, you don't understand. They must be real. And I can prove it. It was a year ago I heard him explain to me where to look for something, something very important I needed to find. And it was right where he described it would be. You understand?"

Mira wanted to believe her. She looked sincere, and her eyes mirrored a plea with Mira to believe, even if it was too far-fetched.

"Claire, what if you forgot where you put it? And one day you remembered, only you assumed it was Charles who told you. What if that's what happened?" Mira didn't feel comfortable playing psychologist, but she wanted to understand Claire.

She shook her head with force. "No. No, I'd know if it were only me who remembered. It was Charles."

Mira recognized it was useless to try and change the woman's mind. And seeing the look of concern on her face, Mira chose to stop. Why deflate the woman's happiness? In truth, her odd behavior didn't hurt anyone.

"I should get upstairs. I'm so tired I'm ready to fall asleep standing in this spot." Mira gave Claire a pat on the hand. "Will you come to bed soon?"

"Yes. I'll be up in a few minutes, but I want to finish my conversation with Charles."

Mira sighed. She didn't reason with her anymore about Charles. Saying good night one final time, she left the kitchen.

When she got to her room, she discovered her phone was blinking. She guessed it was Sean with one of his good night text messages. It made her smile as she walked over to pick it up. The smile turned to a frown when she recognized the number of a missed call and voicemail. Jessica. Mira debated whether to listen. After all of Sean's warnings, she considered erasing it, but curiosity pushed her to find out the contents. Mira opened the message and listened as Jessica's voice sounded like a pale imitation of normal.

Please. I need your help. Someone saw us together, and now Kyle knows. I'm afraid he'll tell Bradley. And if he does...I'm scared, Mira. If you could, tell Sean. He won't answer my calls, but he'll know how to stop Bradley. He's done it before. Please.

Mira spent a few seconds debating what to do before she made the call. "Sean, we need to talk. It's about Jessica."

Chapter Twenty-Five

"No. I refuse to deal with her problems," Sean argued.

"But she sounds desperate." Mira continued to reason with Sean for more than twenty minutes, though she wondered why. She felt tired and wanted to sleep. Yet she carried a soft heart for people in need, people who sounded desperate, like Jessica did tonight.

"I told you; she's paranoid, always has been. She bleeds people to get attention. My hunch tells me what she'll get from Bradley is a tongue lashing on how to stay out of other people's business. It's another thing she's good at."

Mira gave up. She failed to come up with any further argument. Tomorrow she'd call Jessica to make sure she was all right. She'd find peace of mind and be done with it. In the meantime, she planned to sleep. She said as much to Sean and they ended the call.

After hearing footsteps patter down the hall and the faint click of a door closing, Mira settled in under the covers. Before nodding off, she reached out and put her phone on silent. No more interruptions tonight, she decided.

****

Morning came, and Mira fought the idea of leaving her bed. However, it was Friday. Time would run out by the end of the day, and no possible resolution to their problem surfaced. Images of Alex photo-snapped in her head like a slideshow. It surprised her how she wasn't the least bit afraid he'd make a return visit. She might have been ignorant of many things, but certain of one. Alex was a coward. After his encounter with Sean, he'd not take a chance and try with her again, even in one of his insane moments.

Shelving all her worries about Alex, Mira gathered her courage to call Rob. She dreaded it, but figured he'd want an update. Nearly twenty-four hours had passed since their last conversation. She wondered if Rob was aware of Claire's quirky behavior. To be honest, it didn't matter. They faced more important issues. Like what were they going to do, if they failed to stop Bradley Lane? Some kind of legal action must exist to delay the excavation. She handled documents and situations like those on her job often enough. She could do this.

Finally getting up, she reached over to turn her phone back on and discovered a missed call. And another voicemail. Jessica, again. At first, Mira felt annoyed. The woman had turned into the attention-seeking pest Sean described. But she recalled the desperate sound of her voice in the previous message. On a hunch, she opened it to listen. It sounded like the first pleading message with similar words. She reached out to press the button and delete it when a sudden loud scream made her jump.

"What the...?" Mira held the phone away from her ear and stared at it. After a moment, she played the message once more.

I'm sorry to bother you again, Mira, but I tried Sean. He won't answer my phone calls.

And I don't think he will listen to my messages.
I'm going someplace to hide for a while. I
overheard Kyle tell Bradley about our meeting.
I can't wait any longer to see what Bradley will
do. When you get this, please tell Sean I'll be at
our...

In the next instant, Mira heard the scream. She sank down on the bed and stared at the phone again. It shook in her hand as she trembled. She tried not to let her imagination create the horrific scenario nor allow it to force its way into her head. She struggled to settle her emotions and place a call to Sean. Her voice quivered, though she finally steadied it to speak.

At first he didn't want to listen, until she mentioned the scream. In the next second, he ended the call, right after saying he'd be over to hear the message himself. Several times, while Mira waited, she considered a call to the police. She felt responsible somehow. If she'd left her phone on and heard the ring, or called Jessica back after the first message...She sat down and worked to calm herself. Maybe Sean was right. Maybe it was nothing.

****

"I think we should call the police," Mira suggested after Sean listened to Jessica's message several times.

"I don't know. It seems real enough." He frowned as if he deliberated over making a decision. "It could be a trick. Maybe she's working with Bradley to draw us into a trap."

"Oh come on, Sean. Can you honestly say you think it's fake?"

Sean brought his fingertips together and rested them underneath his chin. "I just don't trust her. We should keep our guard up."

"But what if it turns out she's been harmed, and we did nothing to help her? How will we feel then?" Mira shook her head.

Sean remained stubbornly quiet.

"A call to the police won't put us in harm's way, you know." When she saw he still didn't respond, she added, "Fine. I'll call." Mira walked over to Sean and took the phone out of his hand. He didn't stop her, but he didn't encourage her either.

Once the police officer listened to her story, he stayed silent for the moment. Afterward, he asked Mira to come down to the station. In the meantime, he agreed to send someone to the Lane house to see if Jessica was at home. He echoed Sean's comment, agreeing it might be a hoax. Mira was still doubtful.

After deciding it might be awhile before hearing back from the police, Sean suggested they go for a drive. They traveled to the Cape and drove along Route 30 west. Sean kept glancing in the rearview mirror every few seconds.

Mira wanted to ask him why, but he appeared to be preoccupied. They neared the BP station when Sean made a left turn. It led them down a private road where several condos trailed along the beachfront. Sean slowed the car as they approached the last unit.

"Why are we stopping?" Mira said.

"You'll see." He got out of the car. "Come on."

Mira followed and as they passed it she studied a small, dark compact sitting in the drive. She took a quick glance inside. The seat was covered with a stack of file folders. Mira tried to read the writing on one of them, but didn't have enough time. The few words she managed to catch were "Lawrence County." Who carried around so many files in the car, she wondered, but didn't dwell on it as they reached the door.

Sean called out before he turned the door knob. When a large man in a suit greeted them, Sean smiled. "Hey there, Quinn."

Mira stood back as they embraced by giving each other a hard pat on the back before Sean turned to Mira and pointed at Quinn.

"Mira, this is an old friend of mine, Quinn Fairfield. He's come all the way from London to visit me." He turned for a quick second. "Quinn, this is Mira Stanley."

Mira shook the foreigner's hand. His grip was strong, and he held on for longer than usual. His blue eyes studied her intently. "I'm sure the Florida Panhandle is a shock to your system. Quite different from England, isn't it?"

"Yes, but I'm beginning to like it. I've been here less than two weeks, and I do believe I've seen more of the sun than in a year's time back in England. Are you from Florida?"

Mira shook her head. "Ohio is my home. Not much sunshine there, either. Of course, I haven't found much time to enjoy it here."

Quinn cocked his head. "Oh? And why is that?"

Mira didn't think she should explain her business to a stranger, even if he was Sean's friend. But as it was, she didn't need to decline because Sean interrupted.

"I figured we'd stay and visit for a bit, if you aren't busy?" Sean suggested while he took hold of Mira's hand to lead her inside.

"Well, of course. It is your place after all." Quinn passed on through the living room and kitchen, and onto the back patio.

Mira grew confused, as well as curious about Quinn's and Sean's relationship.

After they were seated, Sean turned to Mira and smiled. "I guess you want to know why we're here. And yes, this is my place. Or I should say it's my parents' condo. I inherited it after they passed away a couple years ago. I use it on occasion when I want to get away from the city." He gestured at Quinn. "And since my friend has always wanted to vacation in the U.S., I invited him to stay."

"How did you meet?" Mira expected Sean to answer, but Quinn stepped in.

"Oh, I'm afraid it's a boring story. Sean was traveling through London when we ran into each other. Literally, that is. His car collided with mine. I'm afraid driving on the left side of the road tends to be a bit much for a Yank. Right, Sean? In any case, we struck up a friendship, and it has lasted with the help of emails and phone calls."

Mira caught the look Sean gave Quinn. She wasn't sure what it meant, but she had a hunch this wasn't the whole story.

"Care for some refreshment? It's nearly eighty-something, and I feel parched." Quinn got up to head for the kitchen.

"Seems nice," Mira commented.

"Yes. He is. And very loyal." Sean turned his head to watch Quinn.

Mira found the word loyal to be an odd choice. What behavior merited that? Quinn returned a minute later with something fruity. He asked Mira if she'd ever hunted for seashells.

"You'll find some absolutely beautiful specimens as well as starfish and sand dollars on this beach. Why don't you take this moment to collect some? With the low tide I dare say it's the perfect opportunity." Quinn wore the expression of an excited child on his face.

Mira laughed. "Okay, I think I will. Do you want to come along, Sean?"

"Ha, no. I've collected enough of those. You go on ahead. I'll stay and catch up on things with Quinn."

****

Sean and Quinn waited until Mira walked out onto the sand and down to the shore line. "Now, what did you learn?" Quinn said.

"Not much. Claire Peterson is safe and back in her home. My car is toast after an attempt to murder me as well as Mira, I suspect." Sean stared out at the beach.

"No details on the Lanes?"

Sean detected the strain in his voice. He turned back to see how Quinn pulled at his ear. A habit Sean recognized. "No. Nothing yet. But Bradley's becoming anxious. More than usual, I'd say. Nervous people tend to make mistakes."

"And if he doesn't?" Quinn drank the rest of his punch.

"I'll come up with another plan." Sean responded with confidence. He placed a hand on Quinn's arm. "I made a promise. Didn't I? We both did. And we won't let her down. No matter what it takes. Understood?" He waited until Quinn nodded. Then he waved to get Mira's attention. "And stay out of trouble, Quinn. I know how impatient you can get, but don't do anything rash."

Sean didn't give Quinn a chance to respond. He hurried out to meet Mira halfway. Rather than take a path back through the condo, Sean waved goodbye and led Mira around to the drive and their car. He'd let Quinn work it out for himself. It was best.

Chapter Twenty-Six

As they got into the car, Sean's phone rang. He brought it out of his pocket to study the screen. After a quick glance at Mira, he answered. "What can you tell me, Guárico?"

Mira listened as Sean talked. She didn't like Sean's end of the conversation, but at least she hadn't heard any words about someone dying. Once he got off of the phone, she waited, afraid to ask.

"They can't find her. She's not at home. No sign she's visited any of her usual stops. And Kyle hasn't seen her since yesterday because he's been out of town on business. I know that's legit since one of our biggest clients conducted a merger deal the other day, and Kyle made the trip to Seattle. Anyway, when he arrived home this morning, he figured Jessica was out on one of her shopping sprees."

"Oh, God." Mira's voice shook. Cold from the sense of dread building since this morning made her sick. Once again, she started berating herself with the what-ifs.

"It's not your fault." Sean reached over to grab her hand. "Besides, we still don't know if anything has happened to her."

"Will you stop? You know very well something is not right. First, the scream, and no one's seen her since yesterday? Something's just not right."

"You can't assume the worst. Let's be patient and hope to find an explanation that doesn't involve injury or worse. Okay?"

Sean looked concerned, but Mira failed to decide if it was for her feelings or his worry over Jessica. She figured they both deserved his attention. She refused to be jealous at a time like this or become a basket case when what he needed was her level-headed support.

"You're right. I need to keep calm. Can you think of what else we can do? There must be something, some place you know of where she—wait! Remember? In her last message, she started to say where you could find her, but then the scream interrupted. Something like going to *our* place. She used the word *our*, Sean. Can you think of where it might be?" Mira grew a little more encouraged.

Sean's brow wrinkled for a moment. "I know one place she might go, if she got the chance."

Mira guessed Sean's memory traveled back to another time, perhaps when he and Jessica still loved one another. Though it bothered her to picture him with another woman, she sympathized with his loss. She knew it wasn't easy to erase those memories. Still, maybe a person shouldn't want to erase them since past experience helped to prevent making those same mistakes.

She reached over to place her hand on his arm. It brought him back from daydreaming. "Where to?"

"The Cape marina. We own a boat dock and a storage garage for my family's boat. Jessica and I used to go there to, ah, when we wanted to be alone."

Mira heard the embarrassment in his tone and figured out what he meant. She smiled. "Might as well check it out, right?"

Without further conversation, they headed across town and arrived at the marina in a matter of minutes. It looked deserted for a Friday. Sean explained this was normal though. As a routine, boaters came after work and spent the weekend out on the water, then returned home on Sunday afternoon.

Sean pulled the car onto the gravel drive behind the boat storage and parked. He glanced over at Mira. "Maybe you should stay in the car and let me check things out first."

Mira shook her head. "No way. I'm going with you." He protested, but she planted a stubborn expression on her face to stop him.

"Fine," he said. "But you stay behind me, just in case."

She didn't want to imagine what the "just in case" might be.

As soon as they reached the back door, Sean pointed to the broken lock. It hung by its hinges. He reached behind him to pull a gun from his pocket.

Mira figured after yesterday's event at Surf and Suds, he wouldn't confront any more situations empty handed. She took a deep breath and grabbed hold of his arm.

He leaned in, his ear pressed against the door to listen. After a minute, he nodded at Mira and folded his hand around the door handle. The door groaned in protest as he opened it. Sean winced at the sound and motioned for Mira to stay back.

She waited while he panned the room for any movement. Stepping onto the wood planking, he reached out his arm behind him to take hold of her hand.

"No matter what, stay behind me," he whispered.

They moved further into the building using cautious steps. Each became aware of the quiet, no sounds of the ocean, of the birds; nothing penetrated the room. Sean stiffened and stopped abruptly.

"What? What is it?" Mira tried peeking around his shoulder.

"I think you should go back to the car, Mira."

Mira recognized the tone in his voice. "I'm coming, and that's final."

Sean sighed. You shouldn't see this."

Mira forced her way around him to look. "Is it Jessica? I need to know if—oh my God." She covered her mouth with the back of her hand and moved once more behind Sean. "Who would do such a horrible thing?"

"I'm not sure, but I want you to stay put while I get a closer look. And *that's* final." He turned around to face her. His lips narrowed into a tight line. This time she didn't argue.

Mira stayed behind while Sean hurried to where the body of a man hung by ropes from the rafters. Sean's gun, gripped in both hands, darted side to side as he went. When he got there he leaned down and turned his head sideways to look at the face. As he straightened up, his hand pointed to a paper attached to the man's chest. He nodded at Mira.

"It's a note, and with any luck, a message for us."

Mira imagined she'd played the helpless female long enough and hurried over to where Sean stood. "What's it say?"

"This is what happens to people who meddle in my

business," Sean read aloud.

Mira raised her eyebrow. "Well, this certainly points in one direction."

"You mean toward Bradley Lane?" Sean stared at the body. "Considering who's hanging here with a bullet hole in his forehead, yeah, it seems likely." He stuck his hand inside the back pocket and pulled out a wallet.

"When did they let him out of jail, I wonder?" Mira opened her mouth to comment how Sean shouldn't tamper with evidence, but stopped as she recognized the Ohio Buckeyes jacket stained dark red with crusted spots of blood on it. "And how long he's been here?" The sour taste of nausea filled her mouth and she shifted her eyes toward Sean.

"I'd guess sometime early yesterday evening. I bet they didn't keep him more than an hour before Lane bailed him out." Sean shook his head and read off the driver's license. "Joe Broski. Poor bastard didn't make it home, I'd say."

"How can we be sure it was Bradley Lane's doing? I mean, plenty of people might want Joe Broski dead." Mira supposed anyone who went around blowing up cars and kidnapping little old ladies must travel in dangerous company.

"It may seem a bit too convenient, but you don't know some of the facts. I went straight to Lane's office after our near miss with death and told him off. He acted like he didn't know what this was about, but I didn't buy it. Oh, he's guilty all right. Of that and a lot more."

Mira shivered. She detected the bitterness in his voice as well as the loathing. She wanted justice for

Claire Peterson, and wanted Bradley Lane to pay, but she didn't carry Sean's brand of hatred for the Lanes. Too much emotion led to careless behavior. She hoped he didn't make that mistake. Another thought came to her. It's what brought them here in the first place.

"This still doesn't tell us where Jessica is," she reminded.

Sean frowned and looked away from the body. "No. But I think maybe we can guess what happened."

Mira waited, not sure where he was headed.

"Let's say Jessica came here to hide. When she walks in she sees the body of Broski while she leaves the message on your phone, and she screams."

"But where is she? Why didn't she call the police to report it?"

Sean shook his head. "She's scared and doesn't know who to trust. She realizes Bradley Lane's arm of power reaches far and wide. So she runs."

"Yes, but we can't dismiss the possibility she ran into the killer while he or she was still in the building."

"And was taken away by the killer," Sean finished.

Mira guessed he didn't want to suggest she was murdered, too. "If she did get away, do you think she'd try to contact you?"

"I think if Jessica's scared enough, she'll stay hidden for a while, at least until she feels safe." Sean walked toward the other side of the building and kept his eyes on the floor.

Mira wanted to say something encouraging, but nothing came to mind. If they found Jessica, maybe she could tell them who killed Bradley's man. If she hadn't met with harm, that is.

"What's this?" Sean bent over and extended his

hand to the floor. He picked up a bracelet and examined it. He twisted it to look at the inside band and then held it out to Mira. "There are initials inscribed. It's Jessica's."

"What do you think it means?" Mira formulated her own ideas, but wanted Sean to voice his first.

"Maybe she dropped it on purpose to leave a clue," he suggested.

Mira nodded. "Let's hope." She hadn't erased the guilt over not answering Jessica's call.

"I need to call Guárico," Sean announced and headed for the door.

Mira studied the room a second longer. After one final glance at the body, she stepped outside to follow Sean. He stood by the car with the phone to his ear.

"Yes. We'll be here. See you in a few minutes. And thanks for your help with the other matter." Sean ended the call and looked up at Mira.

Mira reached Sean and gave his hand a squeeze. She wanted to do more, but at the same moment became aware of how strange she felt. The sounds in the background with the wash of waves on the beach and seagulls crying played like a recording that suddenly muted, only seconds later to resume. She suddenly recognized that life carried on out here and death back inside, death and quiet.

The ambulance and police cruisers turned off Cape road. Sean and Mira watched them approach and people file out of their vehicles. Guárico, followed by the group of officers and paramedics, crossed the drive. After a brief introduction, Sean led them inside the building while Mira waited in the car. The image of the body hanging from the rafters remained with her; she didn't need to see it again.

Within five minutes Sean came back outside and made his way to the car. They left the authorities and paramedics to their jobs and headed back to town.

"I'll take you back to Claire's, but I can't stay," Sean said.

"But shouldn't we plan what to do next? Claire only has until the end of today. Bradley will keep to his agenda and order the workers to start the excavation at first light tomorrow."

"That's why I'm heading back to the office. I'll get a court order to delay the work permit."

"But I thought Lane kept your uncle in his pocket."

"My uncle isn't the only judge. I've made some friends high up in the court system myself, one of whom happens to hate Bradley Lane with a passion. Don't worry. I can get this postponed until we find a way to win." Sean leaned over to give Mira a kiss on her cheek and remained quiet for the rest of the trip.

In many ways she wanted to believe Sean would do what he promised and for the right reasons, but Mira remained skeptical. After Sean drove away, she ran inside the house to grab her bag and keys. She hollered a quick good-bye to Claire as she went out the door. She might be able to do a few things herself. In any case it wasn't in her nature to sit idle. Not while the fate of Claire remained uncertain. She entered in the name Port Saint Joe Tribune into her Garmin and the screen popped up with her directions.

"Next stop, Stan Thomas." Mira turned her car onto the road, headed for Port Saint Joe.

Chapter Twenty-Seven

Mira arrived at the Tribune charged up and ready to move. Once inside the building she didn't waste time finding Stan's name plate and desk. Her face fell when she saw his seat was empty. She looked around to find the closest warm body.

"Do you know where Stan Thomas is at the moment?" At first the guy who hovered over his computer didn't answer, as if to ignore her.

"Coffee break," he mumbled. Without looking up, he pointed to the back of the room.

Mira spotted the doorway, and beyond it was a counter with a coffee machine on top. After a word of thanks, she headed in that direction. She found several people, both men and women, standing in the break room as they chatted and sipped their coffee. Not sure which of the men was Stan, she stayed a short distance away to study each of them. At last one of them broke from the circle and walked in her direction.

"Excuse me, but I was told I'd find Stan Thomas in here." The tall, lanky fellow stretched a smile across his face and nodded.

"That would be me, ma'am."

Mira stifled the urge to laugh. Stan's accent was pure southern drawl. She held out a hand. "Glad to meet you, Mr. Thomas. My name's Mira Stanley." He immediately clutched her hand and gave it a firm shake.

"The pleasure is certainly mine, Miss Stanley. And what brings you to brighten my day?"

Mira smiled. She suspected she'd get along well with the reporter. She hated to crush his happy mood by mentioning Jason, but it needed to be done. "I don't know how to ease into this, but I'm here about your cousin and Bradley Lane."

Mira tensed as his face transformed. The anger in his eyes heated up like embers in a fire pit. She hoped he wouldn't refuse to discuss such a painful issue, and she worried Stan might misunderstand her motives. "Look, I'm trying to help a client of mine, Claire Peterson. Maybe you've heard of her late husband, Charles Peterson? He, too, experienced a run-in with Bradley Lane and his company."

Stan appeared to calm somewhat and opened his mouth to speak. "Yes. I'm aware of the Peterson deal, along with many others Lane Developers supposedly made. All legal and proper, as the arrogant asshole told me every time I chanced to confront him. I tell you, Miss Stanley, that man has more ways to spin a story than my great granddaddy ever dished out. And it's a sight wider and longer than most could. If I counted the times I almost nailed him for all those wild tales and such, the numbers would fill this room."

Mira digested all the information Stan offered to share, but his last words left a discouraging taste in her mouth. If Stan, after all this time, hadn't stopped Bradley Lane, what hope did she hold in doing so?

"I wish my words shed better news. I can see you're disappointed. You know, I did come close once. I held a document to prove Lane's wrongdoing right in these very hands." Stan looked around to see only two workers remained in the room, but they were engaged in their own conversation.

He leaned in closer to Mira and lowered his voice. "I'm not too proud of this, but please understand, I was plenty desperate. My cousin passed on a year before. Charles Peterson followed. Before his passing, Jason told me about the evidence. My thirst for justice drove me to find it. I suspected from a conversation between Peterson and myself, right before he died, that Lane tried to bully him into selling the property. Peterson wasn't comfortable with the deal, however he didn't tell me any more than that. He only mentioned he'd taken certain precautions to make sure his wife was able to protect herself after he died, in case Lane tried to cheat him."

Mira considered how Charles meant to protect Claire and with what. "What did you manage to find?"

"Well, this is the part where you'll judge how unethical I am, but as I explained, I was desperate. I went to the Peterson property and spoke with Mrs. Peterson. I'm blessed with the gift of gab—it's a reporter's prime talent—which I used to charm the dear woman into telling me all sorts of things, including where she stored all of her husband's important papers after his demise. Odd as this may sound; she told me Charles instructed her to put them in the shed. She was extremely clear on this point, mind you. Told me he gave her the orders *after* he died. I must admit, this threw me back and shook me up some. Still, I feel it best not to debate the delicate protocol of communicating with the departed. I left and came back much later that night to take a look at the shed." Stan paused as if waiting for Mira's reaction.

"*You*! You were the one who broke into the shed!" Hearing how loud her voice had grown, she added, "How clever to break into the shed that way without a key."

Stan smiled at her awkward moment. "In any case, I found the paper without a hitch—other than tipping the chair and breaking a few plates—and figured I'd finally put Lane where I wanted him. But then," Stan snapped his fingers, "just like that I lost it."

"How? I mean I know from Claire's story you got away because the police didn't find anyone."

"You're right. I got away, but not before getting knocked over the head and losing the paper."

"I don't understand. Did you bump into something? Lose your footing and trip?"

Stan shook his head. "No. I didn't cause it. The bump was made with a club. I'd guess a baseball bat. Someone hit me over the head with it and took the paper."

"Who? Who hit you? Did someone follow you to the Peterson's?" For someone with the gift of gab, his story wound and twisted in so many ways, it left her confused.

"It must have been Bradley Lane. I don't know how he knew, but he or someone working for him followed me, most likely all the way from my apartment, waited for me to find the paper, waited for me to get clear of the Peterson property, and managed to take it from me."

"How fortunate for him," Mira commented.

"Yes, indeed. I awoke an hour or more later, lying on the beach. Must've been dragged there by the thieving bastard." Stan's angry and bitter look returned.

"What was in the document, Mr. Thomas?" Mira grew anxious.

"Oh, it was worth every penny of my efforts. I found that a contract agreement, an addendum of sorts, to the original deed transfer was made. It states if Claire Peterson decides to retain ownership of her house after her husband's death, the deed transfer between Charles and Lane Developers becomes null and void. However, if she should decide to sell, Lane Developers shall pay in full two million eight hundred thousand dollars for the property."

Mira whistled. "It's a sight more than I figured it was worth."

Stan nodded. "Yes. Of course, the only reason Bradley Lane would agree to such an amount, I figure, is because he planned to destroy the document before Charles was cold in his grave. Problem was he didn't find Peterson's copy, and he worried Claire might know about it."

"But she didn't."

"I assumed the same thing until I talked to her that day. When she used the words 'Charles promised me I'd be well-taken care of when he was gone. You wait and see,' I wondered what he meant by that comment."

"Do you think she understood? Or did she quote her husband without realizing what he meant?"

"She did come across as, shall we say, eccentric in her behavior? In such a case, I'd never assume what is real and what is fantasy to the dear woman. To go so far as saying whether she understood what her husband meant would be purely conjecture on my part." Stan scratched his chin and became quiet.

Mira remembered another topic she hadn't brought

up, and Stan failed to address. "Someone mentioned you suspect foul play in your cousin's death as well as in Charles'. Why? I mean, they both died of heart attacks according to the coroner's report."

"I'm afraid my suspicions and deep-seated distrust for Bradley Lane may have influenced the direction of my theory. I know what they reported, but there are ways to induce heart attacks. And for two men who lived relatively in good health, how do they both end up with heart problems?"

"It sounds a bit paranoid." Mira remembered her conversations with Dr. Faithful and later with Jessica Lane. One person having these suspicions might be labeled paranoid, but two? And only one came up with more than conjecture.

"Maybe, but when you look at the lifetime accumulation of scandalous deeds Bradley Lane and his family created—and I dug deep to find each and every one—murder seems very convincing."

"Have you ever heard of a drug called cisapride?" Mira said.

Stan grew silent and shook his head. "What is it for?"

"It used to be prescribed for patients with heartburn."

"Used to?"

"It was taken off the market more than ten years ago. Reports confirmed its usage may cause an increase in heart arrhythmia, and in some cases heart attacks." Mira waited for the reporter's reaction. His brows drew together in a question.

Mira held up a hand. "Wait. Let me finish. At first, I questioned how this drug might be the connection to your cousin and Charles Peterson, until I learned a bottle of cisapride was found in Kyle Lane's possession," she added.

"And you know this how?" Stan leaned forward once more, as if intent on hearing every word.

"Jessica Lane asked to meet with me a couple of days ago. She brought the bottle with her. It's in my bag. Supposedly she spoke with a friend of hers who happens to be a pharmacist. He identified the drug, but that part isn't important. Bottom line, after some digging, she learned Bradley Lane's doctor prescribed it to him years ago for heartburn. Somehow it found its way to Kyle."

"I find it hard to believe Bradley Lane was ever affected by any minor ailment such as heartburn. He has a steel interior."

"That's what Jessica said." Mira tapped her fingers on the counter as she mulled over details. Looking up at Stan she added, "Let's take a look at this. The two men who crossed Bradley Lane end up dying from heart attacks. And by coincidence, Lane has a medicine prescribed for heartburn, which was taken off the market years ago because it can cause heart attacks. Of course, the question is how could Lane manage to get Charles and your cousin to take an unhealthy dose of cisapride? It seems farfetched." Hearing all the evidence aloud, Mira felt its impact and how inconceivable it was.

"Some coincidence. In my opinion, in Bradley Lane's life coincidence doesn't exist. With him it's cold, calculated, deliberate action."

Mira nodded and wondered where all this would take them. They hadn't connected all the information yet. It made it difficult to decide what to do next.

"You know, I'd bet the coroners who diagnosed cause of death didn't find any traces of cisapride, even if it existed, because they weren't looking for it. I'd bet they figured heartburn in a man his age was normal enough to explain traces of any heartburn medicine."

"Possibly. I'm not a doctor and couldn't be certain, but I remember my cousin's cause of death was announced without any delay. Unless they suspect the death involved something other than natural causes, a complete autopsy is not called for. Again, I'd say it's possible."

"Maybe if we spoke with the coroner we'd get them to consider exhuming the bodies." At once, Mira recognized the amount of time and the effort to persuade authorities might be a wasted effort to help Claire. No, they needed quicker results.

"I already tried and was met with a firm no. They won't exhume anyone without concrete proof." Stan shook his head. "I'm afraid the one recourse remaining is to do it on our own."

"All right, I will find the evidence myself," Mira announced.

"And how do you plan on doing this, little lady? Lane's a dangerous man. If you get too close, you might end up like my cousin and your friend's husband, six feet into the cold ground. I don't want to see that happen." A hint of sadness covered his smile.

"You've tried for quite a while and you're still alive," Mira argued.

"Yes, well I'm used to sneaking around and finding evidence. It's part of my job."

"It's part of my job, too. We lawyers tend to nose

our way into some pretty uncomfortable situations. I've always managed to get out in time."

"Again, you deal with the likes of Bradley Lane. Not such an easy task, is it?"

Mira reflected on his words and knew he was right. She needed to be careful. Picturing Claire's sad face when she spoke of losing her home, it was enough to give Mira stubborn courage. No, she wasn't about to give up.

"I can take care of myself. I promise." Mira held out her hand. "Thank you for your time and help."

"What will you do? Maybe I should go with you." Stan paused and then nodded. "I can see you're determined to do this on your own. Very well, I guess I should be used to the independence of the new age woman. It's my chivalrous demeanor refusing to lie down."

Mira smiled. "I'm glad to see it still exists in some men. It's a wonderful quality, Mr. Thomas. Don't ever lose it, even if women turn it down at times."

Stan placed her hand in his and leaned over to kiss it. "You are most welcome, dear lady. And do be careful. It's a vicious world Bradley Lane belongs to."

"I'll be fine. And again, thank you." Mira left, anxious to get on with the investigation. She considered her next move, but she needed the right timing. And that's where Sean's help came into the plan. However, this meant she must find the courage to trust him completely and believe he stood on Claire's side and not Bradley's. It wasn't easy for her. She always remained somewhat guarded. Life and all its hardship made her behave that way. It was time to change, she told herself.

Chapter Twenty-Eight

Sean arrived back in the office knowing he'd find Kyle there. Kyle wouldn't waste time worrying about his wife; not with work in the forefront. And Sean learned one thing for sure over the years. The Lanes were all business.

"You hear from your wife, yet?" Sean emphasized the words *your wife*. He never got used to what happened. No reasonable explanation for Jessica's decision, other than the Lane family fortune, came to his mind. She always loved her baubles and beads. He could never compete with that kind of money, but at least he figured they loved each other. It should've been strong enough. As much as he wanted to think of their relationship as genuine, in reality, his love had created a wall. During their marriage, never once did he face the truth.

"No, I haven't. Have you?" Kyle turned to Sean and narrowed his eyes.

They never got past this, Sean thought. "I looked. One of the places I searched was the family boat storage. She wasn't there."

Kyle nodded.

"But we did find a body," Sean added.

Kyle dropped the file from his hands. "A body?" He bent over to pick up the papers scattered around him.

"Yes, a body. Appears to be one of the guys who kidnapped Claire Peterson. Does the name Joe Broski mean anything to you? I figured it might since your brother probably hired him. He and his partner also happen to be the ones who blew up my car. Quite a busy pair. Anyway, this Broski character was hanging from the rafters when we found him, a bullet hole in his head and a note attached to his chest."

Kyle managed to seat himself behind his desk and place his hands on top to steady them, but he didn't speak.

Sean rested back on his heels and brought his arms up to cross his chest. "I'm sure you want to know what the note says, right? It gave a warning. Something like, this is what happens when you meddle in my business. Whose business do you think the note is referring to?" He watched Kyle become more anxious as he drummed his fingers on the desk top.

"Look. I don't know what you're getting at, but if you believe I'm guilty of any wrongdoing, you're wrong."

Sean shrugged. "Maybe not you, but it smells rotten. So, what do you think? Will your brother fabricate some convenient alibi?"

"I don't speak for my brother. You know as much. I don't own a gun, and I could never shoot someone. " Kyle's voice rose as his tension mounted.

"Yeah, but maybe you gave someone else the order to do it. Keeps your hands clean, right?" Sean smiled at Kyle.

"I'm telling you I didn't—see here, where do you get off acting righteous? You've done your share of things I'm sure you're not proud of."

"What I've done is nothing close to murder." Sean stood up straight and glared at Kyle. "Besides, if you dropped your brother as a client after that very unpleasant lawsuit, as I strongly suggested, things might be different."

"Bradley may be callous and spiteful at times, even committed unscrupulous acts, but he is my brother. I'd never turn my back on him when he needed my help."

"I wonder if you can say the same for his loyalty. Hmm?"

Kyle leaned back in his chair and smiled, his composure regained. "I'd say you've no right to judge anyone in my family. And what goes on between me and *my wife* is none of your business. You lost the right to concern yourself with Jessica's wellbeing when she chose me instead of you."

The words stung. After several years they still hurt him. He didn't respond though. Instead, he turned to leave and called over his shoulder as he stood in the doorway. "For your sake, I hope she's all right. It would be a real shame if you lost her." He didn't wait to hear Kyle's response.

Chapter Twenty-Nine

The traffic back to the house grew heavy. Friday and the plans for weekend excursions to the beach put out-of-towners on the roads passing through Port Saint Joe, either travelling to the Cape or farther on to Saint George Island. Mira steamed with energy and determination as she weaved in and out of the line of cars. Of course the exchange of angry horn beeping followed, but Mira didn't care. She tried to call Sean when she first got in the car. She hoped to avoid wasting time with a return trip to Claire's and instead go straight to Bradley Lane's office. However, Sean didn't answer.

She turned into the drive and discovered his car. He was getting out of it as she pulled in behind him.

"I called you," she said and walked over to give him a hug.

"I forgot I turned my phone off. Sorry. You look like you're ready to burst. What's going on?" He led her up the front walkway.

"I spoke with Stan Thomas. He's Jason Thomas' cousin. You know, the Jason who made a deal to buy Charles and Claire's property, but then the sale didn't go through? Anyway, he managed to tell quite a story." Mira went on to divulge what Stan had told her.

Except for the contract addendum Stan found in Claire's storage shed none of this surprised Sean. "Why isn't a document this important put away in a safety deposit box or at least somewhere in the house?" he commented.

"Yeah, I figured the same. But this is Claire we're talking about. She doesn't always seem level headed about matters, does she?"

"True, but if Charles had this written up before he passed away, why not put it someplace safe? Why leave it to chance?"

It made sense. Mira wondered if they overlooked some relevant detail. More relevant than the contract, something Charles considered important enough to protect his wife with after his death. And where would he hide it?

"I think we need to explore this more," Sean suggested.

Mira couldn't help but smile. "Yes, I think we should, but where do we start?"

"Not a clue. But we should ask Claire." Sean grinned.

"And who knows? Maybe she has a reasonable answer." Mira laughed. "Did you find out anything?"

"I talked to Kyle. He claims to have no idea where his wife is, but he may be hiding it from me. I can't put it past him. His lack of concern is a bit much, even for him."

"You figure he really loves her?" Mira's head tilted.

"I guess. More like a possession he values, I'd say. The Lanes think in terms of commodities and assets."

"Which means Jessica is a possession he'd rather not lose, but isn't too concerned if he does." Mira tried to sum it up.

"Yeah, sad isn't it?" Sean started up the porch steps, and Mira followed alongside him.

"I'd like to ask another question." Mira hesitated, not sure how he'd respond. "First, what if I told you I figured out a way to discover, as you said, what Charles may have been hiding?"

"Okay, I'm listening."

"Good, but please answer without all the protest I know you'll think of to make." She waited until Sean nodded. "Could you find a way to get Bradley away from his office for a short time, or maybe provide a distraction?"

"Oh, no. Mira, I can't let you—"

"Eh! No protesting, remember?" Mira cut in and wagged her finger at him.

"No. I can't and I won't. See? No protests. Just me saying no." Sean gave her a stubborn glare. They entered the house and on through the living room to reach the kitchen. A note on the table told them Claire had gone upstairs to take a nap.

"Sean, if we don't find evidence soon, Claire will be homeless and Bradley will win. Can you accept that?" Mira needed to ask. She needed to push Sean into a corner and see which side came out fighting. Her instincts told her if he refused to help her with this plan, he might be motivated by something other than her safety. She watched his brow wrinkle as deep creases drew his forehead together. After a minute, the lines disappeared and he shrugged.

"All right. It's against my better judgment, but I'll do it. Only because I know you'd go it alone to try your crazy scheme without me, and most likely get caught.

"I'll call Bradley and make up some story. I'll say

we need to talk because...because I learned the police discovered something that concerns him. How's that sound?"

Mira nodded. "Perfect. Now, I need to figure some way to get past his secretary." Mira tapped her finger against her lip. "Oh! I've got it. I'll call you when I'm on my way up the elevator. Then you call the office and tell Gwen that Bradley has been hurt and she needs to come downstairs right away."

Sean shook his head. "I'll be with Bradley, remember? How am I going to call Gwen?"

"Shoot. Okay, how's this? I'll call from the lobby and say Bradley asked me to let her know he's stuck in traffic and needs her to deliver a contract down to the first floor office. Afterward, I'll come up and sneak into Bradley's office."

Sean shook his head again. "What contract? You don't know about his contracts. Besides, once she's down there, she'll find out it's a bogus call, and be back upstairs within minutes. Bingo. You're caught. Bad idea."

"Why don't you come up with something?" Mira snapped, irritated with all his criticism.

Sean remained silent for a minute and then nodded. "Okay, how's this sound? Pretend you're calling from Port St. Joe Pharmacy and Mr. Lane's prescription needs to be picked up right away."

"But what if she says Bradley never gave her any such instructions?"

"You explain how you received a phone call from him, how he didn't have time to pick it up, but his secretary can do so."

"Hmm. Makes sense because Bradley Lane likes

others to take care of menial tasks."

"Exactly. After the call, you'll wait until you see Lane come out of the building. I'll be waiting at the café a block away. You contact me as soon as he starts down the street. Then you call Gwen. Got it?"

"What if she doesn't leave the office right away?" Mira's nerves worked on her and caused her to think of all the possible holes in their plan.

"Let her know the pharmacy is closing within the next half hour. Mira, that's as good as it gets. We do it this way, or we don't do it. I think we shouldn't do it. You don't know what to look for, or where to look for it. Maybe we should switch roles. You meet with him, and I'll sneak inside."

"No, it won't work. I'm too afraid I'd crumble in front of him and blow the whole thing," Mira argued. With her calculating lawyer mind overpowering her, she struggled to erase suspicion that if Sean found something, he might try to hide it. She hated how she still harbored doubts.

"Okay. Let's get started," Sean announced and opened his phone to place the call to Bradley Lane.

****

"There you go. No turning back." Sean's face remained somber as he put an arm around Mira. He kissed the top of her head. "I still don't feel comfortable with this." They moved back into the living room and settled onto the sofa.

"I know." Mira spoke in a muffled tone as she snuggled next to him and buried her face in his chest. Her mind filled itself with a myriad of fears. The insecurities she battled against left her tired and confused. Yet, in her heart she experienced nothing but compassion and love. She admitted she was falling for him with a rush of emotion that took only a few days to consume her. Never in her life had she experienced anything like it, and it frightened her. Being with Sean like this was the only time she relaxed.

Sean placed a finger under her chin and tilted it upward. "Don't make any risky moves. I couldn't stand it if anything happened to you." He whispered the words. His lips brushed her face. Every word caressed her, the sounds of them forming wisps of warm air that lightly touched her skin. "You know, I think I'm falling in love with you, Mira Stanley." He kissed her before she answered, with each kiss more sensuous than the one before it.

Mira struggled to respond, and though a tiny part of her worried how Sean might react, she found the courage to finally tell him. Besides, they came to the point where it was unfair not to. "Sean?"

"Hmm?" His lips continued to explore her neck, and it managed to distract her for a moment.

Mira put a hand on his chest and pushed him away. "Sean, I'm ready to talk."

His forehead wrinkled into a frown. "Oh?" His eyes widened. "Oh! You mean your mysterious visitor."

"Yes. Him." She sat back against the sofa cushion and took a long, calming breath. "I want to tell you about Alex."

"Alex? Is he the ex?" Sean started.

Mira sighed. "Yes. Alex Renfeld. He and I were in a relationship for a couple of years, and it got somewhat serious. No, correct that. It got very serious."

Sean slid closer and reached down to squeeze her

hand. "It's okay. I'm here for you. You can tell me."

Mira smiled. "I felt things moved along without any problems. We were so happy. It was total bliss. I mean, I honestly believed we…well, you know. We set the date and made plans for the big day." She paused. Her teeth bit down hard on her lower lip to stay composed.

"Like all was right with the world. I get it. More than you know, I get it." Sean's voice lowered to a somber tone.

Mira understood and squeezed his hand in return. "Okay, here comes the burst-your-bubble moment. We took the step to move in together after the date was set." Mira laughed. "Playing house was great. Like I'd always imagined it to be." She tried to go on, but her voice refused to cooperate.

"Mira?" Sean whispered.

This was it, she figured. "I came home one evening after work and found everything in the apartment gone. Everything valuable, that is. Television, DVD, stereo, my jewelry, his jewelry. You name it and it all disappeared as if it had never been there."

"You were robbed?"

"It's what anybody would think, right? Of course, I called the police. Then I called Alex, but he didn't answer. Two officers came to the door, recorded what I had to say, what was missing, and then left." Mira tilted her head up to the ceiling and let her heart beat several times before speaking again.

"I sat there in the apartment, alone. I sat there until dark, waiting and waiting. I called him and left messages. I worried maybe something happened, something bad. Like maybe Alex had been there when the thieves came. Maybe they took him, or he went after them. My head screamed with worry."

"And later he called, or came home?" Sean's eyes grew anxious.

Mira nodded. "He called."

"And?"

"And…" Mira laughed again, but with a bitter edge to the sound. "He had one interesting story to tell."

"Good story?"

Hope filled Sean's eyes. Mira wanted to reach out and hold him in her arms. She wanted to, but the story needed to be finished.

"Not really. You see, he explained the robbery was not your typical heist. This was a loan-shark-gets-even moment. Alex owed this big time crime lowlife thousands of dollars, but he didn't have the money to pay him."

"Oh, Mira," Sean whispered.

"Can you believe it? For a brief moment I actually felt sorry for him. I asked him why he didn't use the money in our wedding account to pay the goon. That's when he confessed the account was empty. He'd blown all of it on some stupid horse race." She let herself cry. Whether from sadness or embarrassment of being such a sucker to fall for Alex, she didn't know and didn't care.

"I'm sorry, Mira. I know how it must have hurt being betrayed." Sean leaned closer to Mira and placed soft kisses on her cheek.

Mira wanted to tell him what she knew. She wanted to say Jessica Lane had to be a fool for leaving him and hurting him that way, but she didn't. He owned the right to keep his feelings to himself and tell her about Jessica when he was ready.

"What happened then?" Sean said.

"We broke up, of course. All those lies and deception. Once the reality of the situation hit me, I despised being in the same room with him. The apartment was his. I packed what hadn't been stolen and left before he got home. I found a place of my own and vowed to move on with my life.

"As it was, he called me several times, and I refused to answer. I had nothing left to say. A few nights later, I heard someone pound on my front door. I got out of bed and something told me—it was only a hunch, mind you—but it nagged me and filled me with fear. He continued to pound on the door and shout." Mira could almost feel the heat of Sean's body as his face grew angry. He must care, she thought, and it touched her heart.

"While I called the police to report an intruder, I heard the door break open. Footsteps pounded and hurried closer. I tried running to my bedroom, to lock myself away from the intruder.

"When his voice shouted my name, I knew for sure it was Alex. Right before I reached my room, he grabbed my arm and shoved me against the wall. I screamed for him to leave, but he shouted back at me. He insisted we needed to be together, how he couldn't stand to live without me. I kept telling him it was over. I didn't…couldn't love him anymore. But he kept shouting and shouting. His eyes. I can still picture how crazed they looked. Anyway, the police arrived. When they took him out of my house, he was still screaming." Mira finished with a long, drawn-out sigh. She waited and after an uncomfortable, awkward silence, Sean spoke.

"You're here, now. With me. Nothing can or will hurt you again. I promise," he whispered and kissed her.

"To tell you the truth, I'm not worried about him any longer. Alex is a coward, and I think you scared him plenty the other day." Mira made a weak attempt to laugh.

"About that. I have a confession to make." Sean leaned back, and Mira recognized the sheepish grin.

"What did you do, Sean Thorndale?"

"After he showed up here, I called my buddy at the precinct and had him run the license plate on your ex's car. Turns out it was a rental. I called in a favor to do some digging, find out his identity, and put a tail on him," Sean confessed.

"I guess you know about the restraining order." The warm blush washed over her again. She felt ashamed. She didn't want to be the sort of person who needed to file restraining orders against boyfriends.

Sean nodded. "He won't be bothering you any longer. In fact, I'd say he'll stay in Ohio for a long while where authorities there can deal with him."

"I never wanted to involve you in this." Mira attempted an apology.

"Shh. I *want* to be involved. I want to be in every part of your life, Mira. Every single part," Sean whispered while he held her close and kissed her once more.

After a half hour, Sean suggested they go outside. From the deck, they enjoyed the calm scene of the Gulf water as waves sloshed on the shore until at last he announced, "It's time to go."

Without another word they got up and walked around front to the car. Sean nodded to Mira before he shifted his car into gear.

Chapter Thirty

Once on the road, they headed west toward Port Saint Joe. Mira's mind raced as she tried to create a mental image of her plan, all the steps and precautions she needed to take. Once in town, they'd park the car a block away from Lane Developers, and she'd walk to the coffee shop across the street from Lane's where she could watch from the store window. The minutes would drag, she figured, waiting until she saw Bradley come out of the building.

She found the coffee shop almost deserted. Two other customers sat back in the corner. As she walked over to a window table, the waitress spoke.

"We're supposed to fill up the back section first, if you don't mind."

Mira turned to see her motion with her arm to point where the other two sat. "I'm sorry, but I need a window seat because I'm supposed to watch for a friend," she explained. Seeing the puzzled look on the woman's face, she added, "He doesn't know I changed meeting places. He thinks I'll be across the street at…" Mira made a quick glance to read all of the store front signs. "At Marco's." She finished and her face flushed with heat.

The waitress smiled and nodded as Mira became aware she mistook her red face for embarrassment. Mira chose to play along. "You see, I don't want anyone finding out. So I take precautions, you understand," she whispered.

The waitress patted Mira's shoulder. "Don't you worry none. We women got to stick together. Your secret's safe with me, honey. You go ahead and pick whatever window seat you like, and I'll be right over with some coffee."

Satisfied, Mira sat down and placed her concentration on the business structure across the street that housed Lane Developers. A glance at her watch revealed almost twenty minutes had passed since they left Claire's. Bradley should be walking out within the next five, Mira calculated.

The stream of traffic was steady, just like the pedestrians. They crowded the sidewalks and kept Mira's eyes busy. She could easily miss seeing Bradley exit, if another person crossed in front of the doorway at the same time. As it stood, she didn't allow herself the luxury of blinking. When the waitress came to refill her cup or take her order, she continued to keep her eyes trained across the street while she spoke. Mira figured it helped her look the part of a desperate lover who waited for her date.

After ten more minutes passed, Mira began to worry. She picked up her phone to call Sean and ask what they should do if he didn't come out, when she spotted him. She gave it another few seconds to make certain Bradley headed in the right direction before dialing Sean.

"He left the building and is walking your way."

Next, she called Gwen. This one made her nervous. She needed to sound like she knew what she was doing. She practiced her speech on the way into town.

However, that was rehearsed. She only speculated how Gwen might respond.

"Yes, this is Port Saint Joe Pharmacy calling. We're holding a prescription order for Bradley Lane that needs to be picked up. He called a few minutes ago and explained he couldn't come himself because of a meeting. Anyway, he asked us to call you to say he'd like you to stop by for the order." Mira hoped it didn't sound too rushed. Her heart pounded; she barely heard Gwen's response.

"Sounds like Mr. Lane," she laughed. "Okay, I guess I can stop by on my way home this evening."

Mira jumped in. "I'm afraid we are closing early today, within the next twenty minutes as a matter of fact. Perhaps you can come now? He insisted it was important he get the medicine today." Mira shut her eyes and held her breath. She heard Gwen sigh.

"Very well. I need to stop by the cleaners anyway. I'll come for the prescription first. It will take me fifteen minutes maybe to get there. Is that acceptable to you?"

Mira heard the clip of impatience in her voice. "Oh, absolutely. Thank you for being so accommodating." Mira hung up and waited for Gwen to come out the door. She caught the movement of the waitress from the corner of her eye and saw the critical stare. Mira ignored her, indifferent at this point as to what the woman thought. She dug into her wallet and set down a twenty, five for the coffee and doughnut and fifteen for a tip. That should make her happy, she guessed. In the next second, Gwen exited the front door and walked at a fast pace in the opposite direction Bradley had taken.

Mira hurried across the street. Once inside the building, she went up the elevator to the second floor. Sean had given her a key to the office in case she needed it, which he assured her she would. She didn't ask why he carried it, and she didn't want to know. This was a detail she hadn't considered when she came up with her plan. In her job, she drew the line at breaking into buildings when searching for evidence in a case.

In front of the Lane office, Mira first looked from side to side to make sure the hall was empty. She then tried the door, but it didn't give. She quickly got out the key and put it in the lock. Relief flooded over her as the door opened. After one last glance at the empty hall, Mira stepped inside the office. In the darkened room her hand slid over the wall until she touched the switch.

The lights blinded her for a second, but as soon as she adjusted, Mira crossed the room to get into Bradley's office. The clock on the wall told her Bradley left the building almost ten minutes ago. Sean stressed he could give her a half hour at most. She figured that left twenty to twenty-five minutes to get the job done. The realization left a sense of panic rise in her. She forced herself to remain calm by picturing Claire without a home, no fireplace mantel to rest Charles' urn upon, and no familiar rooms to remind her of him and their moments together. Relaxed, she started for the file cabinet, but after a few steps she stopped.

"If I were Bradley Lane, where would I hide important papers? Papers I didn't want anyone else to see, not even my secretary?" Mira deliberated aloud while she walked around the room. Her eyes searched, stopping at every object to consider it before she moved on.

"Voilà," she exclaimed as she felt underneath Bradley's desk and found several buttons. She knelt down to crawl under the desk and to take a look. She discovered each labeled button served a separate function. One called for Gwen, another triggered a projector screen to descend, yet another ejected a bar from behind a sliding wall, and one appeared unmarked. She pushed it with one finger and held her breath to see what would happen. At once a small drawer slid silently out from the bottom right corner of the desk.

When it opened Mira found a stack of papers, all neatly arranged. She pulled them from the drawer to examine. Most of them were recent deals, which hadn't been finalized yet. She figured he wanted to keep them close by for convenience. By the time she went through all of them Mira became discouraged. She found no suspicious or incriminating document connected to Charles Peterson or anyone else.

She placed the papers back in their secret hiding place when she noticed a small, black notebook resting at the bottom of the drawer. With a quick glance at the clock, she realized only ten minutes remained before she needed to escape back downstairs. She set the papers on the desktop and grabbed hold of the notebook.

At first glance it read like a diary of sorts with dates and comments that stretched over a period of several years. Mira started to put it back, guessing the search was a wash when she found Sean's name scribbled on one of the pages. She took a closer look and read the entry.

Sean Thorndale: 7/21/06 — Discovered

he's been meeting with Guárico often. Not to be trusted; 7/29/06 — My source found out S.T. had been fired from previous job before moving back to Florida; 1/23/07 — Bribed Judge to release records — S.T. was adopted by Gretchen and Frank Thorndale; birth mother was Lois Thorn, but who is the father ????

The book slipped from Mira's hand to the floor. Sean adopted? Scrambling to pick it up, she examined the entries more closely. Each name was described with unfavorable information, information that might be used as blackmail, she guessed. With no time left to study it further, she threw the book back in the drawer along with the pile of papers. She gave the drawer a shove to close it securely before hurrying to the door. When she heard voices, her steps froze. Her breath held along with the rest of her body as she listened.

When her phone vibrated, she snatched it from her pocket and silenced it. As she tiptoed to the far corner of the room, she could see Sean's name still lighted the screen. With a frantic glance she searched for a place to hide. The voices grew louder, and she recognized one of them as Bradley. The other with its higher pitch was clearly female. Her eyes darted across the room in a last desperate attempt when she saw a door behind her. She reached out to turn the doorknob and relaxed as the door swung open. Inside, she found a small closet that didn't hold much more than her slim figure. With no time to reconsider, she slid in and shut the door seconds before Bradley and the female companion came into the room.

"I won't accept that, Bradley. Always, you can find a way, if you put some effort into it."

"Mother, I most certainly put effort into it. More effort than you'd imagine, but Thorndale is too clever. Enough to trick me into believing him," Bradley argued. "Even my plan to scare off Mira Stanley by bringing that ex of hers to town backfired because of Thorndale. I underestimated him, but it won't happen again. I need a little time to figure out what to do."

"Well, it's not good enough. You need to act on this today. I believe you can order one of your people to take care of the whole sordid mess by tomorrow morning. Call in another favor or whatever it is you do to get things done. I don't have the time or energy to waste on this," Vivian insisted.

"It's not that easy. You don't understand."

"What I understand is if we don't stop this, someone will go to jail. Do you want to be that someone? I know I don't. Take care of it, Bradley. No more excuses."

Mira heard the door shut with a resounding thud. Frustrated, she got out her cell phone and opened it. After a quick text a message to Sean, she stared at the screen and hoped he'd answer right away. Seconds later, the phone lit up.

I'll figure a way to get him out of the office. Gwen might be back any minute. Get out as soon as I text you.

Mira waited, the minutes ticked by like hours. She listened as Bradley shuffled papers and opened drawers. Her mind went through a series of "what ifs." What if Sean didn't find a way to make him leave? What if Gwen showed up before she left Bradley's office? What if, what if. The sense of panic in her rose until she feared she'd explode and run out of the closet screaming, until she got out of the building.

All at once, Mira became aware she wasn't imagining herself screaming. The sound she heard was on the outside. She smiled as she recognized the shrill high pitch of a fire alarm.

"Well, for the love of God," Bradley exclaimed.

Mira heard his steps fade from the room. She counted another few seconds and then eased the closet door open. By this point she saw her phone light up again and looked down to read it.

Hurry, right now! Exit the back.

And she did. She sprinted out of the office and through the door, only to find the lobby empty and the elevator lights dimmed out. She headed for the stairs and descended, praying she'd find no one familiar to meet her. This wasn't the way the plan was supposed to go, she realized and wondered what she'd been thinking to come up with such an idea.

The first floor lobby was empty by the time she reached it. She slowed to a walk and turned down the back hallway to look for a rear entrance. Once outside, she found Sean pacing back and forth in the alley. He looked up as soon as he spotted her.

"Thank God. I wasn't sure if I was in time." He reached her and pulled her to him.

"I didn't know how much longer I could spend in that closet." Mira kept her voice steady, not wanting to give into her emotions. His arms held her tightly, and she heard the pounding in his chest as she rested her head against him.

"Let's get out of here," he said and led the way out of the alley and to the street behind Lane Developers.

While Mira followed Sean, she mused over the black notebook and its contents. She struggled with the decision of whether to reveal what she discovered, yet wondered if he already knew about any of it. In one way, she wished she had never found the notebook. However, no time remained to deal with the issue because they had reached his car. They hurried to get inside, and within seconds they were back on the highway headed toward the Peterson estate.

Chapter Thirty-One

"I don't know what to think, Mr. Bradley." Gwen's voice shook. "This woman on the other end of the phone claimed she was from the pharmacy. She explained you had asked for me to pick up a prescription. I went there, but of course I found nothing waiting for you and no one claimed to have made that call."

"And someone pulls the fire alarm, which gets all of us out of the building. I swear whoever this person was, he or she broke into my office." Bradley continued to pace back and forth.

"Sir, nothing is missing, and I found no evidence of tampering with the office door." Gwen spoke in a soft voice.

"It's too much of a coincidence. Too much." Bradley walked back into his office and slammed the door. As an afterthought he pulled it open once more and leaned in to say, "If anyone calls or comes in, I'm not available. Understand?"

He waited until Gwen nodded before he retreated once again to his office. He reached into the bottom desk drawer and pulled out a bottle of brandy. If any occasion called for it, this one did. Of course, it failed to erase his uneasiness. Nothing could.

Chapter Thirty-Two

"Well, that was exciting," Mira quipped and gave Sean a meek smile as they walked into Claire's house.

"It was stupid. How I ever agreed to such a crazy plan, I don't know. Stupid," Sean grumbled. He remarked more than once on the trip back to Claire's.

Mira smiled and shook her head. "I'm okay, Sean. It's over."

"No, it's not. And that part worries me. We haven't gotten to the bottom of this yet." He frowned at Mira. "Promise me, no more hare-brained schemes."

Mira nodded. She chose to keep how Alex ended up in Port Saint Joe a secret for the moment. Sean already despised Bradley Lane. One more miserable act added to the list made no difference. Instead, she walked away from Sean and into the kitchen, but didn't see Claire in her usual spot at the table. "I'm going upstairs to check on Claire."

"She's still napping, I bet," Sean suggested. "I'll go ahead and make us a late lunch."

Mira climbed the stairs and walked to Claire's bedroom. As she neared the doorway, she heard drawers opening and closing. She found Claire with piles of clothing all around her.

"Oh, my! You startled me." Claire looked like a child caught in the act of doing something wrong.

Mira smiled. "Sorry. We just got back, and when I

didn't find you in the kitchen, well, anyway, what's this? Spring cleaning?"

"Not really. This memory grew inside my head and nagged at me. Something Charles mentioned started it. We had another one of our talks while you were gone, you see." Claire nodded.

"Oh? And what did he say?" Mira had learned to play along.

"Well, for one he suggested I get rid of his clothes. He told me the needy had more use for them than he did. Of course, he's right. I'm a foolish old widow who hangs on to things I shouldn't.'"

Mira stood quietly as Claire stared down at the piles of sweaters, pants, and shirts. After a moment, she spoke. "It's not foolish, Claire. It's sort of romantic. You love Charles and don't want to give away any part of him. I get that."

Claire smiled. "You are such a sweet young lady. I thank God for sending you to me. I must admit, before you came I hadn't realized how alone and apart from everything I'd been. It feels good with people like you and Sean to talk to."

"Well, we feel the same. About talking to you, I mean." At moments like this Mira worried Claire might revert back to a recluse once she and Sean weren't around.

"I'd hoped to get this mess sorted out before you returned." She gestured toward the bed and dresser. "Did you enjoy your outing?"

"Let's say it turned out interesting." Mira didn't want to frighten her with details. "Maybe you'll take a break and come downstairs for some lunch? I can help you with this afterward."

Claire nodded and followed Mira to the kitchen. Sean finished heating soup on the stove and preparing sandwiches. They sat outside on the patio to enjoy the afternoon sunshine. Once settled, and with everyone quiet while they ate, Mira sorted out all the events and information which filled her head. She tossed out the irrelevant and focused on the details that merited attention. Questions still needed to be answered. The two people sitting there with her could probably help with a few. However, Mira wasn't sure how to start. She glanced toward the beach and found a man with a clipboard and pen in hand standing a few yards from the shore.

"Oh, great. Another one of Bradley's men is snooping around. I'm inclined to go give him a piece of my mind," Mira exclaimed as she rose from her chair.

"Sit right back down and rein in your temper. That's not Lane's man." Sean grinned.

"Oh? Who else needs to go traipsing across Claire's property?" Mira frowned.

"Remember the judge I mentioned earlier? The guy standing over there is his friend from the county environmental agency. It so happens he's come to survey the property and write a report, which will claim —and I quote—the land needs to be shored up before any excavating proceeds, as its current state may cause flooding to the adjacent properties. At least I think that's the way the judge put it," Sean explained.

Mira sat up straight in her chair, the excitement in her voice evident. "Is this what I think it means?"

Sean pointed toward the worker. "With this guy's report, the judge will put a stop to all work orders on this property until the problem is fixed. And I'd say the job would take at least another week."

"How wonderful!" Mira got up and ran over to give Sean a hug, and then a kiss, and another kiss until she remembered Claire. With an apologetic smile she went back to her lunch.

"This means you can rest easy because by the time they finish the work, Mira and I will figure out how to get your property back," Sean added.

"Oh, I wasn't worried. Charles always promised I'd be fine. He made sure of it. And I trust my Charles." Claire gave them a confident look.

Mira and Sean's eyes met for a second. "Still, it's nice to know Sean's friend is helping," Mira added.

Claire continued on as if she hadn't heard Mira. "Charles had this way about him, you see. He knew how to read people. I used to tell everyone, five minutes after meeting someone, Charles knew if a person was honest or not, kind or cruel."

"Are you thinking of someone in particular, Claire?" Sean's brow wrinkled.

Claire blinked, as if at once she remembered Sean and Mira were there. "I should finish cleaning the bedroom." She got up to go back inside.

Mira threw Sean a concerned glance. "I'll come with you." She picked up her plate and Claire's, and followed her into the kitchen.

****

"There are a lot of nice items, Claire. You're a kind and generous person to do this," Mira commented as she folded clothes and packed them into boxes.

"Yes, I suppose. It's not as easy as I hoped it would be. Letting go, I mean."

"At least you carry on your, ah, talks together."

Mira looked around the room and added, "How many years have you lived in this house?"

"Going on forty. We came back home after living overseas for a short while."

"Home? You're from this area then?"

"Oh yes. In fact Charles and I first met in elementary school." Claire laughed. "He was such a mischief maker and always getting sent to the office."

Mira grinned. "And when did you start dating?"

"Funny, but I refused to tolerate him for the longest time. I used to tattle on him every chance I got. This was in our third grade class. Of course, he charmed the girls, even at that age. As I recall, Vivian and Lois were two of them with stars in their eyes for my Charles. No, I didn't look at him with anything but disdain until high school."

"Vivian? You mean Bradley and Kyle Lane's mother? And Lois Thorn? I didn't realize all of you carried such a long history together." Mira wondered if any contact among them over the years occurred.

"Yes, I know. With all that has happened, it feels rather strange to recall how at one time we were kids who played together."

"Did you keep in contact over the years?"

"Hardly. The Lanes traveled in the privileged social circles. The Thorns weren't much different than them, just not quite as rich. We were worlds apart when it came to money, you understand," Claire explained.

Mira wasn't surprised. The Lanes didn't seem like the kind who accepted people outside their country club set. The Thorns were another story. She didn't know them. Sean was Lois Thorn's son, but he'd been raised by her cousins. Maybe they weren't close. Sean didn't seem pretentious. He hadn't made any condescending remarks about anyone in the brief time she'd known him.

"Though I do remember a time after Lois disappeared when Charles met with Vivian. I'm not sure why, but she called and wanted to speak with him. At first, he refused to go, but reconsidered when he figured she must be suffering. She'd lost a close friend. Funny, he didn't mention it to me, never once a word about their meeting."

"Friends? You mean Vivian and Lois were friends? But I thought—didn't Curtis have an affair with Lois?" Mira grew confused.

"Yes, I know. Strange, isn't it? But they were friends long before that happened. I imagine it's what hurt Vivian all the more; someone she trusted suddenly betrays her. And with her husband no less."

Numerous scenarios sprouted up in her mind. If Mira considered Lois met with foul play, Vivian looked like a major suspect. Or any of the Lanes. Mira wanted to talk to Stan again. Thinking of him reminded her of another question.

"Claire, I spoke with Stan Thomas. He's Jason Thomas' cousin. Remember Jason Thomas?"

"Yes. Why wouldn't I remember?" Claire shoved more clothing into the box.

"Well, he told me a remarkable story. I'm not sure how you'll take this, but…" Mira grew anxious as she explained the confession of Stan's midnight caper. "Stan is the burglar who broke into your shed that summer night."

"Why ever would the cousin of Jason Thomas want to break into my storage shed?"

"Do you recall a visit from Stan Thomas? He claims he spoke with you not long after Charles died."

Claire stared at some place beyond Mira, quiet for a spell. "You know, I do remember someone from the Tribune who came to interview me for an article he was writing. Or at least it's what I assumed."

"Most likely it was Stan. He explained you told him how you had moved most of Charles' papers and belongings to the shed. And this gave him the idea."

"But why? What could he possibly want from my shed?"

"This is where it gets complicated. He followed up on a tip Jason had given him. Jason believed Charles found evidence that proved Bradley Lane's involvement in illegal dealings. Stan learned Charles never completely trusted Lane. It's why he had made sure you were well taken care of after his death. Afterward, Stan was determined to search your shed and see if he'd find the evidence and use it to prove Bradley Lane's guilt."

"Oh my," Claire exclaimed and sat down on the bed. "It does explain a lot. Do you think he found what he wanted?"

Mira nodded. "He found it all right. Stan described it as a contract between Bradley and Charles, an addendum of sorts to the property deal originally made. It states you control the decision of whether or not you want to sell. However, if you do, you get two million eight hundred thousand for your property." Mira waited to see Claire's reaction, and she was glad the elderly woman had sat down beforehand.

"But that's not what Mr. Lane claimed. And his lawyer came to visit me. He claimed it was worth no more than eight hundred thousand in this depressed market. I kept the quote he gave me."

"Well, it's certainly Bradley Lane's habit, not telling the truth."

"And where is this contract addendum? Maybe I can stop the sale. I don't care how much they offer me. I want to stay where I belong with my Charles."

Mira regretted breaking the news. "I'm sorry, Claire. Stan confessed Bradley Lane must have followed him to your backyard. They struggled, and Lane managed to knock him out and take the contract." The look that transformed Claire seemed to take the life out of her. Mira worried for her health. She was too old to deal with these problems.

"He told me, Charles assured me I needn't worry. He promised he had taken care of it. I don't understand." Claire sat there mumbling and shaking her head.

Mira remained troubled. She mulled over Stan's claim how Charles never trusted Bradley. Why sell him the land? What pushed him to make the deal in the first place if he didn't trust him?

"Claire, can you think of any idea what Charles meant by protecting you? I mean, do you think he referred to that addendum?"

"I guess it's possible, but how can I be sure?"

Mira's shoulders dropped. It didn't matter if it was, since they didn't possess the document. She pulled the last of the clothes from the drawer she emptied and gave them a brisk shake. An object fell out and clattered on the floor. "What's this?"

Her hand reached down to pick up a cassette tape labeled with a word and a date. *Evidence—Dec. 3rd,*

2009. She held it up. "Do you know what this is?"

Claire walked over and leaned forward to take a closer look. "Hmm. What does it say, dear? I don't read well without my cheaters." She pointed at the writing and squinted.

Mira told her, and it was as if Claire lit up all at once.

"Oh! The tape. Yes, I remember. Charles gave me the tape and told me to keep it safe. He stressed how it was extremely important evidence. I recall putting it in the storage shed for a spell, but a couple months after Charles passed away, he came one night and told me to move it someplace close by, someplace near me. So, I brought it inside and placed it in his drawer. That's safe, isn't it?"

Mira nodded, speechless.

"At the time I figured the tape must deal with one of Charles' business clients. Now I wonder if this was what Charles meant would protect me?"

Yeah, I wonder. Mira suspected Claire would continue to spout off more surprises. The way she recalled information when everyone least expected it left no doubt. "Do you own a cassette player? We should take this downstairs and…" Mira stopped and remembered the black notebook. After all she'd learned about Sean from a few entries, it made her worry what might be revealed on the tape. "Do you keep one in the bedroom? We could listen to it first, just you and I."

"Yes. I remember storing one away somewhere." Claire rummaged through the bottom drawer of her desk.

Once Claire found the player, Mira placed the tape inside. Both women sat quietly and waited to hear what the "evidence" revealed. At first, Mira was confused. The conversation between the two men seemed all about business. And though she recognized Bradley's deep, throaty sound, she didn't know who the other voice belonged to.

"Oh, my." Claire's eyes widened as her voice grew low and soft.

Mira glanced up, and seeing the tears well up in Claire's eyes, she surmised the other voice must belong to Charles. She turned back to look at the tape player and focused on the conversation.

"I guess we'll draw up the deed transfer according to your conditions. I must say if I didn't want your property so badly, well, I must give you credit, Peterson. I've never agreed to pay that much for any real estate, let alone a private property."

"I only want to make sure my Claire is happy and well taken care of when I'm gone. I worry about her, you know. She's very fragile. She can't cope with the world, not without...I need to make sure, you understand."

Mira heard the quiver in Charles' voice.

"Of course you do. Now, I don't mean to hurry you out the door, but I have another meeting in a few minutes."

"You'll call tomorrow? About the contract?"

"First thing tomorrow morning. And again, you are doing the right thing, considering your circumstance."

Mira and Claire listened to the silence that followed. They waited until the sound of a door closed, only to open seconds later. It became clear to both of them someone new came into the conversation, along with Bradley.

"You're late."

"I had to swing by the courthouse and finish up a case."

Mira's heart stopped for several seconds. The other voice belonged to Sean. Her instinctive reaction from earlier, not to let Sean hear the tape, turned out to be the right call.

"Well, here are the papers Kyle wants. And I need you to sign this."

"What is it?"

"A deed transfer for the Peterson property."

"Wasn't that Charles Peterson I passed in the hall?"

"Yes. And he agreed to sell to me after he passes."

"I don't want to know how you managed it. Especially at...under a million? That's cheap, even for you, Lane."

Mira listened to the crackle of paper changing hands and the scribble of writing. She guessed Charles had brought and left the recorder behind, hidden somewhere close. What she couldn't figure out was how he had known something would be worth taping.

"Why isn't Peterson's signature on this?"

"Just some minor conditions he insisted I add. Then he'll sign. Of course, I told him I refuse to go any higher on the price. The fool has no idea."

Mira heard Bradley's cruel laughter.

"What? That you would've gone higher?"

"Hell no. I'm talking about something far more important, but it's not your concern. Right now, I just needed your signature."

"Someday your luck will run out and you'll find yourself in jail."

"I've managed up to now. You should know better than most. No one crosses me without consequences. This deal only ties up one of those loose ends."

"Loose ends. That's a good one. Well, if a time comes when one of your loose ends includes murder, be sure to count me out."

"Really? Well, I'd say you've dirtied your hands plenty."

Mira held her breath. She didn't want to hear the rest, but she knew listening wouldn't change matters, if Sean was that deeply involved with Bradley and his actions, as it appeared he was. Her heart sank into that black void of distrust once more. She had done it again. Her choice in men left her with nothing but betrayal. They were all filled with lies. Why leave herself open to heartache? Never again, she pledged and let the recorder continue to play. Might as well know the worst.

"I don't think..."

The sound of footsteps pounded down the hall to interrupt them. Mira quickly reached out to turn off the recording.

"Mira? Claire?" Sean stepped into the bedroom. "I think you'll want to come outside and see this."

Mira and Claire followed Sean back downstairs. He explained as they went along.

"I heard the sound of an engine turn on while I was in the kitchen. When I discovered the bulldozer out back, I ran outside to find out what was going on. That's when I learned my dear uncle, the judge, appears to be sharper than I anticipated. After only a few hours he managed to find a loop hole in the stop order. To make matters worse, Lane is retaliating by having the men start the excavation of the beachfront early. I tried to reason with them. I approached one of the workers and argued with the guy. I told him this can't be right."

They reached the kitchen, and Sean pointed to the backyard. "As you can see, I didn't get him to listen. So I called the courthouse. The judge told me there is nothing more he can do. You'll receive a court order on Monday, giving you until the end of the month to evacuate your house. But we still might have a chance."

Mira puzzled over what Sean meant, but quickly set that concern aside as she turned to look out the window. A large trail of upturned dirt led from the beach and almost halfway into the backyard. Her eyes widened as they settled on what mattered most. She heard Claire gasp behind her.

"My garden! Please, not my garden," Claire cried.

Mira looked once more at Sean and her shoulders fell as she sighed. "Oh, no."

"Come with me and take a look. It seems someone found another way to stop Lane's project," Sean announced and opened the patio door to walk outside. He motioned them to follow.

Mira, Claire, and Sean continued across the lawn to reach the garden with its upturned roses. Next to the bulldozer, the driver stood with his arms crossed. Sean picked up his step and met the worker. As they spoke,

Sean glanced back at Mira and Claire. Before they reached him, he ran back over.

"I know this will sound bizarre, but the bulldozer uncovered something," Sean started.

"Yeah, like what? A body?" Mira stared at the worker for a moment and then at Sean. She blurted it out, a wild hunch that surprised her, but in her gut she knew she was right.

"How did you...? Yes, as a matter of fact, it looks like human remains."

Mira wanted to believe his reaction was genuine, but the taped conversation continued to play in her head. "Well, I guess we should call the police. I can't wait to suggest they start their investigation by questioning Bradley Lane."

"Already done. They are on the way. And you're right. Without a doubt Lane has some explaining to do, like why he wanted to buy this property."

Mira studied the upturned soil. "What was the worker thinking? If he entered at the back of the property line, I mean. Why make a path directly up to Claire's garden?"

Sean rubbed the back of his neck. "It's strange, I must say. The driver claimed the bulldozer took off. Says he couldn't get the brake to stick until he reached the garden. So, he started digging there since the whole area needed to be done anyway."

"Oh my. Charles, look what you've done," Claire whispered as she stood close behind Mira.

Mira gave her a nervous glance before turning back to face Sean. "Did you catch that? The guy seems somewhat on edge." Mira nodded toward the worker who shuffled his legs back and forth. He faced them while talking on his cell phone, but when he noticed Mira and Sean were staring, he pivoted around on his heels.

"It's a hunch, but maybe Lane gave him instructions that if anything unusual turned up, he should keep quiet and continue his job," Sean suggested.

"And get paid a tidy sum for his discretion, no doubt," Mira added but wondered how much Sean might be getting paid for his own silence and cooperation. A sick feeling grew inside her stomach as her suspicions of him grew once again, and all because of that taped conversation. It made her confused and uncomfortable. She moved away from his side and turned to Claire.

"Maybe we should go back inside to wait. We can fix something to eat. It's almost dinner time." Mira took Claire's arm, and without so much as a glance at Sean, she led the distraught woman toward the house.

Chapter Thirty-Three

The police arrived, and the forensics team followed shortly after. Mira and Sean filled in the back story for them and explained why the bulldozer was there. The worker didn't say much, only shrugged his shoulders and responded with "I don't know" to the detective's questions.

Claire, of course, stayed inside the house. The shock of seeing her ruined garden with its prize roses in rubble was enough to unhinge the poor woman, Mira commented. And the body of some poor soul unearthed beneath it added more stress than the strongest person could handle. Mira gave her a sedative and sent her to bed to rest.

As gruesome as it turned out to be, they had discovered a way to stop the excavation, just like Sean predicted. She stood peering out the kitchen window as a team of men and women with their hands covered in plastic gloves pulled out the human remains and placed them in evidence bags.

A lot needed to be answered; Mira didn't know where to begin to sort it all out in her mind. Though discovering the identity of the body should take priority, Mira concentrated on one thing: Sean's involvement, or at least her suspicion of his involvement. She couldn't seem to take that leap of faith, to trust he was a good person and would never harm anyone.

"Why don't you go lie down and get some rest, too? I can stay and watch. They shouldn't be too much longer," Sean offered.

"It's okay. You can go. I'm sure you have other things to do." Mira found it difficult to look at him. More than anything, she wanted him to leave so she might be able to relax and deal with the situation. And it didn't include asking him any questions. Not yet, anyway.

"Mira," Sean started and reached over to touch her.

"I think you should leave." Mira backed away from him. His face revealed a mix of hurt and confusion. She didn't need to say more because he turned and left without another word.

****

Once again, Mira and Claire sat down to listen as the tape recorder rested on the bed between them. Sean's voice came across, clear and confident.

"I don't think you could imagine what I've done. But then again, you don't even know what goes on in your own family, do you?"

"I know everything about everyone. You can count on it."

"What you can count on is what I said. I don't hurt people or kill them. And if I find out you've crossed that line, I'll call the police myself, no matter what it costs me."

They heard the sound of footsteps and a door closing. Mira wanted to believe Sean meant those words. She reached over to turn off the player when Bradley spoke again.

"Yes. Peterson was here...No, he agreed to

it. Now, stop worrying. He's old and frail, on borrowed time. And if needed, I'll help him along. Trust me. No one will discover she's buried there. I made sure of it...Mother, I tell you we have nothing left to do. I'll talk to you later."

This time the tape ended. Mira figured if Charles had returned the next day to sign the contract addendum, he retrieved the tape recorder and kept the tape for security. She merely speculated as to why he didn't give it to the police. Perhaps discovering whoever was buried on the property wasn't as important to Charles as his deal to secure Claire's future.

"I had no idea." Claire finally spoke.

Mira gave her an understanding smile. "This is why he meant for you to keep it safe. Unfortunately, Lane destroyed the addendum. No wonder Charles took such precautions. Weren't you curious to listen to this?"

Claire nodded. "I forget too much nowadays. Since Charles passed, my mind seldom carries a thought from one day to the next. I put it away; I remember that." Claire shrugged and grew quiet, leaving both of them in silence for a moment.

"I'm sorry. Your rose bushes are ruined." Mira hesitated to mention them until now.

"Oh, they're only flowers, after all." Claire chuckled. "I must say, Charles seemed to feel it was a necessary sacrifice."

Mira nodded. "You think he caused the bulldozer to move so the body would be discovered." Somehow it didn't surprise her Claire believed it.

"I guess this explains why my roses continue

winning blue ribbons, doesn't it?"

Mira shook her head and waited for an explanation.

"The soil. The uniquely rich soil in my garden, as I've been told. Lots of minerals in bone, you know." A smile came to the surface.

"Oh! Oh my, Claire. That's awful." Mira tried not to look shocked.

"Yes, but however wicked it may be, it's somehow satisfying."

Mira started to think Charles truly underestimated his wife and her ability to cope. Once more, she examined the tape held in her hand.

"We must take this to the police," Mira stated and didn't hear any protest from Claire. She needed to tell Sean. After all, Sean signed the contract just as he claimed. All at once she remembered one of the things Sean mentioned on the tape. "Sean said under a million for your house, didn't he?"

Claire frowned. "And didn't you say Stan told you the addendum he looked at stated I'd receive over two million?"

Mira shook her head. "No wonder he wanted it back and out of Stan's hands before anyone else saw it. Stan is lucky Bradley Lane only knocked him out and didn't kill him."

They left the bedroom, Mira with the tape securely in her hand and Claire walking right behind her.

Chapter Thirty-Four

"Book me on the next flight out of the country. I don't care where to. Got it?" Bradley hung up and gathered the last of the files. He checked his watch again. More than a half hour passed since Floyd called from the Peterson lot.

At the time, he froze and couldn't think for several minutes. The shock of it floored him. He always anticipated the possibility, even prepared himself for it, but somehow never believed the discovery of Lois' body would happen. Certainly not this way.

"Gwen, I'll be out for the rest of the day," Bradley announced on the way out the door. He heard her sputter some words of protest, but he ignored them and pressed the button to send the elevator down. As the door slid open he stepped out into the lobby.

Once he reached the revolving door, his cell phone started buzzing in his jacket pocket. He entered the glass vestibule and pushed the bar forward to exit the building.

"Hello?" Bradley waited with impatience for the voice on the other end to respond. He figured it was Vivian wanting to know if he'd left yet. She planned to follow on a later flight, after he'd left town.

All at once his arm tensed as the revolving door came to a stop. Puzzled, he pressed hard against it, but it refused to give. It was then he noticed the tall, lanky man who'd exited right before him. He stopped outside the vestibule and turned to nod at Bradley with a curt smile before walking across the street.

Bradley puzzled only for a second and then returned attention to his own problem. "Damn worthless piece of—Hello? Who the hell is this?" He gave the bar another hard push; the stubborn resistance of it sent a line of jarring pain from his wrist up to his shoulder. He turned to glance back toward the lobby and rapped on the glass window, short, rapid jabs, to get the building manager's attention. The crackling sound on the other end of the phone faded into a long drawn out hiss. Confusion overcame him as he brought the phone away from his ear to stare at the screen. "What the...?" He glanced up. His heart sped to a rapid pace. For a brief second, he viewed everything around him like the flashes of light with a camera shooting images at warp speed: the concierge behind the front desk smiling, two beautiful and slender ladies who carried bags from the boutique Della Rose swinging from their arms, and the tall, lanky gentleman now seated across the street at Finoli's Café. Bradley blinked as the stranger lifted his glass and tipped his head to nod. The smiling concierge, the beautiful ladies, the tall, lanky gentleman, all paused for a few precious seconds as Bradley stared down at the blank screen.

The charge of an explosion shot from all directions around Bradley. Glass shards flew. The slivers of plastic and glass pierced him everywhere on his body, though he mostly felt the pain enter his eyes, mouth, and his neck. As if splintering knives broke the surface, pinpricks of heat seared and melted his skin. The force knocked him backward, sent him careening into the wall of his glass prison. Like voices in a tunnel, he heard the hollow echo of crying and recognized in a final moment of clarity that one voice, the loudest voice, was his own. Amidst the screams and shouts all around him, he slid down in a slow, deliberate motion to the floor; his body with its expression in red smeared him from forehead to chest. As he released his last breath, files scattered at his feet, his life's work spread out in meshed colors of black, white, and red.

Chapter Thirty-Five

An hour passed. Mira figured she should check on Claire. With all that happened in a short time, she worried how Claire might handle it. She started for the woman's bedroom. At the sound of her voice, Mira paused outside the doorway unsure of whether to interrupt.

"It's her, isn't it?...Yes, I figured as much. Oh, Charles, it is too sad, such a horrible way to die."

Mira stepped inside the room to discover Claire standing by her closet. The anxious and worn expression on her face filled Mira with concern. She had finished her call to Rob. He was shocked by the news and insisted on taking the next available flight to Florida. Mira managed to convince him to wait until tomorrow. She figured Claire needed time alone without Rob there to worry and fuss over her, even if he was her nephew. "Claire? How are you holding up?"

"I couldn't sleep any longer. Too many thoughts tumbling around in my head, I guess. Have they gone, yet?"

Mira figured she referred to the detectives who returned to examine the crime scene. "Around ten minutes ago. They assured me of no more visits today." At least she hoped it was true. Claire couldn't handle any more stress.

"Good. That is, I'm glad they're gone." Claire

found her way to the rocker and sat down.

Mira studied her for a moment. "Who do you think it is?"

"Hmm?"

"I heard you ask your husband. I heard the question, and you said you figured as much."

"Oh. Well, a strong feeling came over me when we were outside. Evidently, my instincts seldom prove wrong." Claire pushed off on her toes to rock the chair.

"And your hunch?" Mira encouraged.

"Yes, needless to say I can't be one hundred percent sure, but Charles and I believe the body in our backyard belongs to Lois Thorn."

Mira stared at Claire and measured the logic of her assumption to see if it fit in with all she knew about Lois. And in many ways, it did. However, she needed to know how Claire came to such a conclusion. "Why? Why do you think it's her?"

"Let's see. First, we have the falling out between Curtis and Lois when he learned she had stolen so much of his money. Then, we can't forget the breach between Vivian and Lois. I knew when all of it came out, the whole sordid, ugly affair would lead to trouble. Very, very dangerous trouble."

"But it doesn't explain how or why the body of Lois ended up buried on your property," Mira argued.

"No, it doesn't. And this is where Charles comes into the picture." Claire fidgeted with the fringe of her shawl. She twisted the ends of it between her fingers. After a few seconds she looked up at Mira with a weak smile.

Mira smiled back but puzzled as to why. She waited for her to continue.

"When Charles eventually told me he suspected Bradley Lane's ill doings and how he didn't trust him, I believed him. I've come to realize the Lanes always put money first. Nothing or no one gets in the way."

"Why didn't he trust him? Was it because of the way he pushed to get your property?"

"Oh, no. I mean, yes. That was one thing, but nothing to do with Lois. You see, Charles spoke with Jason Thomas. He told Charles that Bradley Lane kept a dark secret, serious enough to put him in jail for a long time if it were discovered. When Charles asked him what it might be, Jason claimed a certain woman who disappeared and assumed to have left town may not have made it out alive."

"Lois."

Claire nodded. "Who else?"

"But how does Bradley figure in all...?" Mira's eyes grew wide and she gasped. "Are you saying Bradley Lane murdered Lois Thorn and buried her on your property?"

"No. I can't say for sure, but Jason told Charles he suspected the reason why Bradley Lane wanted his property and ours. He claimed this was Lane's way to hide what could destroy his family."

Mira looked at a photo of Claire and Charles sitting on top of the dresser. She guessed the couple to be in their twenties or thirties. It was a shot taken on the beach. They looked happy and so young, Mira thought.

"Why didn't you tell us this before?" Mira waited with a puzzled look.

Claire folded her hands in her lap and stared down at them. "I'm ashamed to say I was afraid someone might blame Charles. After all, her body is on our property. But now, well, it's too late, isn't it? No point in hiding from it."

Mira reached over and patted the woman's shoulder. "You loved him very much."

Claire looked up to meet Mira's eyes. "And still do. I realize by telling someone what I suspected might finally stop Bradley from trying to get my property, but I couldn't bring myself to hurt Charles that way."

Mira sighed. Claire continued to think of Charles as being alive. It was sad and sweet at the same time. She still hadn't figured out how Jason knew that much about Bradley Lane's involvement with Lois Thorn's disappearance, but she believed in her gut it was what contributed to his untimely death. And not necessarily of natural causes. Stan's as well as Jessica's words echoed in her head. It didn't look good for Bradley Lane.

The thought of Jessica reminded Mira how she was still missing. The grim discoveries of the past couple days conjured up an unpleasant scenario. First, Joe Broski's body, and then the remains buried in Claire's backyard. Was Jessica next? Mira shuddered and elected to keep from leaping to that conclusion.

The whole situation had become tangled and twisted with all its lies and secrets. By now, Mira found it difficult to trust anyone, except Claire. She considered Sean for a moment. If only she'd make up her mind whether or not to believe his story. If she didn't care for him, it wouldn't matter. But she did. And her heart refused to settle on a bunch of maybes or what-ifs, afraid to give into her emotions and love him.

Whatever the reason, Mira understood no one else was as familiar with the case and this horrid mess. She elected to take that leap of faith and talk to him.

"Claire, I'm going out for a bit. Will you be all right for a short while?" Mira's eyebrows drew together as she waited.

"Oh, I won't be alone, dear." Claire nodded and smiled. "You run along."

Mira opened her mouth to speak but stopped herself, and with a slight wave she left the room.

On the way downstairs she made a list of places where she might find Sean. As it turned out, she didn't need to. The buzz and vibration of her phone made her stop to check her pocket.

"Hello?"

"Mira. I know for some reason you're angry with me, and may not want to talk, but I have some news," Sean said.

"No, I was being stupid and unreasonable. I do want to talk to you and see you, and I'm sorry for acting…"

"Mira, wait," Sean interrupted. "Listen to me. Bradley Lane is dead."

****

"He's scared as hell." Guárico kept his voice low as he spoke to Sean. They stood a few feet away from the front desk.

Sean studied the scrutinizing stare Alice, the deputy assistant to Chief, gave the detective. She'd been dogging Guárico since the kidnapper turned up dead, probably on orders from Chief who didn't trust the detective. Some of Guárico's methods might be considered a bit unethical according to department standards. However, most didn't argue that he got results. Sean found him admirable.

"He's scared and he's turning himself in. For protection, I'd imagine. It doesn't mean he'll talk," Sean said.

"Well, he has to give us something. This isn't a motel. Without evidence, we can't hold him. He should realize that."

"If I know Kyle, it won't be much. He won't take the blame for murder," Sean argued.

"We've worked this case too long, Thorndale. We can't let it slide now."

Sean narrowed his eyes and tilted his head to gesture behind them. "Be careful."

Guárico smiled. "Don't worry. I'm too good to get caught. Besides, Alice has the hots for me."

Sean laughed. "More like she's got eyes for the chief."

Their conversation ended when Kyle Bradley walk through the front door. His unkempt appearance surprised Sean. Yet, it made him realize how rattled he must be.

"Kyle." Sean nodded. "Sorry to hear about your brother."

Kyle glared and in a few steps skirted around Sean without a word. Then he turned. "You better hope you and your friends had nothing to do with this, or…"

"Or what, Lane?" Guárico stepped between them. "Is that a threat? Should I add that to the report?"

Kyle gave them one final, defiant stare before he turned back to face the desk and Alice. "I'd like to turn myself in. I know things about the kidnapper's murder."

Alice looked puzzled. "We don't arrest people for that, but I'll get someone to take down your report. Then you can be on your way."

"No! I mean I, ah, there's more." Kyle looked back at Sean and Guárico before he leaned over the desk to whisper, "I think my life is in danger."

Alice scowled at Kyle. "I'll call for someone to write down what you want to say, and afterward they'll decide what to do. Okay?"

Kyle didn't have an opportunity to answer, as another man came up to the desk and interrupted.

"I'd like to turn myself in. See, there's this crime I'm wanted for, that is, me and my partner, only he's dead cause somebody knocked him off. I don't wanna end up the same way, so if you could set me up in one of those cells, that'd be just fine."

Guárico recognized Alice's expression when she scrunched up her forehead and looked like a bulldog. It meant she was ready to blow. He smiled and jabbed Sean in the side. "Watch this."

"What the hell is going on here?" She turned her head from side to side, glaring first at Kyle and then the other man.

Kyle opened his mouth to protest, but stopped when he saw the face of the man next to him.

Sean detected how the eyebrow lifted, and he had a hunch Kyle recognized him, or at least figured out who he was. In either case he shifted his attention back to Alice.

"Just get somebody to take my report, will you? I haven't got all day," Kyle snapped.

"Well, aren't we the king of demands. See here, I'll get somebody when I'm good and ready. You just sit your keester over there and…"

Guárico stepped up to the desk. "It's okay, Alice. I'll handle this." He told Kyle to follow him.

"I don't think Chief would want you to do that," Alice started to protest, but grew silent as they continued to walk away from the desk and down the hall. She turned to give Sean a questioning stare.

Sean shrugged. "Don't look at me. I can't get him to do what I want, either." He walked to the exit, leaving Alice to deal with Joe Broski's partner.

Chapter Thirty-Six

When the phone began to ring, both Mira and Claire only stared at it. After hearing of Bradley Lane's death, neither one wanted to hear more bad news. They waited for several rings before Mira rose from her chair.

"Might as well answer," she mumbled and crossed the room in long strides to grab the receiver.

While Claire appeared to wait patiently, Mira carried on the phone conversation with no more than an occasional "I see" or "Yes." After a few minutes, Mira hung up and stared out the window.

"Well? What is it, dear?" Claire's eyes reflected concern.

"Forensics found some ID on the victim. I guess whoever buried the body didn't bother or care to hide who she was."

"It's Lois. Isn't it?" Claire spoke in a subdued tone.

Mira nodded. "We don't need to wait for the DNA evidence after all. They still need an official exam for their reports, though." Mira didn't finish, but instead walked back over to Claire and patted her hand as she sat down next to her.

"It's sad, isn't it?" Claire looked at Mira with tears in her eyes. "To die alone? No husband, no children, and a selfish old brother, the judge, callous, selfish old fool." Claire shrugged. "Sorry, I don't mean to be harsh."

Mira chewed on her lip, thinking of how to say what came next. "Claire, I know this will be a shock, but I found something important. I'm not sure if I should say anything, though."

"Then I guess since you brought it up you must want to talk about it. So why don't you tell me what it is, and perhaps I'll know how to help," Claire suggested.

Mira sighed and patted Claire's hand once more. "Lois did have a child. A son."

"Oh my, do you know who?" Claire's eyes blinked.

"Yes. Yes I do. And that's the important part." Mira smiled. "It's Sean."

****

Sean observed through the interrogation window while Kyle spilled every detail about his brother's actions and the Lane debacle. Guárico questioned Kyle for over an hour. To hear the man tell it, he was lily-white and clean as they come.

"Bradley always did whatever it took to protect the family. I told him he'd go too far someday," Kyle confessed.

"And of course you are an innocent victim in all of this." Guárico's lips pressed into a fine line.

"I told you, Bradley's sole agenda was for business profits. He'd do anything to keep anyone from getting a penny of the Lane fortune."

"And that includes murder."

"Yes. I suppose. I'd never commit such an act, but this doesn't mean someone else would look at it that way. After all, I'm a Lane, too."

"You think whoever murdered your brother might come after you?"

"Exactly. Which is why I'm here. I want police protection." Kyle sat back in the chair and crossed his arms.

"Yeah, well, I guess it sounds reasonable." Guárico reached over to turn on the intercom. "Tell Stokes to see who's on duty tonight. I got somebody who needs—Wait a minute." Guárico put his hand over the microphone and stared at Kyle.

"What? What are you waiting for? Tell him," Kyle urged.

Guárico smiled and took his hand away. "Hey, I'll call you back in a minute."

"What the hell? Why did you...?" Kyle stopped and narrowed his eyes. "Okay, Detective Guárico, what game are you playing?"

Sean smiled and leaned forward closer to the window. He knew how his friend operated.

Guárico pulled out a cigarette and lit it. He hovered over Kyle's shoulder until his head was inches from Kyle's. Taking a drag, he blew the smoke into his face.

Kyle stifled a cough but he responded in a raspy tone. "I asked you a question."

"Yes, you did. And I'll answer it this way." Guárico got up and paced the room. When he stopped, he stood behind Kyle. He took another long drag on his cigarette and leaned over until his lips reached next to Kyle's ear. "You're a gutless liar. And I'm going to prove it." Raising his hand, inches above Kyle's neck, the cigarette held between his fingers, he flicked the ashes loose.

Kyle jumped and grabbed hold of his neck. "You

lunatic!" He rose from the chair, but two strong hands shoved him back down.

"Let's try this again," Guárico growled. "What do you know about Joe Broski's murder? And where is your wife?"

****

"I'm going to have to file a report, you know," Alice announced. She shook her head at Guárico and pointed at Kyle. "Unless you've got some reasonable explanation for that cigarette burn on his neck."

Guárico shrugged. "I told you. He wanted a smoke, got careless, and burned himself. It happens."

"Ah huh. Since when do we allow smoking in the precinct?" Alice reached out to pull a form from the tray, not taking her eyes off the detective for a second. "You fill this out. I'm talking to Chief about this before I do anything."

"Got it. Thanks." Guárico took the paper from Alice's hand, and with one final glance at Kyle, he walked away.

Sean bit down on his lip to keep the laugh subdued.

"Hey! I thought we had a deal. Where's my damn protection?" Kyle shouted, and then snapped at Sean. "What the hell do you think is so funny?"

"Watch your mouth. This is a public office, you know," Alice scolded. "I say you get out before I arrest you for profanity. There's a law against that. Of course, you should know that, too, counselor."

Kyle started to say more, but shut his mouth. Instead, he turned and stormed out the front exit.

"Have a great day. *Counselor*," Sean called out before he turned back to the counter and Alice. "What? Can't a guy have a little fun?"

****

"That's right. She's on their family yacht. It's docked at the marina. A few yards down from yours as a matter of fact. I'll be there in five. You wait for me until then. You hear me?"

Sean heard Alice shouting at Guárico in the background, but he ignored her. Instead, he explained to Sean how Kyle admitted to receiving a call from Bradley. He told him Jessica was on the yacht. He'd put her there to keep her quiet. Sean hoped quiet didn't mean killing her.

****

Sean and Mira arrived at the marina within ten minutes of Guárico's call. They found no cars parked nearby the Lane's yacht, which meant they needed to wait.

"Let's give him five minutes. I'm sure he'll show up." Sean slowed the car to a crawl as he moved closer to the *Maiden Vivian*, an impressive seventy foot silver, white, and blue vessel.

"I take it Curtis bought the yacht early in their marriage when he was still madly in love with his wife?" Mira's voice couldn't hide her bitter view of the senior Lanes.

"No. I mean yes, he did buy it when they were young, but his cavorting with other women didn't stop after they married. It seemed he believed marriage shouldn't change his habits and that his behavior didn't measure how much or how little he loved Vivian," Sean explained.

"Why bother with marriage, then?" Mira scowled.

"Money. Her family possessed lots of it, and that meant adding to the Lane fortune."

"Like the damn aristocracy built their empires, one marriage at a time."

Sean laughed. "Yes, well, I guess you're right."

"Look. A car is pulling into the marina," Mira announced.

They waited patiently as the familiar black compact drove up and parked next to them. Guárico got out and walked over to Sean's window. Another car with the Port Saint Joe Police logo painted on the side pulled up behind him. Two deputies exited the vehicle and followed.

Within five minutes they were walking across the dock and boardwalk, which led up to the *Maiden Vivian*. The quiet was unnaturally serene, only to be interrupted by the sloshing of water hitting the sides of the yacht.

Mira's heartbeat pounded like a hammer against her chest. She hadn't rid herself of the guilt. She'd taken Jessica's concerns too lightly. If any harm came to her, Mira would feel somewhat responsible.

The deputies had gone ahead of them to search the deck. After circling around, they came back to report.

"No sign of anyone topside, Sir."

Guárico nodded. "Let's head down below then."

Everyone followed the detective as he descended the short flight of stairs. They found three bedrooms and the galley left to search. Guárico and one of his deputies covered the front half, which left Sean, Mira, and the second deputy to explore the remainder.

The deputy, Sergeant Collins, with his revolver held above him in a tight grip between both hands, led the way. The three of them treaded down the hall; each searched from right to left, alert to the slightest sound.

Sean heard the whimper first. "There." He pointed to the galley. Despite Collins' protest, Sean hurried past him and entered the small room.

Mira watched him disappear. In seconds, she and Collins heard the soft cry of a woman. They walked to the doorway to find Jessica seated in a chair. She rubbed her wrists as Sean knelt down to untie her ankles.

Collins backed up and shouted to Guárico and the other deputy that they found her and she was alive.

It dawned on Mira how the idea of Jessica being other than alive hadn't sunk in, until now. Her legs wobbled a bit, and she leaned against one of the walls inside the galley to steady herself. She observed Jessica when she rose from the chair, a bit unsteady on her feet. Her body trembled as she sobbed and shook her head.

"I didn't think anyone would come to help. I thought...I thought if Bradley returned with those men, I—Oh, Sean." She seemed unable to finish.

Mira wanted to add how sorry she was for not answering Jessica's phone call, when Guárico spoke from behind her.

"Move your ass, Collins, and let me through."

Mira turned to see him approach. As he reached the doorway a smile erased the serious expression on his face.

"Well, I'll be. Surprises sure never cease, do they?"

Mira twisted back around to catch Jessica giving Sean a kiss on the lips.

"I should have never left you, Sean." She rested her head on his shoulder. "I still love you."

The words hit like a hard, emotional blow to the stomach. Mira stared in silence as Sean rubbed

Jessica's back and kept a tight hold on her. He didn't say a word, but he didn't need to. His actions said it all. It took no time or thought for her to decide what was next. She turned to place a hand on Guárico's chest.

"Please, let me by," she whispered. She hurried up the stairs and off the yacht. One of the deputies stood alongside his squad car with his back to Mira. He talked on his phone and paid no attention to her as she headed to Sean's car. Her breath held while she searched for Sean's keys. He usually tossed them inside the glove compartment.

She breathed easier when she found them. In one swift move she slipped inside and started up the car. She struggled to keep calm and look like she had every right to be driving Sean's car out of the marina. With a smile and wave she drove by the deputy who dismissed her with a casual nod. Once on the road, she pressed down on the gas and raced toward Route 30 east and Claire Peterson's house. The only thought on her mind and in her heart was to escape, away from Florida and far away from Sean. She struggled to erase the image in her head, the one of Jessica clinging to Sean while saying how much she loved him, and Sean who held on as dearly, never once acting like it was anywhere but there, with his arms around Jessica, he'd rather be.

Maybe this was why she carried all those doubts, she guessed. Maybe in her heart she knew he didn't love her because he hadn't truly gotten over Jessica, and she refused to accept it. Instead, her mind chose to mistrust him and suspect his loyalties remained with the Lane family. Little did she realize the Lane she needed to factor in the most was Jessica, not Bradley. It didn't matter whether Sean spoke the truth and acted with sincerity toward Claire or not. The law had found their evidence. If Sean turned out to be a part of it, he'd pay. As far as Mira was concerned, he and Jessica could have each other.

Chapter Thirty-Seven

Mira wiped the tears from her eyes as she pulled into Claire's driveway. If she hurried, she could pack in a matter of minutes, call for a cab and be on her way to the airport before Sean discovered she or his car was missing. She figured that was fine, too. She didn't want to see or hear from him ever again.

"Mira, why you look upset," Claire exclaimed as she opened the door. "Is everything all right? I mean is Jessica okay?"

"Oh, she's just peachy. In fact, I'd say Jessica Lane is as happy as she's ever been. She and Sean both." Mira stretched an uneven smile across her face and walked into the kitchen. She pulled the bottle of vodka from the cupboard hiding place and poured some into a glass, then gulped it down.

"Are you...all right, dear?" Claire stood behind Mira with a frown of concern on her face.

"I'm great, Claire. The case is solved. Your home is safe and—Oh, I'll call your nephew and let him know the good news. He'll be happy. Everyone will be happy. Now, if you'll excuse me, I've packing to do and a plane to catch." Mira skirted around Claire to get to the hallway, but Claire grabbed her arm.

"Please, tell me what's wrong," she whispered.

Mira shook her head. "I can't. I ah, I'll call you later, when I get settled in back home. We'll talk then, okay?" She patted the woman's hand and then pried it loose from her arm. She ran up the stairs and threw her clothes in the suitcases as quickly as possible. Within minutes, she talked to the Port Saint Joe cab service. They promised to send someone out within minutes.

Her next call went to the Panama City airport. If the cabbie got her there in less than two hours, the airline employee promised Mira would be home before nightfall. She'd make arrangements for her car later. No time for second thoughts, she admitted. She grabbed hold of the suitcases and after one last glance at her room, Mira went downstairs to wait for her ride. With any luck, she'd be on the plane before Claire had the chance to tell Sean she'd left, giving him no opportunity to voice those excuses or explanations she no longer believed.

As she said goodbye to a confused and distraught Claire and rode away in the cab, Mira comforted herself knowing she accomplished what she came for, no more and no less. Life would go on as usual and that suited her fine.

****

"What do you mean she left?" Sean shouted at the deputy who looked puzzled by Sean's actions.

"I mean she drove by, smiled, and waved like it was totally normal for her to be leaving."

"Maybe she wanted to get back to the house. After all, we were done here. Besides, you and Jessica acted like you wanted to be alone," Guárico teased and tried to hide a smile.

"We did not want..." Sean started and then shook his head. He turned his attention back to the deputy. "Did she happen to stop and say where she was going?"

When the deputy shook his head, Sean walked over and got into Guárico's car. "Take me back to the Peterson house."

"Sure thing, boss. Got any other errands you'd like me to run? Get your groceries? Pick up your dry cleaning? Shine your shoes?"

"Shut up and drive," Sean growled.

"What about the little lady?" Guárico gestured behind him to the back seat where Jessica sat with her arms crossed, a sullen look on her face.

"Take me home first, if you don't mind. I'd like to see my *husband*." Jessica glared at Sean as if her eyes bored holes into him.

"Drop me off first. She can wait." Sean spoke in a low tone. He worried if too much time passed, he might be too late. As they pulled out of the marina, he silently hoped with all he felt for Mira he had enough of that time. The alternative seemed all too bleak.

****

"Thank you." Mira smiled and handed the cab driver the fare along with a generous tip. He had driven to the Panama City International airport in little over an hour, breaking all speed records to get her there before the next flight north. She figured he deserved the money.

She managed to get both of her suitcases onto a carrier and wheeled her way into the airport terminal. She was scheduled on Northwest Airline for a flight to Memphis and a connecting flight to Ohio. Photo images of her apartment flashed in her mind, leaving her somewhat comforted with the familiar.

Mira moved through the crowd of travelers as she perused the neon signs to find the right one. Twenty yards or so ahead, adjacent to the Delta airline terminal, Mira frowned as she spotted the familiar outline of a man and the face of the woman he spoke to. Vivian Lane smiled and laughed while talking with Quinn Fairfield. He appeared to be quite intimate with Vivian as he touched her arm and embraced her once or twice. Mira couldn't imagine why. The picture with the two of them together didn't add up when she considered how Quinn was supposed to be a good friend of Sean's. How did he know Vivian Lane? And why was he friendly with her? It didn't make sense to Mira.

Forgetting all about finding the Northwest Airline terminal, Mira moved closer to the couple to see if she could hear any of their conversation. She figured it was easy enough to blend in with the crowd and not be noticed or recognized by either one of them.

Now within ten feet she hid behind a pillar to listen. Frustration settled in as she discovered with all the chatter of the passersby, she didn't understand a word coming from Quinn's deep baritone voice. But then Vivian laughed and slapped Quinn in a playful gesture on the arm.

"Oh, George, you are such a charmer. I must say I can't wait to visit you in your quaint little village along the Rhine. Germany is lovely this time of year, isn't it?"

"George?" Mira said under her breath. For a second she figured maybe she was mistaken. Someone who looked like Quinn from behind, but in fact was a friend of Vivian's named George. When he turned around, Mira saw his face. It was Quinn Fairfield, unless he had an identical twin, she admitted.

"Thank you for the gift. I love poetry, especially the work of Rimbaud. How flattering you remembered." She clutched the leather volume to her chest for a moment and then placed it in her bag. "You are more than welcome to stay at my place whenever you come back to Florida," Vivian continued on in her high-pitched coquettish tone. "Sleeping in a motel room is not the way for a baron to live."

"Baron?" Mira exclaimed, this time a bit louder. She winced and slapped a hand over her mouth. What was Quinn up to, she wondered. None of it made sense. Quinn was British, not German. She'd heard it with her own ears. And with a title? Someone needed to do a lot of explaining. Mira watched as the baron gave Vivian a hug goodbye. Vivian waved and walked toward the terminal gate entrance.

When a voice announced the call for the next Delta flight, the crowd thinned out around her. Mira worried Quinn might spot her. She worked her way back toward the airport entrance. One of her lawyer hunches nagged at her. She didn't know what was going on with Sean's friend, but if he disguised his true identity from Vivian, he might be trouble. Though it surprised her, Mira considered only one thing to do. She needed to warn Sean.

"Why, if it isn't Mira Stanley!"

Mira stopped when she heard the voice. Her shoulders tightened as she recognized it, the lilting, bubbly sound of Nadine Wiggins, local Realtor. The sound came across loud enough to compete with the airport intercom system. Anyone could hear it. And anyone included Quinn Fairfield.

Nadine ran to catch up with Mira. "How wonderful it is to see you again. Are you leaving us so soon? We didn't get a chance to dine together and chat."

"Yes, it's a shame you are leaving."

The low tone of Quinn's British clip came from behind Mira. Tiny prickles of nerves ran up and down her spine. Why didn't she ignore Quinn and Vivian? If she had continued on to her gate and boarded the plane, she wouldn't be facing an uncomfortable encounter.

"Mr. Fairfield. What a surprise. And yes, it is unfortunate, but I must get back home right away. Work and all, you know." A nervous twitter escaped her and she sidestepped, moving closer to Nadine. After a quick introduction she added, "But I might find time for a drink on my way to the airline gate, if you want to go now, Nadine."

Nadine shook her head. "Oh, I wish I could. My flight leaves in a few minutes."

Mira's heart sank. This was not going well. If Quinn suspected she had eavesdropped on him and Vivian, he might be inclined to act on it. And that may not be a pleasant experience, she figured.

"Yes, well, I guess I should check on my reservation, too. I didn't realize how late it is. My flight is supposed to leave soon." Mira started to walk away with Nadine, but Quinn caught her arm.

"Might I speak with you a moment in private, Miss Stanley?"

Mira turned and smiled. "I really have no time. You know how the airlines can be." She tried to pull her arm loose when she winced at the stab of a hard object in her side.

"I suggest you come along. I don't want to hurt a lovely lady such as you." Quinn kept his voice low as he spoke.

Mira let her eyes shift down for a second. A dark

metal barrel pointed at her waist. She managed to keep from screaming and gave him a slight nod. With a glance at Nadine she said goodbye.

"Next time you're in town, be sure to look me up, sweetie. Nice meeting you, Mr. Fairfield." Nadine waved and moved into the crowd.

"Let's go," Quinn ordered and pushed the barrel into her side as he grabbed her arm to move toward the exit, leaving her luggage behind, next to the pillar.

****

"Claire, she must've said something, anything," Sean urged, but the woman kept shaking her head.

"She refused to tell me much, other than to say she'd call later, after she got home and settled in. I must admit though, she seemed quite upset." Claire sat on the sofa with Delilah snuggled up next to her.

Sean suspected why Mira became upset and he prayed for a chance to explain. His love for Mira heightened the fear of losing her. It scared him more than a little. It's why the panic inside of him grew. "Did you happen to catch the name of the taxi cab service?"

Claire did. Sean called the service and after some heavy-handed persuasion he learned to which airport the cabbie had taken Mira. Within seconds he was out the door and headed for Panama City. The cab had a twenty minute head start. If he drove fast enough, he might make it in time before her flight left. Sean wasn't about to let Jessica ruin his life a second time. He'd get Mira back, even if he needed to follow her a thousand miles north to Ohio.

Chapter Thirty-Eight

"It's unfortunate, isn't it? I hoped to finish my business here and leave for England without a hitch." Quinn glanced at Mira with meaningful eyes. "But I think perhaps fate played its hand."

Mira leaned against the passenger door, as if distancing herself from Quinn would help her escape. Although Quinn didn't say, she guessed from the familiar signs along the road they might be heading back to Port Saint Joe.

"I merely wanted to do what was right, you know. My life has been nothing but focused on that one goal. It's almost done. After she's gone, it will be. At last, justice will shine, and Lois will be at peace."

Lois? Mira sat up and became more attentive, no longer focused on her predicament. "You said Lois. Are you referring to Lois Thorn?"

"We're almost there. I suggest you consider what you'll say to him when you see him. We seldom get a second chance at love, you know. And I'm giving you that chance, Mira."

Mira turned to study Quinn's face. His expression forced its way to the surface, perhaps to unveil the suffering and pain hidden for so long. It took but a moment for her to guess the "him" he referred to was Sean, and it irritated her.

"Why do you think I want a second chance? He

loves someone else, not me."

Quinn's head twisted around. "Do you honestly believe that? I've seen the way you two look at one another."

"No. I think you're mistaken, Quinn. Or should I call you Baron?" Mira didn't want to think about Sean any longer. Besides, she had more important matters to discuss.

Quinn laughed. "Baron. Yes, it is a stretch of the imagination. Only an egotistical old fool like Vivian Lane would believe such a fabrication. Give her sort a little flattery, a bit of attention, and you've hooked a great catch."

"I don't understand. Why do you want to impress someone like her? She's despicable. She's the mother of Bradley and Kyle Lane, and they certainly aren't the kind to be proud of, not to mention her deceased husband who always cheated on her."

"How right you are, Miss. The Lanes belong under a rubbish pile, in my opinion. And it's been my job to put them there." Quinn turned once more to stare at Mira with a soulful look.

Mira shivered for a second. An indefinable chill overwhelmed her. "Put them where?" she whispered, afraid to ask but also to hear his response.

"As far into the ground as I can get them." The words came out cold and hard in tone.

"Bradley…" Mira started.

"Bradley Lane was a ruthless money-monger who put no value on life. His sole agenda was how to increase his fortune and gain power. It's a pity to all who crossed his path and stood in his way, for they found no chance to survive."

Mira took shallow breaths and her heartbeat raced. Without any doubt, she knew Bradley died at Quinn's hand. Justice for Lois? Weren't those his words?

"I loved her more than anyone could love another mortal. She left me once. I convinced myself I'd never get her back. My life was empty without her. Do you understand?"

Mira nodded though she remained confused. She kept quiet with the hope to keep him talking. She caught sight of the welcome sign to Port Saint Joe and realized they approached the turnoff to the Cape.

"And then I found hope, as if in a moment my life rekindled, reborn if you will. She wanted to come back to me. It was our second chance."

Mira heard the catch in his voice and turned to watch his shoulders quake. He began to sob and it grew louder as he lost his composure. In the next instant, Quinn slammed his hand against the steering wheel. Mira jumped in her seat, unprepared for the abrupt change in mood.

"That bastard and his family took it away. My chance, *our* second chance at love. Don't you see? We could have lived out the rest of our days with each other. But they took it away. I couldn't let them. They needed to pay, you understand."

And Mira did. Or at least she had a pretty good idea. Quinn and Lois. It must be the answer. Somehow Quinn learned of Lois' demise and Bradley Lane's involvement. And he wanted revenge, or justice as Quinn liked to call it. She wanted to ask questions, but wasn't sure how he'd respond.

Before she was able to decide, the car pulled into the drive leading to Sean's beach condo. She found no sign of Sean's car, which made Mira somewhat nervous. Quinn was unstable. He brought her to the condo, and she had no clear idea as to why. He'd told her to prepare what to say to Sean. So where was he?

Quinn got out of the car. He came around to Mira's side and opened the door. "Let's go inside." He pulled on her arm and led her to the back door. Once they entered the living room, he directed her to sit down.

Mira wanted to confront Quinn and ask what he planned to do, when he turned his back to her and spoke into the phone.

"Sean? It's Quinn...Yes, I heard." Quinn turned to look at Mira. "I think you should come to the condo... No, you don't need to go anywhere else. She's here, Sean. Mira is with me." Quinn ended the call and sat down in a chair next to Mira.

"They've identified Lois. A bracelet around her wrist has an engraving on it. It says—and I know this by heart—it says, 'My love for you is beyond any mortal's, your soul mate forever, Quinn.' And I meant every word of it."

"How did you meet her?" Mira found the courage to ask. She hoped to keep Quinn's mind occupied. She figured if Sean started from Claire's, he'd arrive in less than five minutes.

"Oh, we were college mates. Both of us attended Oxford. We fell in love and married within a year." Quinn's smile suddenly faded. "Later, Lois chose to travel to the states and see her family. I fully supported her, but I had work commitments and didn't go along."

"And she never returned, did she?" Mira guessed meeting Curtis Lane may have stopped her.

"No, she returned, after a year. Such a long

vacation, but I accepted it since I loved her and trusted her. However, her trips back home became too frequent. In fact, after four years passed, I put my foot down. She never wanted me to come back with her and I found it unnatural."

"And what did she say?"

"She didn't. Lois made her choice and left. She didn't return. The next I heard from her was by phone. She told me she wanted a divorce and why."

Quinn lowered his head to rest in his hands. Mira waited to ask for the true story of how he met Sean.

"In any case, I didn't stop her. I signed the papers and never heard from her again. Until five years later, when she called and asked if I'd take her back, if I found it in my heart to start over again. Of course, I was elated. Our second chance, you know."

"But she never came." Mira figured it was around the time, twenty years ago, when Lois disappeared from Port Saint Joe.

"I assumed she changed her mind, had second thoughts or doubts about us. I tried to get in touch several times, but my calls were ignored. I considered flying to the states to confront her, ask her why she changed her mind. But the humiliation...I couldn't handle it."

"And then you met Sean?" It seemed an appropriate place in the conversation to ask her question.

"Yes. Oddly enough and it proved quite fortuitous. It happened a few years ago, during my visit to New York for a lawyers' convention. I was a keynote speaker at one of the workshops. Sean attended, we spoke, and after a while I realized who he was and our connection."

Mira found it too contrived, but didn't question it. Stranger things had happened in her life. Why not this? "How did you come to the conclusion that Lois met with foul play?"

"Simple enough. One day, Sean shared the story of Aunt Lois' mysterious disappearance. I always assumed she chose to stay in Port Saint Joe. To find out she no longer lived there and she hadn't for nearly twenty years? Too coincidental, I'd say."

Mira nodded. "And that's when you took the path to play detective and find out what happened."

"I started by hiring a detective agency to search coast to coast for Lois' whereabouts. I guessed it was possible she moved elsewhere. At least after I discovered she'd had the affair with Curtis and how he publically humiliated her, it seemed a likely choice."

"But you didn't find out anything."

"No. Feeling quite frustrated at the time, I asked Sean to help. He started searching for information almost three years ago, for any detail that connected Bradley and his family to Lois' fate. He was already in partnership with Kyle, so getting close to the Lanes proved easy enough."

Mira knew the doubt she carried threatened to destroy any feelings for Sean. And the moment with Jessica managed to finish it, but she still needed to know how deeply involved he was. "Did Sean do anything to help carry out your, ah, agenda?"

Quinn seemed to read her mind. "Oh, no, dear child. This was my burden, my vendetta to complete. I couldn't ask him to get involved. He has his entire life ahead of him. As do you. And your love should keep you together. At least I will have satisfaction knowing that."

Mira ignored the last message. "Why murder? I mean, wasn't jail for Bradley Lane justice enough?" Mira glanced at the clock on the wall to see forty minutes had passed. What took Sean so long?

"I tried, but Bradley Lane proved as cold as steel. I believed the notes I sent him would break him, make him slip and reveal what I knew he had done. I admit the crime of murder isn't difficult when you carry motive like a burning ember inside you. I strongly believed when the police found Joe Broski in the boathouse with that warning pinned to his chest, they'd point fingers at Bradley. But no, it wasn't enough. He would get away, like all the other times. I refused to let it happen. A bit of tampering with his phone and, well, the rest was easy." Quinn stood when he heard the sound of a car pulling into the drive. Peeking out the window, he smiled. "He's here. Finally I can bring this to an end."

Mira's eyes grew wide at Quinn's words. End what, she wondered. At once she recognized her fear for Sean's life, as well as her own.

"Sean! Watch out! He has a gun," she shouted and got up to run to the other room, but she was too slow. Quinn grabbed her arm.

"Sit down, miss. We must finish this."

Chapter Thirty-Nine

Sean recognized Quinn's vehicle parked in the drive. What he couldn't figure out was why Quinn brought Mira along. Mira was supposed to get on a plane and fly home. He'd been on the road, more than half way to Panama City, when Quinn called. How he'd managed to arrive while driving at least ninety miles an hour without any cops to stop him was pure luck. He hoped luck held out and Mira was okay. Quinn's actions didn't make any sense.

In the next second he heard Mira shout something about Quinn and a gun. "Mira?" Sean ran for the back door. When he entered, he found Quinn on the sofa next to Mira. The look on her face warned him not to over react. "What's going on, Quinn?" He kept his voice calm and walked slowly into the living room.

"Why, your lady friend and I were having a nice chat. Weren't we?" Quinn hugged Mira.

Sean didn't like what he saw. Quinn acted tense. His words, clipped and sharp, came out in rapid succession. "Why don't you and I go outside and sit on the deck? We can continue our talk there, alone." Quinn shook his head.

"And leave this beautiful young woman? Not a chance, dear boy." Quinn stood up and crossed to the bar. "But I'll fix us all a drink. It should calm things down a bit."

Sean motioned for Mira to come stand by him. She got up and with light steps sprinted over to him.

Quinn turned. "Whatever did you do that for? You don't think I'd ever hurt her, do you? She's your love, your soul mate, just as Lois was mine." He crossed the room to hand each of them a glass before returning to the bar to lift his. "Cheers." He downed the brandy and poured another shot.

"What's this all about, Quinn? Why did you bring Mira here?" Sean kept his tone calm.

"I told you. You're soul mates and should be together. That is my parting gift to you." Quinn turned to top off his drink.

"Parting gift, huh? You plan on going somewhere?" Sean looked at his watch. He'd instructed Guárico to wait at least twenty minutes before sending anyone in. That left them fifteen.

"Yes. I'm afraid I must. I've finished what needed to be done. I have nothing else left. You see, if Lois lived, we would have made a happy family. You, Lois, and I. Ah, don't look surprised." Quinn laughed. "I see your lady isn't. You knew, didn't you, Mira?"

Sean felt Mira's hand grip his sleeve.

"Well, maybe you discovered Lois was Sean's real mother, but I doubt you knew I am his father. I didn't find out myself until I received some documents in the mail last month. The detectives I hired years ago found new evidence, one being a birth certificate from the courthouse in Panama City. Your birthday, that first year Lois left me. It suddenly all made sense. The trips back home weren't only for her lover. They were moments to be with her son." Quentin tipped his glass.

"Can you imagine how this destroyed me? She

269

didn't want a family with me. She only wanted Curtis. Enough to give our child away. Oh, I realize her motives weren't pure. Still, I loved her. And I love her now even more. You're looking at a fool, my son. The fool who waited all these years and missed countless opportunities to spend with the only family he had left. Ironic, isn't it? Both of us searched for a lost family member when we had one right under our noses, and neither of us knew it."

Sean wasn't sure how to react. He was stunned by the news. The fact he'd been cheated, all the Christmases and birthdays he missed spending with his mother and now his father. He sensed a renewed hatred for the Lanes.

"Of course, it's too late. I've lost too much. Live and love, my dear couple. You are young, but my time has come and gone." Quinn gulped the rest of his drink and slammed the glass down on the counter. He reached inside his pocket.

Mira eyes grew wide. "Sean! His gun!"

Sean fought to free his arm when Mira pulled on it as she ducked behind the table.

Quinn brought the gun up to his head and in an instant pulled the trigger. The explosive sound rocked Mira back onto the floor.

"Quinn!" Sean ran to the man's side, but it was too late. Quinn's breathing rattled as he tried to speak. Sean leaned forward to listen.

"She was my soul mate, you know," he whispered, and then his head rolled back into Sean's arms.

****

Quinn's body was carried away by the paramedics as Sean, Mira, and Guárico looked on from Sean's deck.

"I guess you'll want to take some time. I can get your statement later on," Guárico said.

Mira detected the sympathy in the detective's voice. It surprised her, but a lot of surprises happened in the past few days.

"Thanks, Guárico. Can you give us a couple hours?" Sean touched the top of Mira's head with his lips and added, "*We* need some time."

Guárico shrugged. "Fine with me. I'll head back to the station. You come along whenever you feel up to it."

Her head leaned against his chest as Mira listened to Sean's heartbeat. His arms tightened around her. She tried to block the image of how he held Jessica like this, only hours ago. He was right. She did want to get away, but did she want to leave Sean? Quinn's words echoed in her head. *You two belong together. You're soul mates.*

****

They endured the drive to town in silence. They had spent a few hours alone together, sitting on the beach, watching the ocean waves without talking. Mira wanted to speak, to broach the subject of Jessica, but at the moment it somehow became small and insignificant. Sean lost a father and a mother in a single moment's confession.

Once they arrived at the police station, Guárico met them at the front door. "Kyle Lane has paid us another visit. I guess Jessica convinced him to talk. He's giving me some excuse how he wants to start over with a clean slate. I can't figure those two out. They're inside and, well, see for yourself."

Mira and Sean found the Lane couple in the lobby. Kyle, with his arms wound tightly around Jessica, gave her pecks on the cheeks and mouth. When they became aware they were being watched, Kyle stepped back from Jessica, but kept his arm around her waist.

"I've come to clear some things up." Kyle turned to Jessica and smiled. "Jessica says it's time people knew the truth and to hell with the Lane reputation. I think she's right."

When they heard Kyle summoned to the other room for questioning, Mira and Sean walked away. "I thought..." Mira started.

"Yes, I know what you thought, but you couldn't be more wrong," Sean murmured and moved closer to Mira. "What's it going to take, Mira Stanley, to convince you I'm falling in love with you?" He brought her lips up to his and kissed her.

"I guess it's a good start," she murmured.

"All right you two. First them and now you. What's this look like? No Tell Motel? No hanky panky in the police station, you hear?" Alice scolded and rapped on the counter with a gavel.

Mira and Sean laughed but did as the officer asked. Guárico called to them from across the hall.

"Hey! You'll want to hear this." He motioned with a wave of his arm, leading them through the doorway.

Inside the windowed cubicle, they faced the interrogation room where Kyle sat. They listened while he spoke to the detective and told everything he knew. Bradley had been doing Vivian's bidding whenever she demanded it. And that included getting rid of Lois' body.

"I didn't know it at the time. That came out later

when Bradley told me our mother killed Lois Thorn. They'd argued over money, you see. Lois extorted a small amount out of Mother, but she came back. She wanted more to keep quiet. Bradley and I figured her affair with our father played itself out, and he'd grown bored with Lois, just like all the others. However, when he found out about the money, he threatened to call the authorities. And it might have worked, if Lois wasn't aware of all the other dirty deeds he committed."

"You're saying Lois changed tactics by threatening Vivian?" Detective Wilson wore a skeptical expression.

"Yes. Somehow Lois couldn't get to the money she embezzled. Father managed to find out where she'd stored the money in those overseas' accounts. He always had his sources. Anyway, when she failed to get the money, she blackmailed our mother. At some point, they fought. Vivian shoved Lois who fell onto a marble statue and cracked her head open. When Mother realized she was dead, she called Bradley to get rid of the body."

"And that's how she ended up buried in the Peterson's backyard."

"Well, Bradley claimed it's what happened. The problem was he buried her at night and after several drinks. The next day he couldn't remember exactly where the body was located, only that it was along a certain stretch of road on Route 30. After some thought, he finally narrowed down the area to two properties, but he remained uneasy about the whole incident. Fortunately around that time, an excavation crew was hired by the county to dump fill dirt on several lots along the shoreline to stop the tide water flooding. Bradley felt relieved as this proved a convenient way to hide the evidence, buried underneath all that fill dirt. But after a few years, he began to worry, you know. With the occasional flood water eroding the land, he figured the remains would eventually be uncovered. It was a chance he'd never take. You understand? That's why he tried to buy property belonging to the Thomases as well as the Petersons."

"Did your brother ever mention Jason Thomas or Charles Peterson? That foul play caused their deaths? Your wife believes so."

Kyle shifted in his seat. "I know Jessica found something in my room and told you about it. But she got it wrong. You see, Bradley asked me to keep this medicine for him, keep it hidden until he told me otherwise."

"What medicine, Kyle?"

"It's called cisapride and taken for upset stomachs. Bradley claimed to use it, then stopped a few years ago. I suspected even then how it was a lie, but I didn't question him. I never did." Kyle shook his head.

"Why ask you to hide it?"

"Mother told him to."

"Why?"

"Because she had done something with it she shouldn't, that's why. Look. I can assure you this doesn't involve what happened to Jason and Charles. They both died of heart attacks. A strange coincidence, I know. Still, Bradley had nothing to do with their deaths, and neither did I." Kyle's voice became agitated.

"Settle down, Mr. Lane. I'm asking these questions to clarify. Can you explain why Bradley wanted you to hide the medication?"

Kyle hung his head and remained silent.

"Mr. Lane?"

"Our father had a serious heart condition in the final years of his life. He took medicine for it. Our mother knew this."

"What else? Why did any of you want to hide the cisapride?"

"After a while, I decided to do some research." Kyle rested his head in his hands.

"Research?"

He nodded. "I found out cisapride can cause an irregular heartbeat and in many cases heart failure, especially for those with a severe heart condition." Kyle's voice remained so soft they barely heard his words.

"That's hardly a reason to hide the medication. Try again, Lane. This time, make me believe you."

Kyle looked up at the detective with hate in his eyes. He spoke louder this time. "We hid it because our mother didn't want the police to find it after our father passed away. She didn't want them to find it." He sobbed, and then managed to ask, "I'm thirsty. Do you think I could get a drink of water?"

Detective Wilson turned to look at the window and nodded. Someone brought in a glass, which Wilson handed to Kyle. "Okay, Kyle. Why didn't Vivian want them to find the medication?" He waited while Kyle downed the water.

"Thank you." He handed the glass back to Wilson and sighed. "Mother changed his medicine. She'd taken the cisapride from Bradley's medicine cabinet, you see. Instead of his heart medication she gave Father the cisapride, right after he confessed he'd carried on the affair with Lois for most of their married life. Usually, his affairs lasted a few months, never years. I imagine it was a blow to her ego when she realized he must love Lois. She continued to give him the cisapride, knowing the danger, until he had a heart attack and died. There. You have the truth. Now, can I go?" He stood up.

Wilson led Kyle out of the room. Mira and Sean remained in the cubicle, speechless over what they had learned. Soon, Guárico motioned them to follow him. He led them back out into the lobby where they found Kyle crying on Jessica's shoulder. They noticed Alice didn't scold this time. Instead she came around her desk and handed Jessica a box of tissues.

"That's not what I expected," Sean said.

"Me neither." Mira watched the couple crying together. "Maybe we should leave them. I feel like we're intruding."

"Not yet." Guárico held up a hand and walked over to speak to Kyle. "I'm sorry to break this up, but after what you told us, we need to act on it. Where is your mother at this moment?"

Kyle shook his head. "I don't know. At the house, I suppose."

"No, I'd say she's in London," Mira spoke up. She explained her encounter at the airport and what she overheard. She recognized her information irritated Kyle as he narrowed his eyes at her.

"I'd like you to call her, Kyle. Ask her where she's staying." Guárico's tone sounded commanding and left no doubt he expected his orders followed.

"No. I won't. She's suffered enough guilt over the years. What good will it do? She's over seventy years old. To put her in jail serves no purpose."

"Kyle," Jessica started and laid a hand on his arm. "You've protected the family long enough. Vivian caused the deaths of two people and covered up both. She needs to pay."

Kyle remained silent for a minute. He looked from Jessica to Guárico to Sean and back to Jessica again. "Give me my phone."

They all waited as he took his time to open the phone and punch in a few numbers. Mira wondered how someone managed to turn in their own flesh and blood, someone who at one point in time showed nurturing and love. For some reason, the image of Quinn as he kissed Vivian's cheek came to mind. She appeared so vibrant and happy at the moment. This had to bring her to her knees, although Bradley's violent death proved bad enough.

It's almost done. After she's gone, it will be.

Quinn's words came to her and took on another meaning as she remembered the way Bradley died.

I admit the crime of murder isn't difficult when you carry the motive...He would get away, like all the other times. I couldn't let that happen.

"It's ringing, but she's not picking up." Kyle frowned.

"No!" Mira shouted. "Hang up. You need to hang up, now!" The image of Quinn as he hugged Vivian, the treasured gift of poetry held tightly to Vivian's chest, it was all Mira needed to guess what might happen next. The end to it all, the deed to finish it, but it was too late.

"Mother? It's Kyle. I wanted to see if..."

The deafening sound from the other end of Kyle's phone was heard across the room. The shocked expression on everyone's face left all of them in

277

silence, except for Mira. "Oh my God," she cried as she held onto Sean's arm. Her eyes followed as the phone slid from Kyle's hand to the floor. It rocked back and forth as everyone stared in silence.

Epilogue

"I guess we're stuck here for a while." Sean kissed Mira once more. They had sat in the front parlor of Claire's house for over an hour. The winds howled and rattled the window panes while tree limbs from the palms slapped at the side of the house, all evidence of the building storm.

"You'd let a tiny hurricane stop you?" Mira teased while she tried not to laugh. "A big, strong man, a Thorndale no less? I must say, I'm surprised."

"Oh, really? Who confessed since a storm headed this way she wouldn't fly under those circumstances? Hmm?" Sean gave Mira a playful poke in the side. She laughed and pulled away.

"This is nice though, isn't it, sitting in the home we helped save?" Mira reached across to grab her wine glass. "Funny how things turn out. I came here to prove the agreement between Charles and Lane Developers was phony."

"And it turned out to be perfectly legal, except for the tiny detail where Bradley destroyed the original addendum."

"True. But at least you were honest about not knowing what Bradley was up to. Thank goodness you don't need to deal with that family any longer."

"Yes, and by the way, I think you owe me an apology." Sean raised his chin.

"Me?"

"Yes, you. *You* insisted I knowingly signed the document to cheat the Petersons."

"I questioned why your name was on the deed, that's all. And you told me you didn't remember signing it. You must admit it sounds weak," Mira argued.

"But I didn't remember. You know how many papers I sign on a daily basis?"

"All right you two. Enough. Help yourselves to some hors d'oeuvres, your choice of crab puffs and shrimp. And cocktail sauce if you like." Claire came into the room and set the tray on the coffee table.

"Thank you, Claire, but please stop going to such trouble. You've been waiting on us hand and foot since this morning. Besides, I thought you were eager to put your garden back together." Mira tilted her head with her eyebrows raised.

"Oh, I will soon enough. Can't ignore that rich soil, can I?" she chuckled. "However, we have plenty of time for that. After all, Charles and I agreed how out of respect for Lois, we should leave the ground in peace, so to speak. At least for a month or more. Charles shared with me how spirits appreciate such things, you know."

Mira opened her mouth to speak, but popped a crab puff into it instead. Who was she to argue with wisdom from the great beyond?

"In any case, I enjoy having someone to cook for, and it keeps me from puttering around aimlessly in this big, old house." The gleam in Claire's eyes shone. "Maybe you'll get used to it and decide not to leave."

"Ah, you clever woman. I recognize the devious

motive in your actions," Sean teased as he munched on the shrimp. "And it's working, too."

"Good. Now, what would you two like for dinner? How about lobster bisque? Or perhaps you'd prefer something a bit spicier. I have an absolutely scrumptious recipe for Cajun gumbo. Charles and I managed to convince a local restaurateur in New Orleans to part with it. Can you imagine? It had been kept a family secret for generations."

"Poor woman. She's so lonely. I think we should stick around a few more days, don't you?" Mira whispered into Sean's ear while Claire rambled on.

Sean laughed. "I do believe you're right. Ohio and your job can wait, can't it?"

"Oh yes. I'd say it can wait as long as it takes."

"As long as what takes?" Sean leaned close and nuzzled Mira's neck, both of them unaware that Claire had left the room.

"Long enough to be sure you'll make an honest woman of me. That's how long."

"Well, it might be a while," Sean breathed into her ear.

"Oh yeah? We'll see about that. And if you…"

"Mira?" Sean tilted his face up to stare intently at her.

"Hmm?"

"Be quiet," he murmured and brought his lips to her mouth, his kiss long and lingering.

A word about the author...

Kathryn Long is the author of the Lilly M. Mystery series, as well as the paranormal mystery, *Dying to Dream*, and short stories published by ezine The Piker Press. She stays actively involved as a member of Sisters in Crime and maintains an author website, blogsite, and Facebook page. For more about the author, visit:

www.kathrynlong.webs.com.

www.ingramcontent.com/pod-product-compliance
Lightning Source LLC
Chambersburg PA
CBHW060518260626
47161CB00003B/702